If you enjoyed this book, why not try one of the following:

Kate Furnivall - The Far Side of the Sun

Christina Courtenay - The Scarlet Kimono

Rosanna Ley - Bay of Secrets

Leah Fleming - The Postcard

Lucinda Riley - The Midnight Rose

Veronica Henry - A Night on the Orient Express

The
TRADER
OF
SAIGON

The
TRADER
OF
SAIGON

LUCY CRUICKSHANKS

HERON
BOOKS

First published in Great Britain in 2013 by Heron Books
An imprint of Quercus

55 Baker Street
7th Floor, South Block
London
W1U 8EW

Excerpt from the *The Tale of Kieu* by Nguyen Du
(translated by Hyunh San Thong) published with the
kind permission of Yale University Press.

A CIP catalogue record for this book is available
from the British Library

HB ISBN 978 1 78206 321 6
TPB ISBN 978 1 78206 454 1
EBOOK ISBN 978 1 78206 343 8

This book is a work of fiction. Names, characters, places
and events portrayed in it, while at times based on historical figures
and places, are the product of the author's imagination.

10 9 8 7 6 5 4 3 2 1

Printed and bound in Great Britain by Clays Ltd, St Ives plc

Typeset by Ellipsis Digital Limited, Glasgow

For Scott

ONE

All that was left of the little lizard was a skeleton. It was trapped behind the browning tape which held the tattered mosquito net across the window. Tail curled, body strained and snaking, it looked like it had struggled to the very end. Alexander and the lizard sat together in the dusty café in Hanoi's Old Quarter, watching people and sharing time. Alexander was stony-faced. Dead teeth bared, the lizard smiled.

Alexander knocked back the dregs of his watery coffee and lit a cigarette. He took a hard drag and ran his finger around the rim of his cup, listening to the stern, tin voice of the loudspeakers crackle in the heat as the Party marched through their evening bulletin. The street was insufferably busy, as were all in Hanoi. The buildings here squatted closer than in any other city he'd seen, and the trees they hid behind were all taller and thicker. His eyes sifted through the mess of brown faces and patrolling government uniforms and snagged on an elderly woman, crouched in a doorway on the opposite kerb. She was bending her head to the bowl in her hand and shovelling rice into her mouth through the gaps where her teeth should have been. A cat paced beside her, rubbing his mangy fur on her shin and flicking the stump of his tail, impatiently. The woman dropped a scrap and the animal chomped frantically at the ground. She paused and watched him, her tongue licking out from the corner of her mouth and her chopsticks upright in the bowl, like incense at a funerary rite. *God, no, not her*, thought Alexander. The lizard smiled.

Dusk was starting to creep in, but the air still boiled. In the searing heat, the sewers sweated, and hot, wet air rose up from underground and soaked the people with stench. All along the tree-lined street, shops and eateries spilled over from their doorways. Women sat on the tiled steps, fanning their children with the latest order of government pamphlets. Faded red flags hung from every awning, and they drooped as though weary of the heat too, and the strain of parading their loyalty. A food hawker wiped shimmering grease from her cheekbones and scraped her ladle around the rim of her broth bowl, calling out to those on the pavement. The thin, breathless whistle of bicycle spokes rang out as a stream of riders slipped ceaselessly by.

Inside the café, the electric lights were a stuttering blue buzz. They gave Alexander a headache. He pulled his glasses from his nose and placed them on the table, rubbing his eyes. When he had lost his glasses in his first weeks of war it had taken him years to replace them. He preferred not to see the faces of the men and boys who stalked him, charged him and lay dead in his way. Sometimes, he still preferred to keep his world blurred. All women looked more beautiful, softly unfocused.

It was right at the end of the war when he finally bought new ones. They had thick plastic rims that rested on the bridge of his nose, and the initials of a former owner were scratched into the corner of one lens in tiny, pointed letters. He had been in Saigon – a thousand miles south of where he sat now – and had bought them from a Frenchman in a reeking back alley. A lucky find, they were the only pair in a suitcase that bulged with knock-off watches and Zippo lighters, dented, tarnishing and engraved with the names of the bloodiest battleground cities. They cost him four dollars and a can of Heineken he had stolen from a drunken marine. He got them home just in time to watch the city fall through the slats of his shutters. He had stood with his face pressed against the dark wood and squinted out, and the low, loud moan of helicopters thumped through his chest. It swallowed the shouts of the looters on the ground, and they mouthed noiselessly at each other as they smashed, pushed and stole their way through the chaotic streets. The Americans were finally leaving, and this was what his victory looked like. Hidden in his room that day, Alexander had shared in the hysterical thrill of freedom.

When he looked back, he was still surprised at how easy it had been to desert the US Army. He had expected to be hunted, but he supposed the generals had bigger things to worry about. He was surprised too, at how simple it was to be a stray American, even after the war had ended. He practised his Russian, he lied and he hid, and he slithered through the shadows, untroubled. He supposed the Communists had bigger things to worry about too.

Alexander took another big pull on his cigarette as a soldier sidled by the café and stared brazenly in. Nothing

itched him more these days, though, than time in Hanoi.
Like nowhere else in Vietnam, the people here were cynical.
The Party's grip was tight and ingrained, and it bred a sense
of urgent devotion. Mistrust had grown competitive; a game
to be played between fearful men who would shop a
comrade quick, lest it be them otherwise. He much preferred
the rebellious South. There were far more men for the
Party to watch there. He hid better amongst their dis-
loyalty.

He waited for the soldier to pass and then peered back
out, across the street. On the corner, a group of women
had gathered. They were chattering noisily beneath a
simpering portrait of Ho Chi Minh, swapping gossip and
rice for gossip and fruit. *No,* thought Alexander, *not them.*
His eye-line inched along the pavement, and red–and–yellow
government banners blazed angrily between the trees. The
Office of Justice and Criminal Punishment. The Central
Committee of the Vietnam Fatherland Front. The Office
of Conscription and Relations with Foreign Aggressors. He
ticked off each escape in his head. A mother sat on the
pavement and scolded her daughter, yanking a comb through
the child's hair. The girl scowled as her mother snatched a
parting along her scalp and twisted her hair roughly up,
pinning a knot on the side of her head. *No,* thought
Alexander, *not them.* He always chose with great care. He
was good at choosing. It had brought him success, selling
dreams to simple Vietnamese women, and selling simple
Vietnamese women to rich, expectant men. He went for
the ones with the saddest eyes, but who looked like they

had potential. An artisan, he blew hot air into thin glass girls and shaped them into ornaments of humming birds and orchids, so they sparkled in the sunlight at market.

The gathering of women quietened, collected their fruit and fastened the ribbons of their *nón lá* hats with scrawny fingers, their faces disappearing into shadow beneath the broad rims of the conical straw. As they moved away, Alexander saw another girl. She was sitting at the entrance of a passageway, with a blue-and-white-tiled 28 above the arch. Her hands were resting neatly on her knees and her head was down. There was a door hanging open in the gloom behind her – just a crack. An official approached and she wriggled awkwardly in her seat, leaning away from him. He spoke and tossed a coin in her lap before striding into the passageway and throwing open the door.

Alexander caught a glimpse of a squat toilet before the door swung shut again. He watched as the girl frowned, glancing anxiously into the passageway behind her and clearly waiting for the man to leave. Her shoulders were hunched and she clasped her hands together, folding them over each other and playing with something he couldn't quite see. A ring? He strained his eyes and watched her tug and twist a band of sickly grey metal around her finger.

He dragged his chair closer to the table and leaned forward, to get a better look. Each time a man approached the squat, the girl shifted in her seat. Her hands jumped from where they had laid on her knees and curled into quick, tight fists in her lap, hiding her ring from the men who paid her. Alexander knew a squat-girl would not own anything of real value; it was her behaviour that nudged at his interest. This is just for me, she seemed to say. As the men left the squat and walked away without a word, or a look, or a thought, her shoulders loosened and her hands slipped back to her knees, her ring proudly facing the world.

From limp hands on skinny knees, the ring shone out, like hope. It shone through the heavy air and foul smells, and across the street, and through the ragged mosquito net with the sticky brown tape, and it snapped Alexander's eyes suddenly into focus. *Yes*, he thought, *her*. He took a last, quick draw on his cigarette and ground it out in the damp at the bottom of his cup. His stare only left the girl for the briefest moment, as he straightened his glasses back on his nose and picked a banknote from his wallet. Clamping the wallet shut with a flick of his wrist, he tucked the note beneath the cup's saucer and weaved out between the tables. He pushed his shirt tighter into the band of his trousers as he left the café, skipped the kerb, and crossed the street towards her. The little lizard watched and smiled.

TWO

Hanh held out her hand. The man yanked at the seat of his trousers and shifted impatiently on his feet. He rummaged in his pocket and threw an oily coin in her palm before hurrying into the passageway. As he jerked open the corrugated tin door of the squat, it rattled dangerously and strained against its weak hinges. Hanh slid the coin into her pocket and wiped her hand on her skirt, watching the man squeeze his lumbering bulk into the tiny space behind her.

In all the time she had worked here, she never became any less surprised by the stream of men who would pay to use the filthy latrine. It didn't matter how desperate she was – even if she'd eaten a hundred rotten mangos – she would never go in there through choice. It was dark, low-roofed and barely wider than she was. Wooden planks lay across a shallow hole, and they were always soaked with urine, slippery and stinking. In the evenings, when she was forced inside to wash the floor, she would clasp one hand tightly over her nose and mouth and bunch her skirt above her knees with the other, pushing the wet rag into the corners of the room and up the base of the walls with the toe of her sandal as quickly as she could. Black flies would nip at every scrap of her exposed skin.

The door clattered shut with a gust of foul air, and Hanh saw the man fumble urgently with his buttons and wrench his trousers to the ground. She snatched her eyes away and stared at the cracks in the pavement, listening to the man groan as he crouched over the seething hole. There was a splash from the water pail and a line of escaping water trickled past her feet, running away from the squat on its regular route to the street. The man emerged from the passage, flicking his wet hands beside him, and tiny specks hit against her cheek and arm.

It was suppertime in the Old Quarter, and all along the street the food stalls were trading. Hanh ran her hand across her stomach, feeling the sharp ridge of her bottom rib. She hadn't eaten anything since breakfast, and it made her feel tired and impatient. Close by, a vendor was pinching pieces of yellow fat between his fingers and smearing them around the bowl of his blackened pan. The fat sizzled and smoke rose in his face. He stepped aside, rubbing his eyes. She watched jealously as he threw a handful of chopped shrimp into the spluttering pan, and her mouth began to water. The rich, salty aroma of *nuoc mam* lifted above all the other smells of the street, tormenting her.

She squirmed, peeling herself away from her plastic chair, and a bead of sweat dribbled down to the small of her back. Another man was walking towards her: a Party official. He stopped close and stood over her, demanding to know how much it cost to use the squat and blowing his rancid breath in her face. Hanh felt her body brace against the back of her seat. When the men talked to her it made her nervous – especially officials. They spoke as though she were nothing better than a dog. She mumbled a reply into the humid air. He snapped at her to speak up, and she gripped her hands tightly together, worrying her mother's ring around her finger. She had argued with her mother again this morning. Hanh hated it when they argued. She tried to hold her tongue and be a good girl, like she was told, but it was difficult sometimes. Good girls did not survive long in Hanoi. Her mother didn't understand.

Hanh hauled up a louder voice to answer the official, and he paid and disappeared into the passageway. As the water leaked along the ground beside her she slipped her grubby feet in and out of her sandals, wriggling her toes. Tonight, she would go to the river and wash, and then she would paint her toenails. She would paint her mother's toenails too. She'd paint them a bright, happy colour. Though her mother wouldn't be able to see from where she lay in her sickbed, she would know they had been painted and they could feel beautiful together.

The pavement was beginning to quieten, and the bicycles that jostled for space on the road were thinning too. Between their merging paths, Hanh could see into the café on the opposite side of the road. It was crowded, as it was every evening, with barely a table empty. Disgusting Dinh was there, drinking beer with the owner, and his bloodshot cheeks were glowing blue in the fluorescent light. The legs of his plastic chair bowed under the weight of his sprawling body, and he raised a fat finger to the waitress, who jumped up and scurried to his table with another full drink. The girl hurriedly wiped the condensation from Dinh's bottle with her apron and fussed around him.

Hanh frowned, bitterly. If Dinh could afford to drink beer all night, he could afford to pay her the wages he owed. It was more than two months now since he'd given her anything for the hours she'd worked at the squat. She even called him Uncle – like he said she had to – but it made no difference. He still wouldn't pay her. Sometimes, when her rations were low and she didn't have money for anything extra, the bubble of air in her empty stomach would cry at her to quit. She knew she wouldn't really, though. The Party would rather let Hanoi starve than allow private business, and what little work existed was entirely corrupt, secret and scarce. Jobs like this were rarer than tigers, and Dinh's thin promise of some payment was better than a guarantee of none. He looked up suddenly and caught her staring. With a grin, he waved and patted his thigh, like he wanted her to sit on it. The owner of the café threw back his head and slapped Dinh on the shoulder, bellowing with laughter.

Hanh looked quickly away, her eyes scavenging over the other busy tables with their bottles of drink and bowls of steaming pho-beef broth. At the far side of the café, there was a man that caught her attention. He had white skin and was sitting alone by the window, watching the street with interest. He was probably Russian, she thought. The only foreign men in Hanoi were Russian, these days; here to trade and prop up the Party. She leaned forward just a little in her chair. It was difficult to see him properly; his table was half hidden from the pavement by a greying net. Was he the man she had seen there before? It had been the day she went to temple with Thuy, and they were laughing about the monkey they had chased away from the fruit at the altar, and Hanh thought she had seen a white man look at her, just briefly. The moment was quick, but sharp as a poker, and she hadn't quite known what to make of it.

The man drained his cup and sparked a cigarette alight. Hanh dipped her head, but kept a curious watch through the corner of her eye. The men she knew rolled raw tobacco, and they stuffed the papers so greedily that the fibres overflowed and stuck to their teeth. This man smoked real cigarettes, and he smoked with confidence. Leaning back in his chair, he stretched his arm out to his cup and flicked the ash away with one finger. He wasn't slouching over the table like Disgusting Dinh, or bossing the waitress, or grinning stupidly. He was quiet and calm, turning the cigarette packet in his hand and tapping it on the table. To Hanh, his eyes stood out. They were small and dark and powerful.

A man butted his foot into the leg of Hanh's chair and called her attention abruptly back to the squat. She held out her hand and took his coin. His sweat-speckled shirt was just inches from her face, stretched tight across his bloated belly, and she pinched her lips together to stop from breathing him in. He sidled into the alley, his gaze lingering brashly over her face and chest as he left, making her shudder. This was what real life was like: rude and threatening. It made her mad just to think of it. She knew she would lie awake again tonight, listening to the cramped rumble of her belly and her mother's deep wheeze and feeling a heavy, choking fear: *This is all I will ever know.*

She put her head back down and stared at the pavement. Another stream of water was escaping across the concrete, down to the street. Once, Hanh tried to tell Thuy how she felt. She told her she pretended that she was that little trickle of dirty water, running away from the squat, down the street, out of the city and into the distance. She told her how she imagined she would reach the sea and be clean and free. Thuy had laughed and Hanh had laughed too, though just with her voice, and not with all her soul.

It was almost dark, now. Hanh was looking at the ground and she didn't see him coming until he was right in front of her. He crept up and surprised her, the calm Russian with the powerful eyes. With her palm upturned and open, and her heart sparked alert, Hanh held out her hand.

THREE

Phuc lived on a street in Saigon where the morning light fell thin and yellowish between the buildings. He crouched on the rooftop of his home, his knees folded into his armpits and a cigarette snagged to his splintering lip. The scrap of tin in his hand was stubborn, but he forced it flat and placed it over the last remaining hole in his rust-gnawed roof. He brought the hammer down with a piercing crack, the nail spat in, and the little shack shuddered like a rice stem beneath him.

His patchwork finished, Phuc sat back and squinted towards the rising sun. Houses crowded over the land for as far as he could see. With brittle brick walls and rippling, sheet-metal roofs, they leaned upon and pushed against each other like sleeping drunks. A group of children darted past him, laughing and hollering as they chased a limping dog, and he rubbed his eyes, yawning. This miserable place had kept him awake again last night. From the house by the junction, the boy with typhoid had howled for hours. Somewhere nearer, tarpaulin had flailed in the wind, and the awkward, irregular steps of drunken feet had dragged along the ground, and he'd heard a slurred curse as someone stopped and relieved themselves against the wall of his home. He sniffed bitterly and cast the stump of his cigarette to the pavement. It nudged through a crack and disappeared into the gurgling black river that gushed through the gutter below.

From the end of the street, the guard was watching him. The boy squatted on the kerb's edge like a perched bird, hook-beaked and glowering. A rifle stood to attention over his shoulder, but he couldn't have been more than sixteen years old. Prison-thin, his tongue was barbed by a sharp Hanoi accent, and his head was as thick as wet wood. Week after week, he soaked up every detail of life from the Economic Zone – every whispered conversation – and dripped it back to the Party. There was a guard at the top of almost every street, these days. It was a wonder there were any Communists left in the capital, thought Phuc, with all the boys they had shipped to Saigon to spy on these troublesome Southerners. He shifted to the edge of the roof and slipped grudgingly down.

Inside, Phuong was making *cháo* with a cupful of stale rice she had saved from last night's supper. Flame stroked at the bottom of the stockpot, and smoke rose and swept across the small room as Phuc tramped in. Phuong used to make their *cháo* with stock, but now it was just water she ladled into the pan, and it hissed and spat as it hit the hot metal. Kieu was helping her mother. She was sitting at the table and preparing the salad bowl, slicing spring onions into thin rings and crushing a handful of peanuts with the flat of her knife.

'He's out there again,' said Phuc, slumping down in the seat beside his daughter.

'He's always out there,' Phuong replied. She wiped her hands on her apron and placed a stack of bowls on the table. 'It's his job.'

'He was watching me.'

'Of course he was. That hammering was louder than gunfire.'

Phuc touched the back of his hand to the teapot, and then poured himself a cup of lukewarm tea. He sipped the dusty green liquid, swilling it against the back of his teeth. The guard ambled past his open doorway and stared brazenly in.

'Shut the door, will you, Phuong?' said Phuc, hiding a scowl behind his upheld cup.

Phuong scurried across the room. 'He's just a boy,' she said, shaking her head as she pulled the door to. 'You can't blame him. He's only doing what he has to do, like everyone else around here.'

Phuc's lips puckered. 'Don't be tricked,' he hissed as a whisper. 'Those weak limbs might belong to a boy, but his mind belongs to the Party. He goes well beyond what he *has to do*. Last week, he sat on the corner and sucked his cigarette so hard he nearly swallowed it, watching that fool Boa sink himself with a drunken speech about how he'd die before he ever referred to Saigon as *Ho Chi Minh City*. Next day, Boa's hauled away to the camps and not a soul on the street has seen him since. Tam said he was barely given a grain of rice in the whole six months he spent at Can Tho. He lived off nothing more than insects and manioc leaves. Manioc leaves, Phuong! They'll send your guts bleeding from your body, if you eat too many of them. Old Boa will never survive that.'

'All right, Phuc,' snapped Phuong, shooting her eyes at Kieu.

Kieu was quietly plucking coriander leaves from their stem and tossing them into the salad bowl. She looked up and smiled at Phuc, brushing her hair from her cheek and tucking it behind her ear with her little finger, just as Phuong did. She was fifteen now, and so delicately balanced between woman and girl. Her almond eyes and plump pink lips filled her face, as if they did not yet know where to settle. Watching Phuong and Kieu cook breakfast was Phuc's favourite way to banish the night. They looked beautiful when they cooked, Kieu especially, her long hair glistening in the firelight. She didn't deserve to live in a slum like this. He reached across the table and squeezed her hand, gently.

'I'm sorry,' he sighed. 'I just can't stand it here . . . this constant surveillance. We're being held hostage by a child, Phuong. It's humiliating.'

Phuong stirred the *cháo* and shrugged at him, sadly. 'That's what you get for being on the wrong side of war.'

The wrong side of the war, thought Phuc. Who'd have believed it? Though it was clear in his mind how he'd got to this point, the speed and weight of his fall still shocked him. He felt as though just a few full moons had passed since he owned a big house in the rich, leafy suburbs. He had been one of the few honest businessmen in the whole of Saigon – and amongst the most successful too – bringing fish from the coast to sell to the city's crowded restaurants.

In the early days, he would wake long before dawn and hitch a lift to the coast on the grain trucks, arriving before the crowds to get the best deals and the freshest picks. Back in Saigon, he would tout his fish around the cafés and markets, and when he fell into bed at night, the muscles in his shoulders would burn from the strain of dragging his fish-cart and his hands would be blistered and raw, but he'd still be awake again before the lazy sun.

By the time the war arrived and the South filled with foreigners, Phuc had more than ten boats with his name on the stern. Every day, he caught crate upon crate of snapper and mullet and eel and crayfish and mottled blue crab. He owned motorbikes too, and employed a fleet of couriers to race his catch from sea to city, in time for breakfast. Regular orders flowed from the smallest bars to the smartest Saigon establishments. Throughout the war, he kept his head down and his business boomed. He fed office workers and school children, fat-bellied American generals, their lapdog government officials, wide-eyed, bloodthirsty foreign journalists and a thousand profiteering mobsters. He liked to joke he owned all the fish in Saigon. 'There isn't a guppy in this town,' he would say to Phuong, 'that hasn't looked up at me from the slab and asked for forgiveness!'

Everything Phuc had, he earned himself. Everything he earned, he gave to his family; he thought he'd been building their future. He bought plum trees for Phuong, which she kept in the courtyard at the back of their home, and they blossomed at Tet. He sent his sons, Thao and Quan, to the best school in the city. He bought a bicycle for Kieu. It was a Peugeot, imported from France. When she rode, she looked like a dove in her white silk *áo dài*!

Phuc couldn't give his family anything now. It was seven years since the Communist tanks had rolled into Saigon and the Party took his business, his boats, his home and his savings. They stood at his door with tight lips and chilling eyes, and they took his dignity.

His family were moved to the Economic Zone at the east edge of the city. From the life Phuc had known and loved, it felt like exile. For years, he was forced to work in the fields. The Party were clearing new swathes of land for the collectives, and they needed the men from the Zones to dredge the ditches. They said new land would ease the famines. It eased it for some, but nothing more found Phuc's table than envy. Though he begged for paid work at the farms and the port, there was never anything regular. The rations could only get him salted meat from the market – nothing fresh – and the rice he fed his children was cheap and grey, with flecks of grit (that stuck in their teeth), from where it had been spread to dry by the side of the road.

Even given a lifetime's thought, Phuc would not have dreamed the South could lose the war; not with all the US men, their choppers and mighty firepower. He never doubted the brutality of the hate-filled, backwards North Vietnamese Army, but he far undervalued their patience. They ran the Americans out with little more than stamina and spite, and every Southern man left behind was a criminal: a traitor who fought against his own blood, worthy of punishment. The South had backed the wrong horse, and they'd never be allowed to forget it.

Over the years, the Party reminded Phuc often; his past was too sweet a temptation for corrupt officials to resist. If they had a roof to repair, or a girl to impress, or a debt to repay, or were just on a power-trip, they would thumb through the records at the Party offices and find a weak link. With the notes about his booming business and big-city mansion scribbled across every page of his file, Phuc stood out like a flame on a hilltop. Sometimes, if he had scrounged work that month, he gave them money and they left him alone. Other times, there was nothing in his pocket but dust and dirt, and he had no choice but to disobey. When he couldn't pay, he was beaten. He'd lost count of the times he'd been smacked by fists, knees or elbows. Once, he was hit on his doorstep with a rock in a bag, and now the lid of his left eye hung down like a dying leaf.

Though he told himself it was the cries of the street that troubled him each night, really, he knew that it wasn't. What kept him awake was the fear in his gut. It wasn't a fear like imminent danger, but a slow fear; a dreadful sense of anticipation, inescapable, exhausting and hopeless, like walking through sand. The Party was watching him, even in sleep. One day, they'd be back.

'Breakfast is ready! Where are my troublesome sons?'

Phuong's shout hauled Phuc from the depths of his stupor. He wiped his face quickly on the cuff of his sleeve and gathered himself, as Thao and Quan tumbled out from the back room.

'Morning, Dad!' said Thao, shoving Quan from the seat beside Phuc and pitching down in his place.

'*Thao!*' cried Quan. 'That's my seat! You sat there yesterday. Dad, tell him!'

'Shhh, boys,' said Phuong, slapping Thao playfully on the back of his head. 'Your father's tired. He was looking for work again last night. He doesn't want to listen to you two bickering like a pair of parrots.'

Phuong took a bowl from the stack on the table and dropped in a small piece of raw fish. She ladled boiling *cháo* on top of the fish and passed it to Phuc. Into all the other bowls she just ladled *cháo*, then she slid them across the table to the boys and Kieu.

Phuc watched as she scooped the last tiny portion into her own bowl and tucked her seat beneath the table. He looked down into his *cháo*. Little chippings of crushed peanuts were sinking into the watery gruel, towards the fish that lay at the bottom. His spoon hovered guiltily above the bowl.

'Aren't you hungry, Phuc? Why aren't you eating?' Phuong asked. The rest of the family were waiting patiently for him to start.

'I don't want you to buy fish any more, Phuong. We can't afford it.'

'Nonsense. I can't expect you face the day with an empty stomach.' Phuong picked up the salad bowl and sorted through it with her fingers, selecting the freshest coriander and passing it to Phuc. 'Besides, if Tam can give you work on the boats like he said, then we'll be fine. You should go and see him again today. Find out if he has anything for you,' she said, smiling.

'Perhaps we should get a wooden fish for Dad,' said Quan.

'Yeah! Let's get him a wooden fish,' roared Thao, walloping his brother gleefully on the back.

'Don't tease your father,' said Phuong.

'Why would I want a wooden fish?'

'Like the story,' said Quan, looking expectantly at Phuc. Phuc stared blankly back.

'You know, the story about the miser who only gave his family rice to eat and nothing else. He hung a wooden fish on the wall above the dinner table and told his children that every time they ate a mouthful of rice they should look at the fish and pretend to take a bite. He told them to make chewing noises and say how good it tasted. The miser's youngest child was very small and didn't understand what his father had told him. He looked at the fish and made loud noises, slurping and slopping and licking his lips for a whole minute long. The miser's face went red and his eyes bulged with anger and he shouted at his son: *I told you to take just one bite! Don't you know how expensive fish is these days!*'

Thao and Quan rolled about the table, laughing.

'Boys! Be good. You know your father isn't a miser,' said Phuong, but she was laughing too.

Phuc stared into his bowl and the table fell quiet, except for the snorts of the boys as they struggled to swallow their giggles. They were all laughing at him. He was worse than a miser. What sort of a man couldn't even feed his family breakfast? He frowned and shoved his bowl to the boys, whose eyes lit up like fireflies.

'You're giving us your fish?' cried Quan. 'Thanks, Dad!'

'You can split it with your sister.'

Phuong looked up, surprised. 'Heavens, Phuc. What's bitten you, today?'

'The Party might enjoy living like dogs, taking sick pride in how thin they can make their children, but mine are going to grow up strong-boned,' he said, ramming his chair back from the table.

'Where are you going?'

'I need another cigarette.'

He fumbled for the packet in his trouser pocket and stamped outside, slamming shut the door behind him.

'Morning, Brother!' called Thinh, raising his hand and waving from across the road. He was leaning against the frame of his own door, one foot in his house and one on the street. A huddle of scrawny chicken pecked at the grit on the pavement.

'Brother!' Phuc cried, pointing down at Thinh's feet, aghast. He was wearing new boots. They were black as a cat in the night, and polished to a shine. 'Who did you kill to get those shoes?'

A smirk spread across Thinh's face. 'I got them at Fán T'án Alley,' he whispered slyly.

Phuc swallowed a cough from the back of his throat. Everyone in Saigon had heard of Fán T'án Alley, but he'd never known anyone who'd been there. It was a wretched cut of a backstreet, scored through the centre of Cholon – Saigon's ancient Chinatown – by mobsters, pimps and black-marketeers. From all over the city, it was where men went to satisfy their vices; a place where the girls were cheap and the games went on in an endless loop, like prayer beads. It was a crook of the town where even the Party was loath to go. 'You won new boots?' he asked, confused.

Thinh laughed and slapped his arm. 'I won a wad of cash as thick as your head, Brother! I'm going again tonight,' he said. 'Come with me.'

Phuc shook his head. 'No way.' He'd heard the stories of dark cellars, unpaid debts and sobbing, widowed women. It was not the kind of place for a man like him.

Thinh narrowed one eye and looked at Phuc, his face a blend of amusement and pity. 'You can't say you don't need the money.'

'We all need the money.'

'So what's the problem?'

'I'm not like that.'

'Phuc! You were a businessman. All businessmen are gamblers!'

Phuc scowled. 'Business is skill and hard work,' he said. 'Those games are nothing more than luck, and luck is for fools.'

'Rubbish! Luck is for everyone! Luck is what makes men equal. The Communists could learn from the gamblers!'

Thinh belched another great laugh and Phuc could see

deep into his toothless mouth. For a moment, he hesitated. It was true; his fortune would be as good as any man's, but he had seen the bosses of Fán T'án Alley eating fish at Saigon's high-class restaurants. They wore red silk and capped their teeth with gold. What money did they have spare to make peasants rich? He shook his head again. 'Isn't it dangerous?'

Thinh shrugged. 'Only for rats, thieves and cowards. You're not a coward, are you, Phuc?'

'Of course not.'

'Then come!' Thinh laughed, and flicked his head to the prowling guard-boy. 'Only the dead are safe in Saigon anyway, Brother. You're the only man I know who doesn't play games in the city. Are you even a man at all? You survived the war, but now you're worrying yourself to death like an old woman. Look at me. Are these the boots of a degenerate?' Thinh lifted his foot and slapped his shoe with the palm of his hand. 'I could buy ten pairs like this, if I wanted. I could buy shoes for my wife too. Wouldn't Phuong like new shoes, Phuc?'

'She wouldn't like Fán T'án Alley,' he muttered.

'Then don't tell her,' said Thinh. He grinned and threw a wiry arm around Phuc's shoulder. 'Listen, just bet the cost of a beer, and if you lose, I'll buy you one. What's fairer than that?'

Phuc glanced at the guard, the offer leaking into him, and he thought of his family inside with their pitiful, fish-less rations. *Just bet the cost of a beer.* That was reasonable, wasn't it? If he won, he could buy them all a proper break-fast tomorrow, like they used to have, like a real man should.

Just for a morning, they could all forget. He ran his hand through his thinning hair and felt a twitch of flesh in his broken eye-socket. What harm could possibly come, he thought, from just one beer?

FOUR

The man looked directly into Hanh's eyes as he spoke. Other men who came to the squat never bothered to look her in the eye. She stared quickly down, embarrassed, and held out her hand for his payment.

He didn't give her any money.

'Can you tell me where to find the Salute Guesthouse?' he said.

His Vietnamese was fluent, but Hanh could tell he was speaking carefully. *I was right*, she thought, *he's Russian*. She recognised the sound of his words, flicked from the roof of his mouth with a pointed tongue. They were short and metallic, like a dripping tap. The first time Hanh had heard voices like this, she didn't know where they came from. Thuy had known, though. She'd been so excited.

'Look!' she had whispered, clutching Hanh's arm as they walked along the busy street and squeezed by two broad-shouldered men with brown uniforms, bright white faces and stern expressions. 'Those men are Soviets!'

Hanh had glanced back as the men marched away. Their voices were loud and their strides long and arrogant. They looked so big and out of place. 'Why are they here?' she had asked.

'They've given the government money for schools and roads and houses. They're going to help us rebuild. Vietnam will be just like Russia.'

'What's Russia like?'

'It's a paradise!'

Hanh wrinkled her nose and frowned. 'If my home was paradise, I wouldn't come here.'

'You're always a miserable donkey,' Thuy had teased, with affection.

Now, as the Russian man questioned her, Hanh stayed silent. She still didn't know what she made of the Soviets. There seemed to be more and more in Hanoi and everyone said they were rich and powerful, but the city still looked a crumbling, shell-pocked wreck. Their closeness to the government made her wary too. She'd heard it whispered that they couldn't be trusted, that they were only here to spoonfeed the Party more myths and hate, brandishing their money and influence around like weapons and cheating the Viet people of what little rice and pride they had left. Though she didn't know if the rumours were true she could see for herself that officials scuttled around them, eager as lice. She knew where the guesthouse was – it was the biggest in the Old Quarter by a stride – but whenever the Party was concerned, it was always wise to be careful. She shifted in her seat, avoiding his eye. His stare was intense and uncomfortable, but something about him was different from Russian men she had seen before. His skin was less pale, his lips weren't tight and he just felt softer, somehow.

'The Salute Guesthouse?' he asked, again. 'Do you know where it is?'

Hanh took a small, brisk breath. She didn't want to keep him waiting. 'Go this way,' she said, waving her hand towards the end of the road. 'It's on Hóa Ma Street. Walk as far as the bus station and then turn left. The Salute is next to a *pho* shop and a tyre store. There's a sign outside. It's very big. You won't miss it.'

'How long will it take?'

'Ten minutes, maybe. It's not far.'

'Great. Thanks for being so helpful.'

Hanh felt pink heat prickle in her cheeks. No one at the squat ever normally said *thank you*.

He pointed at the junction. 'So, I turn left, and walk past the bus station?'

'No. Walk past the bus station and *then* turn left.'

The man nodded and rubbed the dry stubble on his chin. 'I'm terrible with directions,' he said, smiling widely. 'I'd never have found my way there on my own. I'm not from Hanoi.'

Hanh looked at his tallness, his round blue eyes and milky skin, and a laugh jumped through her lips. 'A buffalo could tell you're not from Hanoi!' she said without thinking.

The Russian threw her a blunt, odd smirk. 'What did you say?'

'Nothing,' Hanh cried quickly, shaking her head. She slipped down in her chair and cursed at a crack in the pavement. How stupid and careless she was, to make fun of a Russian! She held her breath and willed him to leave, but he didn't.

'I've seen you before, haven't I?' he said.

Hanh stared at the ground, harder. 'I work here every day.'

The Russian stepped nearer. 'No,' he said. 'I've seen you at the café over the road.'

Hanh's heart gave a walloping kick. She'd been right about the day she was at the café with Thuy, with her hair washed and combed and a happy smile on her lips. A white man *had* looked at her. She hadn't imagined it. She shook her head, again, even more strongly. This wasn't the time to be recognised.

The Russian dipped towards her, looking closely at her face. 'I'm sure I have,' he pushed. 'You were with a friend.'

'It wasn't me.'

He straightened up and gave another, definite nod, then shoved his hand in his pocket. 'What's your name?'

Hanh bit her lip and tried to cool her panic. She had mocked a Russian and now he was going to write down her name and report her insolence to the Party!

'My name is Tran Thi Hanh,' she mumbled angrily.

The Russian pulled his hand from his pocket and held it out, a crisp, new banknote standing upright between his fingers. 'Thanks again for your help, Hanh,' he said. 'I'm Alexander.'

Hanh stared at the money, confused. The Russian wasn't insulted. He wanted to pay her. It didn't make sense. She could feel the hot stare of the clutch of women on the opposite pavement. They were standing on the corner, watching her squirm, and sneering. On the breeze, she thought she heard their whispers. Even though her head and stomach ached with hunger, she didn't want his money. She looked up and met his eye. 'I didn't do anything for your money,' she said. 'I'm not a beggar.'

He hesitated, surprise streaking momentarily across his face, then he smiled again and tucked the banknote back into his pocket. He leaned towards Hanh, so suddenly that she flinched, and she could smell the sweet, laundered freshness of his shirt. 'You have beautiful eyes,' he whispered. 'You should look up more often.'

Before Hanh had a chance to catch a breath, the Russian had spun on his heels and was walking away. He crossed the street with a glance and a skip, and she grasped her hands together in her lap, her mind shock-dazed, and watched him disappear into the bustling dark.

FIVE

As he walked down the street and away from the girl, Alexander couldn't help but smile. She was perfect, he thought. Hanh. At the end of the road, he stepped from the pavement and turned towards the bus station. He already knew where the guesthouse was. He had been lodging at the Salute for more than a month.

Hanoi's sky was darkening fast, and he dipped into a lighted shop-front and picked a beer from an ice bucket. He paid the vendor and tucked the bottle into the back pocket of his jeans, feeling the damp and cool soak pleasantly though the worn denim. He'd done well tonight, spotting Hanh like that on the crowded street. It was worth a beer. She was a good find. Her face was a little plain, perhaps, but she wasn't ugly, and her skin was pale enough that the men would be keen. Pimples had marked her forehead, but they didn't matter much; he could blame her age and not lose too much money. She talked so little that he hadn't been able to see her teeth. He would need to get a better look next time. Teeth were expensive to mend or to pull. He couldn't sell a girl with bad teeth.

He had played their conversation just right, also – he was sure of it – staying long enough to spark her interest, but not to spook her. Success relied on handling girls with a delicate touch. He smiled again, remembering the way she furrowed her brow and chewed her lip as he spoke. She'd been afraid of him, but she had some spunk too. He liked that.

It was odd, though, that she hadn't taken his money. Most girls would have grabbed it away in an instant, and there was something unusual about the way that she spoke. Her voice had been quiet, but there was a splinter of steel to her words. Not that it mattered; he had seen her blush when he thanked her. Such a little thing he gave, but she snatched it hungrily. The hook was in her already, and given a little time and effort, he knew he could become whomever he needed to be to reel her in. Of course he could. With a deft, feather-light touch, he could shape and reshape into any man he pleased, zipping seamlessly into a new skin, to get a job done.

Alexander grew up in southern Kansas, in a town where farms outnumbered offices three dozen to one. His parents were strident conformists. His father worked at the factory on Lincoln Street, attaching blades to the underside of the harvesters, so they hung like rows of pointed black teeth and ruthlessly chewed through the wheatfields in June. His hands were striped with scars – red, pink and white as they faded – from where he caught his flesh on the serrated metal as he riveted it in. In the evenings, he ate pork chops for supper, with potatoes and gravy, then he went to the bars and played pool with Big Buddy Blacker. He assumed and expected that Alexander's life would turn out exactly the same.

Alexander's mother was a homemaker. She spent her days frantically baking, cleaning, tweaking her beehive hair in the hallway mirror, counting the long hours until his father came home from work, then sitting in the rocker at the window and chain-smoking, when he'd go straight back out again.

The only expectation Alexander's parents ever had was for him to fit in. When he was small, he had struggled. He wasn't athletic, so the boys didn't like him. He wasn't smart and he didn't try much, so the teachers did not take to him either. Every morning before he went to school, his mother would crouch to his level and hold his cheeks in her hands.

Try to be good today, she would plead in a whisper. *Promise you'll try to fit in.*

I promise, Alexander replied. Her skin was soft and smelled like the lavender cream that she rubbed on her face when she sat at her dresser. He wanted so badly to please her.

Night after night, he disappointed his parents. They craved a boy who was well behaved; who played sport with the others. A boy the neighbours didn't whisper about at the ends of their gardens when they collected their mail. But Alexander wasn't *good*. He didn't play with the other boys. He was awkward and quiet, so he played on his own. At football practice, he would hide beneath the bleachers and eye them with jealousy. How easily they slotted together. He wanted to a part of their team. They were relaxed and carefree, all banter and backslaps, fitting in without thinking.

Over the years, though, he learned to pretend. The more he studied the boys at school, the more he found he could peel away their details; the way they slouched and swaggered when they walked, or held their smokes between finger and thumb. He collected every feature, stored them up and then played them back, like a movie-reel. Pretending worked, and it made him friends. His parents were thrilled with him.

The new Alexander got girls, too. Girls were easy. Dumb and easy. When he had spoken to girls before, he had felt exposed and anxious, but now he seemed to know just which to choose and what to say to flatter them. He never went for the ones with the shortest skirts or the loudest laugh, but he picked the ones who combed their hair neatly back, who walked to school with their mothers and who looked so surprised when he called them pretty. He knew how to keep hold of a girl's hand when she seemed a little shy and tried to pull away, and he knew just how much pressure to apply, so she'd let him lead her out of the diner on a Friday night to the field behind the factory, where he'd lay her down between the shadowed hulks of broken harvesters and lift her polka-dot dress.

Alexander's skill was the very best thing about him. He loved the fact he could change, slipping between shades to match the background, and belong. He loved the control. It made him smile, how easy people were to fool, and how clever he was for fooling them. At the back of his mind, though, the smallest spur scratched him. The real Alexander was always rejected. He could never go back to being himself.

As he rounded the corner of the road, the tall, narrow silhouette of the Salute Guesthouse came into Alexander's view. It towered above the parade of grubby pastel facades that stretched along the rest of the street, rusting balustrades clamped to their windows like prison bars. At pavement level, the frontage was a wall of glass, and a sign hung down announcing vacancies and a list of rules in severe red letters.

The proprietor was sitting with his feet on the desk, his head tipped back and his mouth gaping open, fast asleep. His young son scampered up from the floor beside him and rushed to hold the door as Alexander entered.

'Hello, Mr Alexander! Hello!'

Alexander nodded, but he didn't stop.

The boy hurried after him with an eager grin. His bare feet slapped flatly on the tiles, echoing in the sparse reception room, and his sharp eyes found the beer in Alexander's back pocket. He grabbed Alexander's wrist and pointed at the bottle.

'How was your day, Mr Alexander? You must be very tired. You want more beer? I can get it! Good price! I'll bring it to your room!' he spluttered in broken Russian.

'I don't want anything,' said Alexander, still walking.

The boy stopped at the base of the stairs and dropped his grip, but his eyes followed Alexander as he climbed. 'If you want anything, you tell me! I'll bring it to you!'

Alexander ran his hand over the pink towels and patterned sheets hanging from the banister. They clashed with the peach-and-red tiles where they spilled on to the floor. That boy was far too nosy, always looking for an excuse to pry. Alexander had made it clear to the proprietor that no one was allowed in his room. Not for any reason. He had insisted the proprietor gave him the guesthouse's second key as well as his own, just to be certain. His privacy was precious. He needed a place to relax. The pretending was tiring, sometimes.

In his room, Alexander locked the door and threw the key on to the bare mattress. He slumped down into the wooden armchair at the window and cracked the bottle cap from his beer with his teeth. He was at the very top of the guesthouse and his view across the city was wide. It calmed him. Twisted metal spires rose from half-built structures and scored his eyeline, and all along the building-tops rust bled into faded paint where the metal speared the concrete. Everything was unfinished in Vietnam. There was always something still to do.

He took a swig of his drink and heaved his feet on to the windowsill. In a jar beside his boots, formaldehyde glowed a dull lime in the low light. He looked at the glistening fluid, and the perfectly preserved baby suspended within it. Distorted by the thick glass, with wet wrinkled skin, she curled up as though she slept. Her long, thin limbs were sharp-boned at their bends, and her hands were balled to rigid fists and tucked beneath her shapeless chin. When Alexander had seen the jar for sale in Saigon's Russian Market, he had bought it without hesitation. He had carried his baby with him since as he travelled throughout the country. They shared uncomfortable journeys, lonely rooms and sleepless, sweated nights. With a scrape of glass on tile, Alexander turned his baby to share his view of the city, through the sealed seam of foetal eyes. He leaned back in his chair and cracked his knuckles.

Winning Hanh would be easy.

SIX

'Kieu?'

Phuc crouched at the head of his daughter's bed and whispered gently into her ear. The sun was only just beginning to nudge against the horizon and the air outside was still misted and cool. It crept through the ill-butted joints of his home, casting a damp haze around the dark bedroom. He whispered again, touching his fingers to the skin on her wrist.

Kieu stirred and opened her eyes – just a glittering crack. 'Daddy?'

'Come into the kitchen, bear cub,' he smiled. 'Don't wake your brothers!'

Phuc slipped past the slumbering shadows of Phuong and the boys and pulled his chair soundlessly out from beneath the breakfast table. The tips of his fingers tapped on the wood, in anticipation. He hadn't slept for a moment all night, but he didn't feel tired. He felt more keen for the day to start than he had done in years. What a stroke of luck he'd had at Fán T'án Alley! In the cellars, he played one game and won, so he played another, and then another. He stayed long after Thinh had quit, betting just a few dong each time, and in a single night he'd earned more money than he would in two months at the port. He couldn't wait to share his reward with his family.

Kieu padded out from the bedroom and sat opposite him, sleepy-eyed and squinting. She was wearing her pyjamas, and she tucked her hands up her sleeves and shivered. Her thick black hair was crumpled about her face, and she pushed it back with her swaddled hand. 'What's wrong, Daddy?'

'Nothing's wrong!' Phuc whispered, excited. 'I have a surprise for you.'

He lifted the bundle of newspaper from his lap and unknotted the string. Slowly and neatly he folded back the layers of black and white to reveal five chunky fillets of pale pink fish. He wiped the print from his hands and sat back, proudly.

'Dad!' cried Kieu, her face suddenly awake and wide. 'You bought fish!'

'Shhh! You'll wake everyone up.' Phuc laughed.

'We should wake them up! This is brilliant!'

'Not yet, Kieu.'

'But my tummy's already growling. Don't make me wait! Let's get them up and have breakfast!'

'Shhh, you noisy bear!' Phuc pressed his finger to his lips and stifled his laughter. 'I thought it would be an extra treat for your mother if we cooked for her. Will you help me?'

Kieu paused and sucked on her sleeve. She threw him a special, mischievous smile. 'Of course I'll help,' she whispered. 'This can be our secret.'

A warm swell of happiness heaved inside Phuc's chest. It wasn't just to cook that he'd woken Kieu up. He had wanted to share his prize with her first, to hold a moment of blissful calm together, before the boys rose and tore through the house, before Phuong started busying and asking him questions, before the dank truth of day nudged in and doused him.

Thao and Quan were the image of Phuong, not just in the roundness of their dark brown faces, but in the way they swept through a room with such vigour and sound. Of course, he loved them for it, but he felt a more kindred spirit with Kieu. She was quieter, balanced by composure and intelligence that didn't always need speaking, and she understood the turns of Phuc's thoughts as though she had walked them all beside him. He remembered the day she was born; her sticky, red face and how she had bawled as the midwife washed her in the earthenware basin. Every day since, she made him feel young and vibrant – as though he still mattered.

He pulled a banknote loose from the wedge in his pocket and held it out to her. Her eyes thinned, playfully wry, and she looked at him sideways. 'What's this for?'

'It's a gift.'

'You don't need to give me money.'

'It's OK. I'll give some to the boys too, later. You can buy yourself a sugarcane drink.'

Kieu shook her head and shrugged, pushing his hand away. 'I don't need it, Daddy,' she said. 'You save it.'

Phuc tucked the money back in his pocket, smiling. Everything his daughter did was so dignified and graceful.

When the Party first came to their home, she was eight. As the soldiers charged through his house, tearing it apart and looking for every last dong of his family's savings, she had sat quietly on the staircase, banknotes wrapped around her ankles and her red socks pulled up to her knees. Banknotes were rolled into a tight coil and hidden in the twist of her chignon. Banknotes had been stitched into the lining of her dress by Phuong's shaking fingers, only the night before. Even when a soldier with a rifle ordered her to empty her pockets, Kieu had been calm. Phuc could have never trusted the boys to do that. They would have cried or sniggered or talked, for sure, but Kieu understood how important it had been for her father – that the family needed the money to survive. He had been so proud.

Kieu stood up and gathered the fish from the table. She went to the stove and plonked herself on the floor, the newspaper bundled in her lap. 'Do you want to be my assistant?' she said, looking back and grinning. 'I'll let you help, if you promise to be quiet as a mouse!'

Phuc and Kieu sat with their shoulders touched together and giggled clumsily at their secret, silent cooking game. Phuc struck a match to light the fire, and it flared with what felt like a roar in the empty room. Kieu filled the stockpot with water, tipping the pan and dribbling a stream down the side of the metal to hush its patter. She hooked a knife beneath the tip of a fish's spine, peeling back a ribbon of thin white bone, and in a moment she'd boned all five and dropped them into the simmering pan.

'I thought I heard whispering,' said Phuong, opening the bedroom door and blustering into the kitchen. She stood beside the table with her hand on her hip and studied them, suspiciously. 'What are you two naughty monkeys up to?'

'Dad's bought fish,' Kieu beamed.

'Fish!?' Thao charged out from the bedroom. He clambered roughly on to Phuc's shoulders and peered down into the stockpot, his mouth already open and dribbling. 'It's a feast!' he shouted.

Quan scrambled up beside him. 'It's a king's breakfast!'

Phuc laughed, lifting the boys from his shoulders and standing up. Earlier, he had separated a cut of money from his spoils and hidden it in the old teapot at the back of the shelf where he kept his nails and penknife and string, and no one would find it. The rest was still in his pocket. He pulled it out and passed it to Phuong.

'Phuc!' she cried. 'Where did you get this?'

'There's a Russian ship in the port, this week. There's a fistful of work for as long as it's docked.'

Phuong's smile widened. 'It's here all week? That's great news! I can't remember the last time you had a whole week's work.'

'I know,' Phuc nodded, 'and the Russians pay far better than the Party. You can buy fish tomorrow too, Phuong – or beef, if you want.'

Phuong tucked the money into the pocket of her apron. 'What a magnificent husband I have!' she said, shooing the boys to the table. 'What do you say to your father, children?'

'Thanks, Dad!' chirped Thao and Quan.

'Thank you, Daddy,' smiled Kieu, now laying the table beside him.

Phuc's slipped his fingers through hers and held them, tightly. His family were proud of him, like they used to be. He didn't like lying, but he wouldn't make a habit of it. Last night was a one-off occurrence. They didn't need to know.

'How long until breakfast is ready?' he asked his daughter.

'Just a few minutes,' she shrugged.

Phuc nodded – there was just enough time to have a quick smoke. He grabbed his lighter and skipped outside.

In the time they'd spent cooking, the sun had yawned up, and now it was weakly leaking heat along the line between the buildings. At the end of the street, Phuc could see the guard-boy talking to the murky silhouettes of three Party officials, and his heart gave a miniature, unsteady skip. It never led to good days when officials came to the Zones so early in the morning. He lowered his head and lit a cigarette, but his eyes crept nervously back to watch them. The guard raised his arm and pointed in Phuc's direction, and Phuc glanced at the street behind him, trying to not seem obvious. There was no one there, just a few grazing chickens and a loitering cat. His stare shot to his feet, panicked, and he drew hard on his cigarette, willing it to burn. He couldn't go back inside before it was done – that would look too suspicious – but he didn't want to wait here either. Through the corner of his vision, he saw the officials leave the guard's side and begin to stride purposefully towards him, their uniforms sharpening into crisp-pressed focus as they neared. Did they know he'd been to the alley already? What else could they want? He heard the crunch of hard-soled boots on dry gravel and he pulled the door closed behind his back and stepped away from the house. Phuong would panic too, if she saw them.

'Good morning, Comrade,' he said, trying to disguise the nervous waver in his voice.

The officials stopped where they met him in the road. They had rifles slung over their shoulders and icy expressions. The one in the middle smoothed the breast of his uniform. 'Mr Phuc?'

'Yes?'

'I'm here on Party business.'

Phuc nodded seriously. 'How can I help?'

'We have been monitoring your neighbourhood. We have reason to believe you are disloyal. We understand that you have been involved in illegal and immoral capitalist activity and that you have arranged secretive meetings for conspirators and spies where you befouled the name of Ho Chi Minh.'

Phuc shook his head. 'Not me, Comrade. I'm a good Communist. I support the Party.'

The official stared at him, unblinking. 'You were a business-man, weren't you?'

Phuc felt a sharp throb of blood through the rim of his old, shattered eye socket. This wasn't about the alley at all. They were here for money. 'It was a long time ago,' he said, firmly. 'Before the war.'

43

The official squared up, stiffening his body. 'You served fish to greedy American soldiers. You fed them up and made them fat and strong so they could fight against your Vietnamese countrymen.'

Phuc shook his head again, more vigorously this time. 'No, Comrade.'

'But you did sell fish, didn't you?'

'Yes.'

'To the restaurants where the Americans ate?'

'Sometimes.'

'So you made yourself rich by helping Americans. You were a traitor to your country.'

Phuc lowered his head, wincing. There was nothing a Southern man could say to win against a Party official, and the more he protested, the more he riled him, the deeper the penance he faced. He hocked a lump of tacky phlegm from the back of his throat and spat at the ground. 'Yes, Comrade,' he mumbled.

The official's lip gave a satisfied twitch. 'So, why would I believe you are loyal now?'

'I'm reformed.'

'A donation to the Party would convince us of your loyalty.'

Phuc groaned and stepped forward, opening his palms. 'Please, Brother!' he begged. 'Look at my home. I have nothing to donate. Believe me, I'm loyal.'

'You wouldn't want me to tell my superiors you're still a capitalist and a traitor, would you?'

'No, Brother.'

'Three hundred dong would secure your position.'

Three hundred dong. The number sparked in Phuc's ears, and lit a sudden idea, deep inside his head. He had more than that amount, today, hidden in the teapot at the back of the shelf. Even with the money he had given to Phuong, he still had more than four hundred dong, wrapped in a coil and tied with string. He cast a hesitant look towards his house. The door was still shut. Phuong and the children were still at the breakfast table. This was his chance to buy their safety and freedom. He could use the money he had won at Fán T'án Alley and pay the official to burn his file, and with it, destroy all record of the man he once was. With no evidence of where he had been and what he had done, no one would come looking for him. He could forget about his stolen business and his family could relax. If he offered enough, Phuc could buy his way free of the Party forever.

He took a small step forward, looking the official directly in the eye. 'To prove how loyal I am, I'd like to give the Party more than three hundred dong,' he said cautiously.

The official paused, his face gripped by suspicion. He glanced at his comrades. 'How much do you want to give us?'

'I want to give you four hundred.'

'And what do you want the Party to do in exchange?'

Phuc held his stare, resolute and steely. 'Burn my file.'

The official sniffed and scratched the scar on his cheek with a long, sharp fingernail. 'It's not possible,' he said, but his eyes were flickering.

Phuc stepped closer. 'Anything's possible, Brother,' he pushed. 'Tell me what I can do for you.'

The official's tongue licked out from the corner of his mouth and back in again, as quick as a thief in the night. 'Give me five hundred dong.'

Phuc's stomach reeled in excitement. He hadn't expected the official to change his mind so easily. He had swung wide open like a greased door! With the money he already had, getting to five hundred would be easy.

'Deal!' he said, and he put out his hand.

The official wrapped his fingers around Phuc's, closing them firmly and squeezing him tight.

'This is more than a deal, Brother. You've made me a promise, and I strongly suggest you keep it.' He brought his face close to Phuc's, and his breath smelled like spicy, aniseed broth. 'Or there will be one new widow and three new orphans shipped to the labour camps.'

SEVEN

The wheels of Hanh's bicycle crunched over the dry gravel as she left the East Highway and swerved down the path to her hamlet. Beneath the canopy of palms, it was dark as midnight. She pushed her feet down on the pedals, speeding blindly forward along the winding track, and cool, black air hissed by her ears. When the trees cleared, she could see her neighbours' houses dotted through the paddies. They were marked only by flickering firelights; snatches of bright yellow warmth, floating above the land like spirits.

At her own home, there was no light to welcome her. The little pile of timber and thatch was sitting silent and shadowy over the paddy's edge, balancing precariously on the rickety stilts that her father had dug into the ground when she was very small. She looked up the ladder to the empty porch and listened for a moment. The insects were crying, straining their throats and squabbling in the grass and air around her. A hidden cicada clicked his tongue in disapproval. She glanced over her shoulder, towards the dark path and the rest of the sleeping hamlet, then began to climb. The rungs creaked beneath her feet as she heaved her bicycle up behind her.

'Mumma?' she whispered, pushing open the door.

Her mother's voice came through the darkness, brittle and dry. 'I'm here, little piglet.'

Hanh rushed to the back of the room and threw open the shuttered door. She stooped to the small clay stove on the back porch, struck a match and pushed it into the nest of brown rice husk. The husk sizzled and, as smoke began to rise, warm light spilled into the room. Hanh saw her mother lying on her side on the bamboo mat, just where she had left her. Her eyes were wide watery pools and she worried the pink-ribboned edge of the mat with shivering fingers.

'Why didn't you light the fire, Mumma? You scared me.'

'How can my daughter be all grown up and sacred of the dark?' her mother smiled. 'It's OK. I was tired, that's all.'

'You're cold, though.'

'I'm fine.'

Hanh bent to her mother's side, lifting her weightless hands and rubbing them gently between her own. 'I'm sorry. You'll be warm soon.'

'Good girl,' muttered her mother, though grey lips.

Though the room where they lived was virtually empty, it was perfectly clean and proudly kept. Between the front and back porches lay the square of space where Hanh and her mother had ate and slept together, for as long as she could remember. There were windows beside the doors at each end, gazing out to the yawning paddies at the back and to the lonely gravel pathway and thick palms at the front. They were open to the whims of the northern air,

48

but covered with strong chicken-wire. It was to keep the tigers out, her father used to tell her, though she hadn't heard tales of a tiger here since before the war. At dawn, the sun would fall through the wire and cast rows of sparkling yellow diamonds across the wooden floor. In winter, when the cold arrived, Hanh would shut it out with blankets slung from nails she had bent to hooks and hammered into the wall above.

In the corner of the room, the laundry that Hanh had folded this morning was still in a neat pile. She took a coarse woollen throw from the top of the stack, shook it out, and spread it carefully over her mother. An insect dropped from the thatch above and scuttled across the faded pink flowers. She brushed it away with the back of her hand.

Her mother sniffed the air and frowned. 'I wish you would leave your bicycle outside, Hanh. I can smell the oil. It makes my head ache.'

'I can't, Mumma. It's not safe outside. How would I get to work if someone stole it? It's too far to walk to the city.'

'Who would steal it? It's only our neighbours in the hamlet. Silly piglet.'

Hanh didn't trust the neighbours any more. Since the rice crop kept failing, everyone was only out for themselves. No one said hello. Chickens went missing. Families shut their curtains when they ate.

'I'd prefer to keep it in here. Just to be certain,' said Hanh and she forced a smile to her face. She stood up and moved her bicycle to the opposite side of the room, away from her mother's view. 'Are you hungry?'

Her mother shrugged.

Hanh went to the back porch and lifted a pan from the stack of dented utensils just inside the door. She scooped it into the water urn outside and crouched at the stove, gathering her skirt to her knees. Wiping her hand across the cool bottom of the pan she drew the drips together and flicked them away before balancing the pan above the heat. She watched as the water began to simmer and took a tapioca root from the basket beside her. It sunk into the water with a satisfying splash. In a rice bowl, she mixed flakes of dry herbs and rock salt, folding them together with the blade of her knife.

Her mother watched from the mat. 'What did you get at the market today?' she asked.

'Tapioca and eggs,' Hanh replied.

'Nothing else?'

'Dinh didn't pay me yesterday.'

'What about our rations?'

'We've used them.'

'Already? Are you sure?'

'I'm sure,' said Hanh, patiently.

'I thought we had plenty left for rice and meat?'

'Not this month, Mumma.'

Water jumped from the pan and spat on the open husk. Her mother closed her eyes and hummed a quiet thought. Hanh glanced down to the basket at the little vial of gold liquid, glinting in the firelight, almost empty. She had swapped their ration of rice and meat for her mother's medicine, and already it was nearly gone. There was only enough left to last a few days, even if she just gave her a drip or two on her tongue at breakfast. The doctor was strict and he wouldn't take credit; Hanh had asked before and been scolded like a thieving dog.

Hanh dragged her eyes away from the vial. 'I saw Mai at the market. Her sister had a baby. A boy. The family are having a feast next week to celebrate. We can go if you feel up to it,' she said, trying to distract her mother from their missing rations. She liked to hear news from the hamlet and Hanh was always searching for new, happy stories to tell her.

Hanh hadn't succeeded in distracting her mother, this time. She opened her eyes and wrinkled her brow. 'You need to ask Dinh to pay you.'

'I have,' said Hanh, frowning too.

'Did you ask him politely? Good girls are polite, Hanh. You have to be polite.'

'I was. He's paid me now,' she lied. 'Don't worry.'

Her mother fell silent. Hanh peered into the pan and prodded the tapioca with her knife. The tip slid smoothly in, so she lifted it from the water, dropped it into a bowl, and went to sit cross-legged by her mother's side. She pulled apart the root in her hand, peeling the flesh from the rough skin and rolling a piece of the fibrous, white dough into a ball between her fingertips. She dipped it in the herbs and salt and placed it on her mother's parted lips.

'Eat, Mumma, it's good for you.'

Her mother ate very little and it frightened Hanh. Lately, her skin had become thin and it clung to her bones, as though it were being pulled tight by a strong hand inside her.

They ate their supper quietly. Eating was a great effort for Hanh's mother. She chewed slowly and deliberately, taking what felt like an age to swallow each mouthful. Hanh pulled her knees to her chest, trying to shrink the empty space in her stomach and battling the temptation to eat more than her share. With aching patience, she rolled the tapioca into smooth pearls and waited for her mother to finish.

The last of the root was cold by the time Hanh put it in her mouth. She looked down at the bare bowl and her stomach growled a dissatisfied complaint. She scored beneath her fingernails and licked the escaped pulp from the tips of her fingers, holding the salty morsels on her tongue and rubbing them into the roof of her mouth, until there was nothing left to swallow.

As her mother's eyelids began to droop Hanh looked around the room, chewing her lip. She saw the basket beside the stove and slid quietly across the floor towards it, slipping her hand in and digging beneath the little earthy mound of tapioca roots. Her fingers found the last mango, and she picked it out and stared at it briefly before cramming it into her mouth. She couldn't help herself. The slippery fruit wriggled in her hand and the juice ran over her skin in sticky yellow streams. She faced the wall so her mother wouldn't see.

'What are you doing?'

Hanh heard the crackle of dry bamboo as her mother

shifted on the mat. She sneaked a guilty look back over her shoulder. 'Nothing.'

'You're eating something.'

'I'm not!'

'I can hear you.'

Her hand fell reluctantly from her mouth. 'It's just mango,' she whispered.

'Hanh! That mango was for your father.'

'But I'm hungry.'

'It's not for you,' her mother snapped, raising her voice. 'Give your father the fruit.' She pointed to the family altar on the floor beneath the window. A browning photograph of a young soldier stared back, straight-faced.

'I'm hungry,' said Hanh again, angrily this time. 'What use does Father have for mango? We can't spare it.'

'Of course we can!' Her mother lifted her hand in the air and flicked it at Hanh. 'Will you be so disrespectful of me when I die?'

'Please don't, Mumma.' It made Hanh wince when her mother spoke of death so casually. 'I'm just trying to look after us.'

'Your father will look after us.'

Hanh stamped her foot against the floor, frustration kicking out of her. 'But we're *starving*!' she cried. 'My bones ache all day, and when I move too fast I see blurred colours like the sun in my eyes. And you're sick, Mother! What is Father doing to help us, now?'

'Why would he help us when you're being so rude? Give him the mango, Hanh.'

Her mother had shouted and a cough burst from the hollow of her chest, like a dog's bark. Her head thudded against the floor and she jerked on to her side and screwed her body into a ball.

'Mumma? I'm sorry, I'm sorry!' Hanh jumped up. She wiped the tacky juice from her chin and dropped what was left of the mango into her empty bowl, hurrying to the altar.

'Forgive me, Father. This is for you. Guide us and bring us fortune,' she said, bowing her head to his image. There was little stub of incense in a bowl of sand and she lit it quickly and watched the smoke rise and trace a line across her father's face. Her mother took in a long, wheezing breath. Through the corner of her eye, Hanh saw her body ease and straighten.

'Poor little piglet,' her mother sighed. 'Come and lie with me.'

Hanh shook her head. 'Not now. I'm going to the river. I need some fresh air.' She pulled her sarong from where it was hanging threaded through a hole in the chicken-wire window. She slipped from her dirty clothes and tied the thin material around her body with a tight knot. Then, she went to her mother and kissed her cheek. 'I won't be long.'

It was just a few minutes from Hanh's home to the river, and as she walked along the paddy ridges she wiped the tears from her face with the back of her hand. She remembered little about her father, having been so young when he left for the war. The few memories she had of him were

54

rooted deeply in these fields. She remembered following him as he worked, tugging at his trouser leg and begging him to tell her one of his wonderful stories. They would crouch in the rice together, and she closed her eyes to listen.

'The Emperor had eighteen sons and he fretted over who should succeed him.' Hanh had listened in wonder as her father's words floated out from the field. 'His sons were all very talented; some were wise scholars and some were fearless warriors. The youngest son had chosen the life of a farmer. He lived in the countryside and tended his land with his family.'

'Just like we do,' giggled Hanh.

'Exactly like we do,' smiled her father. 'One day, as New Year approached, the Emperor called his sons to the palace. "From now until the Lunar Festival you must go out and gather food," he told them. "Whoever brings me the most special dish will be the new Emperor." Immediately, the sons left the palace and spread out across the world, searching for the most delicious food to please the Emperor. Some of the sons went deep into the jungle and caught wild animals and game. Others sailed into the rough sea and caught bright blue crabs and lobsters with purple claws. The youngest son went back to his home in the country-side. He desperately wanted to please the Emperor. That night, Buddha came to him in a dream.

'"Nothing in the world can compare to rice," said Buddha." Let sticky rice steam, kneed it soft and mould it into the shapes of heaven and earth. Bring these cakes to the Emperor and you will celebrate the Lunar New Year as one."

'In the morning, the Emperor's son awoke and he saw that the rice in his paddies was ripe. The stems were long, the grains were golden and a delicate scent filled the air. Together, his family harvested the rice, then he washed the grains and ground them into fine flour. His wife mixed the flour with water and made a silken dough. His children built a fire and wrapped the little rice cakes in palm leaves. In no time at all, they had finished. In front of them lay two kinds of cake; one was as round as the heavens and the other as square as the earth.

'On the first day of spring, the sons returned to the Emperor with their gifts. There were extravagant dishes of steamed fish, giant mushrooms and rare, roasted peacock. When it was the youngest son's turn to face the Emperor, he carried his rice cakes and bowed. "My Emperor, this is Banh Day, a cake to celebrate the heavens. And this is Banh Chung, a cake to celebrate the earth. They are wrapped in palm leaves for protection, just as the people of Vietnam protect each other."

'Seeing his simple offerings, the other sons laughed, but the Emperor smiled as he tasted the cakes. "My son, your gifts are the purest. You have used the soil of Vietnam and toiled with your own hands. Rice is the food of all the people in our nation. You shall have the throne!"

'All the other sons bowed to show respect and congratulate the youngest son. As they celebrated the New Year together, his cakes were made throughout the land, for everyone to enjoy.'

Crouched to the ground and surrounded entirely by their crop, Hanh had trembled with excitement. 'Our family is important, Hanh,' her father told her. 'Our work is noble. We feed the people.'

The memory of her father's story caught Hanh like the wind and she stopped walking. Her father had been so proud of his land. She stood in the deserted paddy, fading into the darkness in her blue-black sarong. 'I'm sorry I disrespected you,' she whispered.

At the river, Hanh sat on the thick branch of the banyan tree. The branch was curved where she sat and hung low over the water, and the hem of her sarong draped down and rested lightly on the water's surface. Vines fell from the canopy above. Thin and grey, they willowed down like her mother's wet hair, enclosing her. As she slipped from the branch to the water, her hair and the frayed threads of her sarong were taken by the gentle current. Her thoughts drifted slowly to the Russian. His voice had been deep and measured, and his walk was tall and poised. He had seemed to be so utterly in control, so certain of himself, so unafraid. And he said she had beautiful eyes. Beautiful eyes! She could barely believe it. The words buoyed her and she lay weightless in the water, staring at the bright moon and the points of silver light that pricked the sky above her. She stretched her arms outwards and felt the heavy tension in her limbs and mind ease just slightly. For a moment, she relaxed. He could have spoken to anyone on the street, she thought. *He chose me.*

EIGHT

Whenever he slept, Alexander returned to the jungle. He felt himself back there, trudging through the thigh-deep mud that swallowed boots and bags and bodies. His glasses fogged in the steaming air and as he pulled them from his face, the soldiers around him melted into the trees. Boot prints in the sludge ahead grew and deepened and became the hollows left by tigers' feet, as big as broth bowls. He smeared his glasses down his sleeve, straightened them back on his nose and struggled onwards through the thorny undergrowth. His mind was lulled by the slosh of the mud as he hauled his body forward.

But when a bullet shrieked past his head it pierced his rhythm of movement. With the crack and thump of each shot, he knew they were coming right at him. He fell to the ground and the wet earth thrashed beneath his body. Bullets raced through the trees, scything down the elephant grass that sheltered him. The sergeant screamed orders and Alexander wanted to scream too, just to drown out the panic that blared in his head. He wrenched his arms from the mud and pushed his finger through the trigger-guard of his rifle. His body was rigid and his finger hovered above the trigger, afraid to touch it. He took short, panting breaths, but he felt as though the sergeant's boot had pressed down on his throat and left him airless. He bit his teeth into his lip until he could taste the warm, wet iron of his blood, then he closed his eyes and pulled the trigger.

And when he stopped shooting and opened his eyes his glasses were coated with mud. He looked at the men around him as they fired into the darkness ahead. They were frantic. Desperate. Hungry. These men were not here with him, he thought. They were not mired in the heat and the filth and the terror; they were old, brown show-reels, flickering as he blinked. Alexander felt completely alone. The sergeant kept yelling and Alexander closed his eyes again. He squeezed them shut and fired blindly forward and the cries of the enemy bubbled up, as if from under the surface of oil.

In other dreams, on other nights, Alexander crouched in shadow at the edge of the trees, where the mud thinned and the land had been cleared by farmers, and he looked up and scoured the trees for hidden snipers. Thick roots stretched along the surface of the ground, reaching for his ankles, ready to drag him back into the deep-green dark. He waited there, where black flies hung in clouds and made him twitch like a bullock, and he looked at the women who worked in the fields. The women put down their baskets and stared back, their eyes raking over him like machine guns. He lowered his head in guilt and shame. Alexander watched until they left, then crossed the paddies. As he crept forward, he saw the stars reflected in the shallow water and they shone like eyes; wet and wide and watching him. Alexander shivered. These were the men who did nothing to him, but whom he had killed because he was told to. Because the army controlled him. Because he was weak. He took his glasses from his face and put them in his pocket, and the eyes sunk back into the watery dark.

Sometimes he dreamed that he lay in his hammock and the darkness was smothering. He stretched his eyes as wide as possible, but there was nothing above or below or beside him but black. The more he looked for anything else, the more blackness he found and the more he panicked. Vietnam was a dark place on the very edge of the world, and here he was in his hammock, swinging out over a great abyss. He lay deathly still. A freezing wind blew in from somewhere beyond the end of the world and if he didn't hold on, it would tip him right over. As he gripped his fingers around the sides of the hammock he felt that he clung to the edge of all humanity. The rain poured down and sounded like the feet of a thousand rats, their claws pattering over the wet leaves as they charged towards him. A smell of damp decay came from the ground, from his mouldering uniform, from his skin as it rotted away from his tattered, blistering feet. He could feel his M16 rifle in the hammock beside him, the metal barrel pushing against his body, chilling him through his shirt. Disgust spread through him, like flame through paper, and he loathed himself so much that it ached. And the wind blew and his hammock rocked and his heart beat faster and faster.

Alexander woke with a gasp. The dawn had not yet broken and for a moment he lay still. His pillow was damp at the base of his neck and he could smell the stale mattress beneath him. He pressed his fingers into the dimples of the bare foam and held his breath, listening to the night. There was hardly a noise from the street below. A sliver of moon was thrown across the sky like a hammock and the stars winked at him. He shot his eyes around the room, into the corners and the doorway, watching the shapes of the furniture form and harden against the silvery light.

Alexander stood and walked to the window. With each step, his feet peeled away from the tiles with the sound of a sticky kiss. He slumped down into his armchair and rubbed his hands roughly over his face, forcing himself to be steady. His memories were waking him with increasing frequency and he wasn't sure why. It might have been being back in Hanoi, with the Party on every street corner and the threat of discovery. It was probably work as well, he supposed; for months things hadn't been going so right. There was also an ache in his gut that wouldn't quite shift, a persistent undertow of unnamed guilt that tugged at his insides and stopped him resting, even in sleep. Whatever it was, it brought the jungle back to life as quick and sharp as a gunshot. He was finding it more and more difficult too, to sift through the nightmares and pull aside the memories that were real. Many morning hours were spent at the window, painstakingly unpeeling reality from the terrible threads of imagination that had laced between them.

Alexander had joined the army on his eighteenth birthday. He had woken, dressed and eaten porridge, before marching heroically to the recruitment office at the town hall and volunteering, thoughts of brotherhood circling through his head. Everyone belonged in the US Army. It was the ultimate act of *fitting in*. His mother and father had been so proud to see their boy in uniform.

It didn't work out like he'd planned, however. From almost the first moment the chopper carried him from Bangkok and he set his polished boots on Vietnamese soil, the all-American boy he'd created began to sag. The pressure of war was exhausting: the lack of sleep, the heat, the filth, the food, the constant state of alert, the relentless shoulder-to-shoulder living, the sense of enforced, uncomfortable, obligatory camaraderie, the imprecise and draining expectation of purpose. He hated every smothering moment. He couldn't keep it up.

It was in the jungle somewhere outside Pleiku – he never knew exactly where – that the illusion he had created about himself finally buckled. His platoon had been sent on patrol through the densest jungle he had ever seen; it lay in a bowl of sunken land encircled by steep hills, where the trees were as tall and brutish as giants. The undergrowth was thick and sharp with bamboo. Low, swinging vines and pitiless rain hampered their movement.

The ambush was sudden. It came at once from the ground, the hills and the boughs of the trees, and his platoon scattered like mice, outwards in every direction, panicked and aimless. Or so Alexander had thought. It turned out that he was the only one who had run. Hours later, when the air support had swooped across the land, they found him cowering beneath the crumbling, overgrown archway of an abandoned shrine, curled in a ball at the feet of a cross-legged Buddha. The Buddha had vacant eyes and a chipped smile. Alexander had his arms wrapped over his head and piss down his fatigues. His rifle was nowhere to be seen.

His sergeant was captured that day: a well-liked man, with three kids at home and a rollicking belly laugh. The Vietcong had snatched him away in the frenzy, and it was four days before they returned him. Alexander found his body, tied to the trunk of a tree by a rope around his neck. His eyes and his teeth had been plucked from his head and the bones in his legs were broken. In the wet, broiling heat his body had swelled, and his decomposing flesh made the pools of rainwater bubble as if it were boiling.

If nothing else, Alexander knew *this* memory was entirely real. The solid column of black ants that marched over the sergeant's body, backwards and forwards, disappearing into his empty eye socket and emerging with morsels of glossy human pinkness held aloft and bobbing above their heads, was seared into the back of his retinas. He remembered how the dead weight and wallowing texture of the sergeant's bloated limbs made him impossible to lift, so they cut him down and rolled him into a poncho to carry him back to their base. They hauled a crude trail through the rough forest floor and up the side of the hilly basin as they walked, and the merciless undergrowth slit the skin on Alexander's arms, legs and torso to shreds.

At base, he washed his hands again and again, rubbing the soap right up to his elbows until his cuts were red-raw and bleeding, but his skin still smelled rotten for days. It was more than a week before he surrendered to the cramp in his empty belly and forced himself to eat some cold, canned meat from his C-rations. He imagined the brutal assessment of the commander's report, sent to the superiors in Saigon, to tell them about the tragic loss of their exceptional sergeant.

Too few men.
More manpower needed.
All hands on guns were essential.
One missing, cowardly private.

The rest of the boys in his troop looked at him differently too, after that. They didn't offer to share their whisky or weed when they sat at the campfire and passed it around each evening. They knew who the real Alexander was now, and they didn't like him. He wasn't their brother. His secret was out. He didn't belong.

It wasn't just fright, though, that had stopped Alexander from fighting. He was sorry for the sergeant's fate – of course he was – but there was something else he felt guilt for too. It was a feeling more urgent, that had gripped around his heart and held him back.

Over the years, on the news and the wireless and from men in the street, Alexander had heard clipped scraps of Ho Chi Minh's speeches. *There is nothing more precious than independence and freedom!* he would say, time after time. The words were a burr in Alexander's skin; he understood them perfectly. The Vietnamese were fighting to be themselves, without apology, or doubt, or self-pity. Who was he to stop them when all he wanted was these things too? He didn't really know what the Americans were fighting for, but he knew the cause would never be so worthy. The thought had lain in his mind, stretched out like a python, since they had found him cowering in the shrine in Pleiku.

In the chair by the window, Alexander breathed in his view of the misty Hanoi skyline and the jungle receded slowly away. It was OK, he thought. It was different now. He was in control. He was atoning.

With one last scratch of his chin, he reached forward and snatched his boots from where they were strewn beneath his chair, pulling them on to his feet and wrenching at the laces until leather gripped his bare skin. He stood up, pausing to smooth his hand across the cold metal lid of his jar, then he grabbed his key from beside the bed, and went out to find the Herder.

NINE

Phuc stood at the narrow entrance to Fán T'án Alley and peered inside. It was barely more than a metre wide, with crumbling brick walls rising high on either side, and as he squinted into the moonless dark he could see the shadows of men and hear their murmurs. The bitter smell of alcohol dribbled out to greet him.

Snatching one last glance over his shoulder, Phuc stepped forward and felt the darkness seal behind him. As he walked, he ducked his head. Peddlers were crouched against the walls like spiders and they held their cigarettes up to him and whispered pleas as he passed. There was a waft of perfume, sweet as rotten fruit, and a young whore slipped from a doorway and pulled at his wrist, mewling. He flinched and yanked his arm away, sinking his hand to the bottom of his pocket. Through the worn leather of his purse, he could feel the coil of tightly rolled banknotes, and he clutched them firmly in his palm. The alley made him nervous. He didn't belong here.

Still, this would be his last visit. He only needed one more winning day and his family would be able to start again. He would take Phuong and the children far away from their worthless shack and give them a house with strong brick walls. They would move to the furthest edge of Saigon, to a road where the buildings hid behind high iron gates, and where nobody cared where they came from. The Party would leave them alone, forever. He would be able to forget. He pushed deeper into the alley, scanning the rows of sunken archways that lined the walls, and he stopped at the one with the small sign in clear purple print. *The game is open day or night.* Heaving the door open, he stepped inside.

'Back again?' said the doorman with a thin, wet smile and a threatening stare. 'I've heard you're a rich man already, Brother. Hold tight to your wallet when you leave.'

Phuc scowled and ignored him; he'd seen this doorman in the Zones before, collecting debts, bullying and spying. He squeezed by and down the stairway, avoiding his eye. He could feel the heat of the cellar rising towards him and the steps were so steep that his weight pounded unsteadily on to the stone.

At the bottom of the staircase, the room was small and dimly lit. A single bulb had been lynched from the ceiling and he pinched his eyes between his fingertips as they adjusted to the gloom. The air was damp with the breath and sweat of a dozen men. They were perched on their stools and hunched over the table like vultures. Above them, a thick sky of cigarette smoke had risen and collected.

'Good to see you again, my lucky friend,' said Cheung Hu, from the corner of the room. His round, Chinese face was as cold and expressionless as the tone of his voice and his silk shirt shimmered in the choked electric light. Phuc couldn't help but shudder; Cheung Hu was notorious. This was the man who owned Fán T'án Alley, and all of the people who came here. He glared at Phuc and the words fell from the side of his mouth, like smoke. 'Long may your good fortune continue.'

Phuc gave a wary nod and took an uncomfortable place on the last empty stool. An enormous, mean-faced minder was standing to attention in the shadow beyond Cheung Hu, and watching him keenly also. On the opposite side of the table, the croupier folded his sleeves back from his wrists and cracked his knuckles. 'The game has begun,' he said.

Phuc straightened his spine, readying himself. When he was a boy, he had loved to play Fán T'án with his friends. They didn't have copper coins to play with like the elderly men who played on the street corners, so they stole dry butterbeans from the open sacks in the crowded markets. How his mother had scolded him when she caught them! In Fán T'án Alley, they didn't play with copper coins either. Nor did they play with beans or buttons. Here, they played with the teeth of men who hadn't paid their debts, wrenched from their open mouths as they pleaded for mercy. He looked at the large pile of chipped teeth – yellow, black and bloodied – in the dish at the croupier's side. He licked his tongue around his dry mouth and over his soft, sensitive gums.

The croupier reached to the stockpile beside him and scooped up an enormous handful of teeth. A square had been scorched in the centre of the table and he tossed them down into the burned shape and covered them quickly with

68

an upturned bowl, before raising his face to the room. 'Place your bets.'

Each side of the square was numbered: one, two, three or four. The men at the table stirred to life, muttering bets and placing payments by the number of their choice. Phuc pulled his purse from his pocket. He tugged a banknote from the coil and added it to the untidy heap by the fourth side of the square. 'Number four,' he said to the croupier, who tipped his chin in acknowledgement.

The croupier waited for the men to fall silent, then lifted the edge of the bowl just slightly. With a thin, wooden rod, he began to remove the teeth from underneath. Phuc dug his hands beneath his thighs and watched closely, listening to the dull tap of bamboo on bone as the rod flicked beneath the bowl and the pile was whittled down, four little teeth at a time. Phuc chewed the inside of his cheek until the croupier stopped, tapped his rod on the table and lifted the bowl. There were three teeth left. 'Three wins,' he said.

Phuc had lost. He clicked his tongue angrily against the roof of his mouth. The croupier whipped the money from the table and quickly counted through it with a roll of his thumb at the corners of the crumpled notes. The man sitting next to Phuc stretched across the table. His fingers curled upwards, brown and withered like dead lotus petals, then snapped shut as the croupier dealt him his winnings. Keep calm, thought Phuc, as he watched with envy. It's just a hitch. The croupier reset the game, shovelling teeth from the stockpile to the square, and Phuc pulled another note from his purse and squeezed it tightly in his palm. His luck would come back. He would win this time.

But Phuc didn't win the next game, either. He lost, again. Then again.

Then again.

He stayed at the table and played until the air in the cellar had thickened into a hot fog and his eyes began to water, and his stomach felt sick. He stayed so long that he saw every man around him win, but his luck still wouldn't join him. He gripped the edge of the table, feeling the wood, worn smooth by worrying hands. A dry lump of inevitability was clogging in his throat.

'Shit,' he hissed, as another useless game came to an end.

Cheung Hu walked out from the corner of the room. 'How many games have you played today?' he asked, staring at Phuc through slitted eyes.

Phuc wiped his brow with the back of his shaking hand. His head was throbbing. 'I don't know,' he mumbled. 'Thirty. Maybe more.'

'How many have you won?'

'I haven't won any.'

Cheung Hu threw his hands into the air. A jade ring flashed on his finger and the smoke scattered around him. 'You've lost thirty games? What terrible fortune! I've never heard of a streak like it!'

Phuc looked away, embarrassed. He could hardly believe such dreadful luck was possible. He shoved his stool back from the table and stood to leave.

Cheung Hu stepped towards him. 'You can't go now.'

Phuc shook his head. 'I can't lose any more money.'

'But you can't go home without anything in your pocket. What would your wife say?'

Phuc flinched at the mention of his wife. It was true. Phuong would be a tigress if she knew what had happened. He thought of the lie he had told her about where he was going this evening, and the scar-faced Party official on his street, and the dangerous promise he had made for his family. 'I can't lose any more money,' he muttered again, weakly.

Cheung Hu cocked his head to the side, looked at Phuc and then slipped to block the stairway. 'There is always something a man can gamble,' said Cheung Hu, calmly. 'Play one more game with me.'

'I can't, Brother.'

'Of course you can, if the stake is worth playing for. We'll run a special game – just you and me – and if you win, I'll give you back ten times the money you've lost today.'

Phuc's head snapped suddenly up. 'Ten times my money?'

'Yes.' Cheung Hu nodded.

'And what do you want if I lose?'

Cheung Hu stepped forward, leaned in and whispered.

'No way,' said Phuc. He shook his head again and tried to move back, but Cheung Hu's minder had shifted behind him. He placed a heavy hand on Phuc's shoulder, and Phuc could feel himself sink back on to his stool. 'It's too big a risk.'

Cheung Hu stepped closer and was staring intently. 'What good has ever come without risk?'

'You're asking too much.'

'I'm offering *ten times your money*, Brother. That must be almost 5,000 dong? Imagine what you could do with cash like that.'

Cheung Hu bent low to Phuc's ear and spoke softly, like a demon on his shoulder. Phuc felt Cheung Hu grip his bicep, and a cool pressure soaked through his shirt. With ten times his money, Phuc could pay his debt and start a new life, far away from the threat of the Party. He could buy a house outside the city. He could build high walls and bolt the doors, and keep his family safe, forever. He could take them on holiday to the sea – like he used to – and they could eat fresh fish for breakfast and supper every night of the week. The boys could go to a far better school. Kieu would find a good husband. If he went home now – without a dong in his pocket – they would all end up in the camps, for sure. The possibilities ripped through his conscience like a squall.

Cheung Hu waited, patiently. 'You can win, Brother,' he said. 'No man can be unlucky forever.'

Phuc felt his head slowly nod. 'Fine,' he said at last, though he still wasn't sure that he meant it.

Cheung Hu spun away from the table and pointed at the croupier. 'Play!'

The croupier hurriedly scooped a fresh set of teeth from the stockpile, dropping them on to the table and covering them with the bowl. 'Pick your number,' he said to Phuc.

The air in the room settled to become so quiet and still that Phuc was sure the men around him must all have felt the shake of his breath. They had perked up and made no effort to hide their amusement, smirking at each other and raising their ragged eyebrows. Phuc took his hands from the table and pressed them together in his lap, kneading his knuckles into his clammy palms. 'Number one,' he said nervously.

The croupier's rod licked under the bowl, and Phuc closed his eyes and drunkenly listened to the click of the tooth-pile shrinking. Was he a fool to have bet so boldly? Cheung Hu's grip had been tight. His fingertips were strong, hooking around the blade of his shoulder and pinching into him. Could he ever have refused? He hitched himself up and cracked his neck with a shunt of his head to the side. The sound of his bones shot through the air and across to the croupier, who paused for a moment before resuming his count. I don't need to be afraid, thought Phuc. My luck is due.

The croupier stopped counting and the room was silent. He placed his rod on the table and his eyes darted briefly to Cheung Hu.

Phuc looked at them both, kicking his stool away from the table with a thunderous scrape on the stone floor. A desperate groan escaped from between his lips. 'Just tell me!'

Cheung Hu nodded and the croupier lifted the bowl. 'Two wins.'

The croupier's words struck Phuc like bullets and he fell against the cellar wall and gasped for air. His eyes were burning with tears and he blinked wildly and tried to steel his focus on the death-black shine of Cheung Hu's boots as they swept across the room towards him.

'I'll give you ten days,' Cheung Hu said, crouching down and whispering coolly.

Phuc cried out and writhed on the floor. Cheung Hu could have given him a hundred days to pay; it would have made no difference. There was no way he could ever pay this debt. He was a dead man now, for certain! Cheung Hu stood and Phuc lurched out and grabbed his ankle.

'Please!' he begged as a huge, rough hand clamped around his bicep and yanked him sharply back.

'Get rid of him,' said Cheung Hu.

The minder nodded and hauled Phuc to standing. He dragged him around the table, across the room, and his feet stumbled and tripped on the steep cellar steps. He could hear himself shouting – pleading, cursing and fighting like he never had before – but it made no difference. The minder forced him upwards, and at the top of the stairs, he rammed Phuc's body into the thick wooden door. The weight and the speed of them both threw it open, and Phuc fell to his hands and knees like a dog in the alley, and vomited over the doorman's white shoes.

TEN

The brothel was an ageing town house, squeezed on to a shard of land on a street at the edge of Hanoi's French Quarter. It rested in shade behind sycamore trees and on days like this, when the wind blew east, the leaves were woken and waved like little girls' hands.

Inside the house, the hush was uneasy. Alexander walked through the hallway and his boots echoed on the tiled floor. Sitting girls lined the walls, their arms linked and gripping each other. As they pulled their legs back from his path, they cast their faces down and hair fell over their sunken eyes. One girl moved her hand over her forearm to hide a blueing bruise. She picked nervously at the polish on her fingernails and little orange flakes fell to the floor, like hot embers. Alexander recognised her. She must have been here a year or more. She was probably eighteen now. She looked it too. They'd get rid of her soon.

As he climbed the staircase at the end of the corridor Alexander heard a shuffling of bodies as the girls untangled, and their murmurs stirred the quiet in his ears. Upstairs, dawn pushed through a threadbare drape and the light in the hall was given a pinkish cast. There were no customers now and the curtains over the doorways hung still and silent. Only their tasselled edges quivered as he passed.

When Alexander was almost at the end of the hallway, his own image caught his eye. A curtain was pinned back and he stepped forward into the room, towards his reflection. He was looking thin, he thought, and tired. He'd been working hard recently. His skin appeared pitted and pocked in the lead-speckled mirror-glass, and he touched his fingers to his face. He saw a girl behind him, curled and asleep on a bowing mattress. A string of fairy lights topped the mirror and as they sparkled, his shadow danced across the sleeping girl. Above her, where the wallpaper was torn and the plaster was bare, small grey handprints pushed against the wall. Alexander took a sharp breath as the girl stirred, rolled over and looked at him, then he left the room without a word. Cramming his hands to the bottom of his pockets, he marched to the only doorway covered by dark, heavy wood, paused, and pushed open the door.

The Herder was sitting at a table by the window, shuffling a deck of cards and dealing them out to the empty seats beside him. This was his brothel: one of the many he owned throughout Vietnam. Alexander hesitated in the doorway. It was always wise to assess the Herder's mood before barging in. He wasn't the sort of man to tolerate barging, but some days he took it worse than others. Alexander didn't like to make him angry. Even when sitting, his size was striking; his body seemed to swamp the tiny wooden table. Tall and broad, his jawbone, his neck, his shoulders and his chest were knotted tightly together and set like a great Russian bear. His hair hung almost to his chin. It was thin and straggly, clumped in rat-tails, and his lips were drawn in by the slimmest of smirks, as if something amused him. He lifted a pile of cards from the table and fanned them between his enormous fingertips, considering his hand for a moment. Then he held his head just slightly down and looked out through the top of his eyes, like a wolf.

'A little early for you, Alexander?'

'Couldn't sleep.'

'Too many women in your bed?'

'No.' He shook his head, as if a scrap of tacky dream still clung to him.

The Herder laughed and looked at him, pityingly. 'Of course not.'

Alexander pulled a chair from the table and eased himself down. He felt better already, just being here. He always felt better, when he saw the Herder. He had known him for years now, but never by any other name. As far as Alexander understood, he had given himself the title. The Herder called his girls straying cows. He found them at the side of the road, in dry fields or empty market squares, and he rounded them up. They were the poor, the unhappy, the lonely and the lost. They had deep-brown, innocent eyes and long fluttering eyelashes. They were trusting. He promised them work or food or friendship, and they always followed him. His skill was masterly.

★

Alexander remembered their first meeting well; it had been in a bar in red-light Bangkok, when the war was still raging. The night was sweltering, the air syrupy-thick with spirits and sickly-sweet perfume. Grunts and leathernecks, still in their military uniforms, sang, staggered and hooted at the girls, who danced on the bar in cheap lace bras, flicking their dark hair and childlike hips in time to the music.

Alexander had sat alone in a booth, awkwardly hunched and uncomfortable on the fake leather seat. Sweat leaked from beneath his thighs and the fold of his knees and it dribbled from the hollow of his back into the crack of his arse. His leg twitched beneath the table. He didn't know where the rest of the boys from his platoon were. The chopper had dropped them in the city on a weekend pass from Pleiku just a few hours earlier, and they had showered, shaved and drunk two bottles of whisky before heading out. They did not invite Alexander.

He stared down and swilled his wine in the cloudy brown tumbler. He had asked for whisky too, but the bar didn't have any. He took a gulp and the Herder had sidled up to him, like a dream. He had sat unnervingly close. Though the music was blaring, he didn't raise his voice. He seemed to strike a tone that wriggled below the sound and swam to Alexander through the thick air, calm and easy.

'You don't look like you are enjoying yourself. Don't you like my women?' he said in his deep Russian accent.

'Not much,' Alexander replied. He felt angry, but he didn't know why.

'Why are you here if you don't want a girl?'

Alexander couldn't answer. He had been drawn to the neon lights, the noise, the crowds of people, the chaos. Not to the women.

With the flick of his wrist, the Herder cocked a Marlboro from a packet of cigarettes. He offered it to Alexander. 'Are you enjoying the war?'

Alexander frowned as he took the cigarette. He wished he was enjoying it. He'd thought he would do, before he came here. He thought he'd enjoy it more than anything else he'd ever done. The Herder held out a light and Alexander leaned in.

'The first kill is like your first love, don't you think? It's unforgettable. My girls are unforgettable, too. A man will only kill if he wants to live. These girls are here to remind men why they should want to keep living.' He paused and smoke was held on his lips and in the hole of his mouth. 'Do you want to live, Soldier?'

'I said I don't want a girl,' replied Alexander, the words sounding flat as he forced them out. He realised his hand was shaking and he placed it on his knee. The Herder stretched his fingers around Alexander's wrist and steadied him.

'My friend, I have something far better for you.'

When Alexander looked back, he saw how easily the Herder had read him — just like he read the girls. Real unhappiness is impossible to hide. It seeps out through the skin and men can smell it. Unhappiness makes for easy pickings.

He was glad the Herder had found him, though. It was

fate. That night in the bar, he offered Alexander everything he needed. Escape and opportunity were placed on the table in front of him, much sweeter and more intoxicating than any whisky. Someone had faith in him too. The real him. They could be a team. He couldn't resist.

The Herder gave Alexander lodgings in a Bangkok suburb; a tranquil, whitewashed room with painted blue shutters, on the tenth floor of a building that faced the morning sun. He had spent many weeks of instruction there, and he learned so much about women. There was more to wooing them than he had practised before – much more than a compliment or a tightly held hand – and he had to learn which ones to pick all over again. His back to the open window each morning, Alexander had listened in silent awe. The breeze had kissed the sores and scabs on his body and eased their itching. He had felt like the war was blowing away.

Alexander soon found that the Herder had bars in Hanoi as well as Bangkok. It was easy to do there; the North respected the rich, strong Russians and with a well-placed bribe or two each month, he could strut around unchallenged. An American was valuable too, though. They could move more freely in the US-held South, and the Herder wanted Alexander to help him expand. They set up a den in Saigon at first – before the war had even ended – and now, the Herder owned brothels across Vietnam. Though he stopped in Hanoi for the most part, he always found time for patrolling between them. Alexander never stopped anywhere much. The Herder didn't let him.

The Herder could sell any girl with ease, but there were some he wanted Alexander to find more than others. He wanted them young and he wanted them virgins. That was where the money was. In the brothels, he would hold on to girls like that for weeks on end. He was a patient man. Alexander had known him to bide his time for many months, until he was offered a price that he thought was right. If he could get a foreign customer, that was best. They would always pay top price for a pretty young virgin. The Herder was not so concerned with the girls after that. He would work them until they were worn as soft as chamois and their value would fall, punter by punter. Most local men waited until the girls were older and cheaper and when a girl was eighteen or so – too old or too used to make him any money – the Herder would cast them on to the street to fend for themselves. Putting them out to pasture, he liked to call it.

The Herder did not keep all the girls he found. The pretty ones for brides, he said, the ugly ones for brothels. Alexander liked selling brides the best. He liked to think his girls were on their way to somewhere happy. He liked to think he helped them. An image rested in the corner of his mind and it winked at him from time to time: a girl sleeping soundly in a strong brick house, her breast rising and falling with her breath, her husband lying beside her, his protective hand on her brown-skinned thigh. Yes, that was the image that soothed him. Helping the girls was as much a lure as the promise of teamwork and brotherhood. All those men he had killed in the war – he didn't know how many – they were husbands, sons and brothers. They were fighting for freedom, just like

Sure, he'd been picky, but he always was. Things had to be right. The Herder never used to be so impatient. Silence sparked quick in the sluggish air, and the Herder stared expectantly.

'Are you going to tell me about her?' he said, at last.

'This one is wife material,' Alexander replied. 'She's not a whore.'

The Herder's lips nipped together, creasing. 'You're a romantic, Alexander. They're all whores.'

'No, I mean she's pretty. Pale skin. She'd be wasted in the brothel.'

'How old?'

'Fourteen. Perhaps fifteen. She looks young.'

'Family?'

'I don't know yet.'

'City girl or country?'

'I don't know.'

'You don't know much, do you?' The Herder scowled. 'Where did you find her?'

'In the Old Quarter. She's a squat-girl.'

The Herder spat a laugh across the table, rolling his eyes and baring his teeth. 'You want to bring a squat-girl to my brothel? You think the punters like their girls stinking of crap?'

'She's a good find. Real potential. Trust me.'

The Herder leaned forward, slowly and deliberately. 'You haven't given me much cause to trust you, lately,' he said. His glare whipped critically over Alexander's face. 'Are you going to behave this time?'

Alexander dipped his head instinctively. 'Of course.'

'You remember what we talked about?'

'Yes.'

'No more bullshit?'

Alexander shifted in his seat. It had not gone well with the last girl he'd found, but he wouldn't call it *bullshit*. It hadn't been his fault. Not really. He'd lined up a girl from the Red River Delta; a sweet little thing – not pretty – but podgy and soft, with slight buck-teeth and blind naivety. She'd have made a good wife. The buyer had been a bastard, though; five 'wives' at home already, chained up to a fence. He lived in the North – beyond Sapa – not far from the border with China, and each day he'd send them creeping over the steep, slender gashes of land between the check-points to smuggle back contraband. Weapons, cigarettes, heroin. Animal bones, ground to fine powder. Ivory. Bear bile in tiny clear jars. Like a schoolboy, he bragged to Alexander about how much his women could hide beneath their hats and in the crevasses of their bodies, and the money they made him. He used to have eight wives, he said, but the soldiers had long-range rifles now: a gift from the Russians. He needed replacements. How could Alexander lead his Red River girl to a future like that? He'd told the Herder she'd fled when she'd seen, and he hadn't been able to catch her. The Herder knew the truth, though: he'd let her go.

'I'll do better this time,' Alexander mumbled, still looking down.

'I should fucking hope so,' the Herder bit back.

'That buyer was a dog.'

'I don't want to hear it, Alexander. No bullshit means

no fussing over buyers and no moaning about where the little whores end up. I don't want to listen to one word of your redemption drivel.'

Redemption drivel. Alexander clutched his hands together to stop them shaking. He could feel the tug beginning again inside him. He desperately wanted to help his girls, to make up for the things he had done and apologise for killing their husbands and brothers and leaving them all alone. He wanted to be sure that wherever they went, they'd end up OK, but he wanted to make sure that *he* would end up OK too. Whenever the Herder was angry at him, Alexander couldn't stand it – it gave him more dreams and more gnawing doubts. The Herder was the first genuine friend he'd had, the only person to accept him as he really was. He knew he couldn't face being alone. He needed the Herder to prop him up.

'I'll behave,' he said firmly. 'I promise.'

The Herder's stare narrowed thoughtfully. He turned the Six of Clubs in his hand and rasped the edge through his dry stubble. Alexander saw him push his tongue against the inside of his cheek and a thin bubble of moisture swelled and then popped at the corner of his mouth. He wiped it away with a rub of his thumb. 'All right,' he sniffed. 'I'll find a buyer.'

Alexander tapped his fingers on his knee and leaned back in his chair, exhaling. 'Thanks,' he said, relieved.

A wide grin leaked across the Herder's face. 'Don't get comfortable,' he said, licking his lips. 'You need to go out and round the little heifer up.'

ELEVEN

The market clung to the edge of the East Highway, stretch-ing along the straight leg of road between Hanh's hamlet and the next, and sprawling away into the dusty landscape beyond. A breeze blew along the stalls and the air was sweet and fresh. Papaya, dragon fruit and mangosteen were stacked in brightly coloured pyramids, and thin chillies rested in a dish, like hot chippings of rainbow. A girl sifted through the fruit, turning each piece in her hand and examining it as Hanh and Thuy walked by.

Inside, the hot air stilled and thickened. Faces of vendors peeped out from behind high piles, and they hawked their goods and chattered amongst themselves. The aisles were narrow and Hanh held her basket to her chest. Thuy was following behind her, chirruping a story about a dog and a rat, but Hanh wasn't listening much. There were only a few tickets left in her ration book, and she was trying not to look at the tables laden with tempting treats. Dried shrimps were heaped on dishes and in bags as big as barrels, the little orange and white curls like babies' fingers. Chickens had been crowded into mesh cages and they quarrelled for the empty dust at their feet. She passed a butcher who hacked at the carcass of a pig. He cleaved through the bones with a crunch and a thud on the wood, and the flies that had settled were thrown into the air in frenzy. A woman crouched at his side, shaving the belly of another dead pig, the razor running along the wiry skin with a rasp. Hanh's mouth began to water and she stared at the pig, her feet slowing. She hadn't tasted meat in months.

'Hey!' A man with a fat stomach shoved past her, knocking her into the table. 'You're blocking the way,' he said, striding down the thin corridor and turning from view.

Thuy puffed out her cheeks and stretched her eyes wide open. 'Fat monkey!' she whispered.

Hanh snorted a giggle. She loved coming to the market with Thuy. Though the tables of food made her stomach moan, she always looked forward to the time they could spend together. Thuy's calm, unworried attitude made her feel lighter. No matter how bad her day had been, Thuy could always make her laugh. It had been that way for as long as Hanh could remember. When they were small, they had spent every day in the paddies, catching crabs for their mothers to boil into soup or knotting strips of grass into bracelets. They would hide in the tall rice and sneak up on birds, making them jump in the air and squawk with surprise!

Thuy's family had always been good to Hanh, too. She lived with her mother, father, one set of spritely grand-parents and four cheerful, boisterous brothers. Their house was always loud and full of energy; it was so different from Hanh's. The past few years in the hamlet had been tougher than any. The Party, the drought and the failed crops had wrapped around the villagers and squeezed them tightly.

87

Hanh's neighbours had withdrawn, too busy with their own struggles to help with anyone else's, but Thuy's family still made her feel welcome. She could trust her. She could relax, just a little, when Thuy was around.

Thuy took hold of Hanh's wrist and skipped on through the market. Hanh's feet were beginning to drag and a thick yawn escaped from her mouth. She had woken early again to sweep the house and prepare her mother's breakfast and had worked in the paddy all morning, with a heavy basket slung on her hip. Now, she had to take the shopping home and check on her mother, and cycle into the city to work at the squat this evening. It would be hours before she could rest. A little muscle tensed in her stomach.

'Do you have everything you need?' she asked Thuy.

'Almost.'

'Hurry up, will you? I need to get home soon.'

'All right, grumpy tortoise. Just one more thing.' Thuy pulled Hanh towards to the spice-seller's stall.

Powdery mountains of ground spice were lined up, red, gold and yellow, like the landscape in the setting sun. Thuy called the woman who owned this stall the Big Stain; she sat all day and chewed on betel, a deep red dribbling from her mouth, colouring her teeth, gums and lips and creeping away in the lines of her skin.

Thuy reached over the table and picked up a small bottle of fish sauce. 'How much is this?'

The Big Stain mumbled a reply.

Thuy wrinkled her flat nose in the middle of her pretty, round face. 'That's more expensive than last time.'

The Big Stain shrugged.

Thuy haggled her down, tore a ticket from her ration book and put the bottle in her basket.

Hanh waited impatiently. 'Are you ready now?'

'Ready,' said Thuy with a smile. 'Let's go.'

As they made their way out of the market, voices were rising at the edge of the road. A young vendor was busying around her fruit stall. Her hands scrabbled frantically between the piles of fruit, on the shaded ground beneath her table, in the little tin box on her stool. She was talking to a man who was slouched in a chair at the stall next to her own and Hanh could hear a fleck of panic in her voice.

'Where is my money?' she said. 'It's gone!'

The man watched with mild amusement. A mosquito buzzed about his face and he waved it aside with a stump of a hand. 'There are thieves everywhere these days,' he replied.

'You said you would watch my stall.'

'I was watching it.'

'Then where is my money?'

'Perhaps you lost it?'

'No. It was here! Someone has taken it.'

'I haven't seen a man or a monkey anywhere near your stall.'

The girl stopped searching and stood suddenly upright. She shoved her messy hair back from her red, crumpled face. 'Then it must have been you who took it!'

The man's voice tightened and the smirk fell from his lips. 'I didn't take anything.'

'You did! You took it.'

'Listen, you scraggy bitch, if you're stupid enough to leave it here, you deserve to lose it.'

The girl burst into tears. 'Please give it back,' she begged, holding the empty tin box in a limp hand at her side. 'I have to feed my son.'

'Didn't you hear me? I haven't got your money. Leave me alone.'

'But my husband—'

'Your husband will teach you a lesson if he has any sense.'

The man stood and kicked his stool at the girl, who backed away like a cornered dog. Hanh stared, anger bubbling in her throat. The girl slumped into the seat behind her stall, sobbing into her sleeve and fussing, trying to arrange her fruit with shaking hands.

'Let's go,' whispered Thuy, touching her arm. Hanh didn't move and Thuy pulled at her harder. 'We can't do anything. Come on, let's go.'

Hanh tore her arm free from Thuy's grasp and marched towards the man, her fingers wrapped into fists. 'Give her back her money!'

'Hanh!' Thuy hissed urgently.

The fruit girl jumped up from her stall and looked at them aghast.

'What's it to you?' said the man, scowling at Hanh.

'She worked hard for that money.'

'Get lost.'

'No. Give it back.'

The man choked a laugh. 'And what will you do if I don't?

Do you have strong brothers I should be afraid of? You must have, to be this bold! That or you're a mad little runt.' He ground his stumpy hand into the cup of his opposite palm. 'I've got strong brothers too,' he hissed.

'Ouch!'

Thuy had twisted the skin on Hanh's arm and yanked her back. Hanh spun around. Thuy's face was horrified.

'Hanh, stop it. You're making more trouble. Please, let's go.'

Hanh let Thuy drag her away, out of the shade of the market and into the road, and she felt the man's stare burn into her back like the sun.

'You can't do things like that, Hanh,' said Thuy. She had linked her arm through Hanh's and was clutching her tightly, as if she thought Hanh might run back.

'He took her money,' said Hanh, swinging her basket angrily at her side.

'Don't worry about her. She's a stallholder. That's a good job. She'll make the money back.'

'But she earned it. He had no right to take it.'

'Maybe, but it's none of your business. Don't you have enough of your own trouble to worry about, without looking for more? She wouldn't have done the same for you.'

Hanh shrugged and exhaled deeply. 'It's so unfair,' she said. She stubbed at the road with her toe and felt Thuy cling a little tighter.

'Disgusting Dinh still hasn't paid you, has he?'

'No,' said Hanh stubbornly.

'You should quit, Hanh.'

'Then I'll never get my money.'

'You're never getting it anyway,' said Thuy. 'You need a man to look after you.'

Hanh screwed up her face. 'I can look after myself.'

'They're not all like the man at the market,' Thuy chirped. 'I'm going to marry someone from the city with a good job and a proper house. I'm going to find a good man.'

Hanh didn't know what a good man was. She couldn't imagine any of the city men she knew, the ones who came to the squat with their greasy coins, grazed knuckles and alcoholic breath, were *good men*. 'Husbands are just more work,' she frowned. 'I have enough work already.'

Thuy laughed. 'That's the way life is, Hanh. You have to accept it.'

Hanh looked at Thuy with affection. She wished she could accept things like Thuy did. 'Besides, if I got married, who would look after my mother?'

'How is she?'

'Not great.'

'Is the medicine working?'

'I don't know. I thought her wheeze was quieter last night, but it's hard to tell. This morning her face was greyer than dishwater.'

'She'll be OK, Hanh. She's a tough old goat.'

Hanh watched the steps of her feet. 'I hate just leaving her. Did you know Mai's family were robbed last week? They came in the night while her family were sleeping, right into the house. Her father chased them away. What could I do if they came to our home?'

'You'll be fine,' said Thuy dismissively.

'That's easy for you to say. Your father and brothers are in your house too. You're safe.'

'I thought you said you don't need a man? You could chase them away yourself, I reckon. With a temper like yours, they'd scatter like chickens!'

'Shut up, Thuy.'

'Not that they'd bother coming to your house, anyway. I wouldn't, if I was a robber. What would they steal? I don't think you have much to worry about!'

'What about my bike?'

Thuy laughed. 'Your bike's a lump of scrap, Hanh. I can hear those wheels screeching from across the paddy.'

'It's not that bad.'

'How would they make their getaway? The whole village would know where they went.' Thuy was still gripping tight to Hanh's arm and taking two skip-steps for each of her angry strides. They reached the fork in the road, where the pathway splintered and ran away to their different houses. They stopped and Thuy gave Hanh's arm one last squeeze. 'Listen, I'll look in on your mother tonight.'

Hanh let out a weary breath. 'Thanks, Thuy.'

Hanh hurried down the track to her home, through the tunnel palms and into the open paddies. She looked up, towards the sun. She would need to be quick to get back to the city on time. Her basket was almost empty; she had never come back from the market with so little. She couldn't afford to give Dinh a single excuse not to pay her. The ladder shook as she rushed up to the porch and pushed open the door.

Her mother was lying on her mat, and she opened her eyes as Hanh walked in. 'Little piglet?'

'Hi, Mumma,' she said, dropping the basket to the floor inside the door.

'You've bought us a feast!' said her mother, grinning. 'What a good girl I've raised.'

'I bought some apples. Do you want one?' said Hanh, already grabbing the fruit from the basket and beginning to slice it into a bowl. She put it on the floor by her mother's side and then crammed another apple into the pocket of her skirt. She went to the stove and lit the fire. As the husk began to smoulder, she took the dirty bowls from their breakfast and swilled them quickly in the urn outside.

'Do you want anything else, Mumma?' she said, shouting in from the porch as she chucked the dirty water down into the paddy.

Her mother took a thin piece of apple from the bowl and sucked it. 'Come talk to me.'

'I'm just cleaning up.'

'Stop rushing around, piglet. You're making me dizzy. You can do that later.'

Hanh came back inside, drying her hands down her skirt. 'I can't, Mumma. I have to do them now. Do you want anything else before I go out?'

Her mother looked up, surprised. 'Where are you going?'

'I've got to go to work. You know that.'

'Again?'

'Yes, Mumma.'

'In the city?'

'Yes.'

'But you went last night.'

'I have to go today too. We need the money.'

'Stay a little longer, piglet. Sit with me while I eat.'

'I can't.'

'I've been on my own all day.'

'I know, Mumma. I'm sorry.'

Hanh stood still for a moment, her mother by her feet. The air outside was quiet and still, and as the light grew deeper, casting long shadows through the little mesh windows, Hanh imagined wiry, leather-skinned thieves drinking hooch by the river, stalking barefoot through the paddies, prowling through her hamlet like grey cats at night. She ducked back to the stove and picked a large knife from a bowl. As she bent to the floor to kiss her mother goodbye, Hanh slipped the knife under the edge of her mother's sleeping mat, leaving just the tip of the silvery handle peeping out from behind the bamboo.

'Thuy said she'd come by while I'm out,' said Hanh as she pushed her bicycle out through the doorway.

Her mother sighed. She lifted a heavy hand and wafted Hanh's words away. 'Silly piglet, don't worry about me. You've already lit the fire and I have enough food. I'll be fine until you're home.'

Neither of them mentioned the robbers at Mai's house,

but as Hanh pulled the door shut behind her she saw her mother's eyes in the firelight, wide and shining, like those of a frightened mouse.

TWELVE

Phuc walked straight to the back of the tobacco store. The woman behind the counter eyed him meanly, leaning on the glass cigar cabinet and polishing a silver lighter with an oily blue cloth. The shop was long and narrow and when he glanced back, he could barely see the street. A clutch of enormous lanterns hung above the doorway and crates were stacked on either side, obscuring his view and trapping him in. He breathed deeply and tried to slow the drum of his heart. From floor to ceiling, box upon box of imported Russian cigarettes stared back at him, flush against the wall and neat as tiles. His eyes darted over them, searching for the giveaway. He scanned the regal gold-on-red of the CCCP packet, the Kocmoc with the faceless silver astronaut floating though deep blue space, the blue-and-yellow map on the Belomorkanal, the world's strongest cigarette. *I'd kill for a Belomorkanal*, he thought.

It had taken Phuc all morning to find this place. He had scoured every alleyway in Cholon, asked every store owner, every street vendor, every wandering man who crossed his frantic path. Nobody knew where it was, they said, and they shifted their eyes nervously aside to avoid his stare. If it weren't for the beggar in the courtyard at Binh Tay Market

– whom he bribed with a bowl of hot broth – he might never have found it.

On the wall of cigarettes, there was one panel wider than the others. It was covered by glass, expensive Sobranie Cocktails sheltering behind in pastel boxes. This had to be it. Phuc felt a chunk of peanut wedged into a molar at the back of his mouth and he chipped it free with his tongue and swallowed it down. His girls had cooked him a good breakfast. With the thought of them both at the front of his mind, he clenched a fist and rapped on the glass. He heard movement. The panel swung open and light flooded into a room hidden behind. Phuc bit his lip and swallowed a gasp. A man stood in front of him, tall and square-jawed, with his nose flat to his face. He wore a suit, but it fitted badly, straining over his broad shoulders and bulging at the seams.

'Get in,' he growled.

Phuc stepped forward and the door clicked shut behind him, like the sound of a pistol being cocked. He spun around and saw that the wall was lined with boxes of bullets, as neat as the cigarettes on the other side, but black and grey, as if they were their shadows. Racks of guns covered the walls around him, Kalashnikovs and Makarov revolvers glinting in the dim light. Grenades hung from nails in the wall, swinging precariously by their pins like unripe fruit. There was a slim, battered metal door directly opposite and he could smell the rust that cowered in its dents. The room was cool as a tomb.

A girl was sitting at the desk in the centre of the floor. Balancing her hand on a wad of banknotes that must have been eight inches high, she stretched her fingers wide apart and carefully painted her fingernails. She didn't look up. The desk was messy, strewn with papers. There were two empty coffee cups, a plate of untouched pastries and a shallow dish filled with little glass vials that glittered like liquid gold. Cheung Hu was sitting behind the desk too. He threw a squinted scowl at Phuc. 'I don't like to be bothered,' he said.

Phuc was silent; he couldn't think of a thing to say. He had planned to threaten Cheung Hu, to charge into the secret room and punch him square on his pale jaw and force him to change his mind. Now, as Cheung Hu stared at him, Phuc felt a weakness as though his bones were melting.

Cheung Hu glanced at the girl as she began counting gold bullets into a small black box. She picked up each bullet between finger and thumb, and the wet red polish on her fingernails shone like blood. Then, he looked back to Phuc. 'Why are you here?'

'I heard you are a reasonable man—'

'Whoever you heard that from was misinformed.'

Phuc hesitated. He had to be braver if he wanted to fix this. He raised his chin. 'I thought that we could make a deal.'

'We already have one.'

'There must be an agreement that would interest you?'

'Our deal is not negotiable.'

'I can get you money.'

'No you can't.'

'I just need some time.'

'I don't need your money.'

Phuc could feel his desperation rising and his hands began to shake. He clasped them together and squeezed. 'Let me work for you.'

'No.'

'I'll do whatever you ask.'

'Why would I want you to work for me? Look at you. You beg like a beaten woman. Any vagrant I take from the street would have more strength than you.'

'I'll work hard!'

Cheung Hu took a cigar from his top pocket and spun it in his fingers. A smile shuddered momentarily at the crease of his lips. 'Did your wife cry when you told her?'

Phuc felt a pain in his stomach, as though Cheung Hu had reached inside him, gripped and twisted. He took a staggering step forward towards the table. The man who opened the door was standing in the corner of the room, hands behind his back, expressionless. The girl kept counting.

'Tell me what I can do,' Phuc pleaded.

Cheung Hu sighed, long and deep. 'You have come here, uninvited. I have been patient. I have listened. But this is not my fault. There is nothing left to say.'

'You can give me your mercy.'

'Go home.'

'Please!'

Cheung Hu nodded to the man in the suit, who removed his jacket and slung it over the back of a chair. Phuc looked at him, then at Cheung Hu and then at the girl, still sorting her bullets without interest. The man in the suit stepped forward and shoved Phuc hard. His body clattered against the metal door at the back of the room. The man moved forward again, cracking his knuckles in his palm and Phuc fumbled with the bolt in panic, orange rust powdering in his hands. The door exploded open and he tumbled into the hot, bright light of an empty back alley.

The man came after him, wrapping his giant hand around Phuc's arm and pulling him to standing, and Phuc scrabbled to steady his footing on the loose-stoned ground. The man gripped Phuc's elbow tightly and yanked him to face Cheung Hu, who now filled the open doorway and hid the room beyond.

'Listen,' he said, snarling. 'Bring me your daughter, like we agreed, or I'll come to your house and take her. If I have to chase you, I won't be pleased. I might have to take your wife as well, as compensation, or have my pick from the rest of your pink-cheeked litter. Don't make me do that, Brother.'

Phuc's mind flashed back to the cellar in Fán T'án Alley, to the heat and the gloom and the anticipation, to the leaden, irresistible pressure of Cheung Hu's hand on his shoulder and the words he had whispered, as cool as ice: *My doorman tells me you have a daughter.*

'Wait!' shouted Phuc, but Cheung Hu was already closing the door behind him. The next thing Phuc felt was a fist on his face like a mule-kick. He fell to the ground with a thump and then there was black.

THIRTEEN

'Are you able to pay me today, Uncle Dinh?'

Hanh looked at Dinh and waited impatiently as he rammed a fat finger up his red nostril and rummaged around. They were standing at the entrance to the squat passageway. The street was bustling and the air was stagnant. Skewers of meat hissed on a grill-pan and smoke rose as they charred. It collected beneath an awning, engulfing the shabby bird that swung in a cage from the corner of the canopy and it thrashed against the bars, its yellow breast puffed out and shrieking. Dinh sucked a breath through the side of his mouth and wiped his shining finger down his shirt. 'Not today,' he said, shaking his head.

Be polite, thought Hanh, remembering her mother's words. Good girls are polite. She blinked heavily; the type of blink that flicked aside a wayward thought. 'What about tomorrow?'

'What about it?'

'Can you pay me tomorrow?'

Dinh took another long, dramatic breath. 'Not sure. The Party's been watching me. You know I can't pay you when the Party's watching.'

Hanh's jaw gritted. 'I haven't had my wages for a long while now, Uncle.'

'We live in difficult times.'

'I've been here almost every day. I've stayed late too, and I always clean the squat after you've gone.'

'After I've gone?' Dinh raised a matted eyebrow, a hitch of surprise in his voice. 'Are you saying I don't work hard?'

Hanh shook her head, quickly. 'No, Uncle. Of course not.'

He scratched his neck and pretended to think. 'I can't give you any money today. You'll just have to manage on rations for now, like everyone else.'

Hanh glanced down at Dinh's belly, and then at the bulge of wobbling fat beneath his chin. He was not a man who survived on rations. The churn in her stomach was more than just jealous hunger. It was more than anger too. It was fear. She thought of the basket she'd brought back from the market and the feeble provisions she had managed to buy. They wouldn't last long and her mother needed more medicine. 'It's been twelve weeks,' she pushed.

Dinh's face puckered. 'It hasn't been that long.'

'It has. Please, Uncle. My mother's sick.'

'What's that got to do with me?'

'She needs fresh food. I can't get enough with the rations, and I have to buy medicine. That's why I need this job.'

'Listen! You're very lucky to have any job.' Dinh held his finger to her face and scolded her, sharply. 'What if I pay you here and someone sees? The Party will find out about my business and they'll shut me down. You'll get no money at all.'

Hanh squeezed her tongue between her teeth to stop herself from shouting. Of course the Party knew about his business; everyone in the Old Quarter knew. Why else would she sit here every afternoon? It was a stupid excuse. Everyone in Hanoi had a way of making extra money. She put her hand behind her back and chipped at the crumbling wall in frustration.

'I know, Uncle. Thank you. I won't make any trouble, I just need my money. You don't have to pay me here. I can come to your house.'

Hanh instantly regretted her words. Dinh's eyes flashed along the length of her body and he glared at her, his face chewed to a squint.

'You'll come to my house?' he said, straining forward.

Hanh's muscles tensed, and she held her breath and braced her spine against the wall. He stared harder and she thought he was going to touch her, but then he jumped, as though his flesh had been suddenly pinched.

'Maybe next week,' he sniffed, and he pushed his finger back up his nose and ambled coolly away.

Hanh kept her breath held and her eyes on Dinh until he turned the corner at the end of the street. Shuddering, she eased herself from the wall and slumped to her chair. She stubbed her toe angrily against the cracks in the pavement. Being a good girl was utterly useless. Dinh would never dare to treat her like this if her father was alive. She glanced along the line of open shop-fronts on the opposite pavement, looking absently for faces she knew, and then slipped her hand in her pocket. Her fingers twitched through the little pile of coins she had collected this evening. Dinh would never know if she took one. She pulled out her hand

and stared at the coin resting in her palm. It was tarnished and grey, but shamelessly tempting.

'Hello, Hanh,' said a sudden voice above her.

Hanh thrust the coin back into her pocket and her head snapped up, startled. The Russian was smiling down at her. She managed an awkward, hangdog half-nod.

'Thanks for the directions yesterday,' he said.

Hanh wriggled in her seat. Had he come back just to say thank you? She hadn't thought for a moment she'd see him again. 'That's OK,' she mumbled, uneasy. He'd remembered her name.

'You know the city really well, don't you?'

Hanh nodded warily. Her head still felt a guilty muddle.

The Russian kept smiling. 'I've been to Hanoi a few times,' he said, 'but I always get lost. The streets are a maze. I was wondering if you could show me around when you finish work?'

Hanh shook her head and threw a heavy frown at him. It was late already. Her mother was at home with the knife slipped under the edge of her mat, and even if it weren't for the thought of the robbers at Mai's house, she wasn't about to go wandering around Hanoi after dark with a strange, unknown Russian. Did he think she was stupid?

He took a forward step and ducked a little, towards her. 'What about tomorrow?'

Hanh felt her face screw tighter. She didn't want to be rude and make him angry, but she couldn't understand what he wanted. There must have been someone else he knew who could help him. She stared up, sceptically. 'You want me to show you around Hanoi?'

'Yes.'

'Around the whole of the city?'

'Yes, or just the Old Quarter. Wherever you like.'

At the bottom of Hanh's belly, there blinked a tiny, curious flutter. She'd seen girls with white men before – through the open doors of restaurants and bars – and she'd always thought they sat a little taller. They didn't have things to worry about like she did. White men were privileged. Rich. They could give girls protection. Perhaps, just for an hour or so, she *could* show him around. What harm would it do, in broad daylight? She could walk beside him, with her chin held high and pretend she was someone else for a while, someone safe and important. Maybe they could walk by the café, and if Dinh was there, she could shoot him a look and make him think twice about robbing her.

'All right,' she said, feeling suddenly brave.

The Russian's smile widened. 'Great! Shall I meet you here?'

Hanh thought for a moment. She didn't want to meet at the squat. Those girls she'd seen in the bars would never have met a man at a toilet! The lake was close by though and would be easy for him to find. She never normally went there; it was surrounded by peddlers and drunk, homeless veterans were always sprawled on the benches, but if she went with a Russian, with his white face and strong arms, nobody would trouble her.

'Do you know Hoan Kiem Lake?' she said. 'It's just south

of the Old Quarter. I can meet you there in the morning.'

'Perfect.'

'At eight a.m.?'

'Thanks, Hanh.'

He said goodbye and Hanh wrinkled her nose in disbelief. He strolled away and she pushed her hands beneath her thighs, to stop them shaking. She wasn't sure what had happened, but it felt exciting. She couldn't wait to tell Thuy.

Skipping up from her seat, she peered into the shop beside the squat; the clock said almost 8.40. She wasn't supposed to leave before nine, but Dinh wouldn't come back now. With a quick look along the street, she slipped into the alleyway and wheeled her bicycle from the shadow at the end, then she cracked the padlock closed across the stinking squat's door and pushed away into the Old Quarter.

Outside the city, Hanh cycled beside the dark, empty paddies, listening to the rasp of the insects arguing. At the roadside, children scrambled like rats around the overgrown graves at the old French cemetery. They froze when they saw her and stared wide-eyed, their sharp cheekbones greased white by the moonlight. The market was deserted, the tables empty of goods, and the space behind them was hollow-black and cavernous. She sped past a lonely rest stop with a shuddering flag and a dozen empty hammocks rocked, ghostly in the breeze. The shadow of a stork slipped silently overhead.

Hanh knew that the world was watching her, listening and judging, but she didn't care. She still felt brave. Gripping tightly to the handlebars, she powered her feet on to the pedals until she couldn't make them spin any faster. As soon as she was home she would cook supper for her mother. Then she could go and see Thuy and tell her about Alexander. She swerved from the highway, tearing down the track to her hamlet and skidding to a stop in the gravel outside her home.

The door creaked when she opened it. Inside, the fire was low, the light was thin and the sour smell of illness smothered the air. Her mother was lying on the mat and her breast was heaving.

'Hanh?' she said, rolling stiffly to face the door. 'I'm glad you're home. I've missed you.'

'Hi, Mumma. How are you feeling?'

'Strong as a bear.' Her mother smiled and flashed her gums.

Hanh tucked her bicycle into the corner of the room. 'That's good. I'm going to see Thuy after supper.'

Her mother pursed her lips. 'We don't have any firewood left.'

'It's OK, we have rice husk. That will do until morning.'

'It's not good to run out of firewood, Hanh. When you have a husband, you won't be able to run out of firewood. What would he think of you? A woman with a cold house!'

Hanh opened the door to the back porch and crouched by the stove, lifting the rice urn from the floor to her knee. She removed the lid and began to stir through the left-overs from breakfast with a wooden spoon. The dry rice flaked apart in the red clay. 'It's warm tonight,' she said. 'You won't be cold.'

Her mother shook her head. 'I think you should collect some wood from the river and then come home.'

'I'll ask Thuy if we can borrow some,' Hanh replied, still chipping at the rice.

Her mother hit her palm angrily against the floor. 'Only a lazy girl runs out of firewood!'

Hanh dropped the spoon into the urn and looked at her mother, hurt. She wasn't lazy. She'd been up since dawn and had worked all day, first in the fields and then in the city. Didn't her mother realise? Dry paddy-mud still lined the arc of her fingernails and the muscles in her back were knotted and raw. She could smell the squat on her hair and skin. She was tired and hungry, and all she wanted to do was see her friend.

'I'm sorry, Hanh,' her mother sighed. 'I feel like I've been spun around and around by the wind. I'm exhausted. My nerves are weak. Please don't leave me alone again.'

'I won't be long, Mumma. I promise.'

Her mother rolled on to her back and closed her eyes. 'A promise must be strong as a soldier.'

Hanh swallowed a tut from the tip of her tongue. She had never understood why her mother said that. The soldiers she'd seen were thin and sickly, not strong. They walked with their heads bent down.

When she was young and the war still thundered, they had passed through the hamlet, often. She would sit on the porch and scan their downturned faces, waiting for her father to return. He'd been gone for months, then a year, then longer. She missed his stories and wanted to show him how well she had tended the rice in his field. Bombs had fallen in other paddies: giant, terrifying rocks that shook the earth and exploded into golden fire when they landed. They demolished the crops, leaving deep craters that filled with water when the rains came, and nothing would grow for seasons. Hanh had kept watch on her father's paddy, though. Every night, she had sat on the porch and guarded it until long after dark, when she couldn't hold her heavy eyelids open any longer. Her father's land was important. She kept it safe for him.

Sometimes, the soldiers who passed through the hamlet would stop at her neighbours' homes for food and shelter. Only one ever stopped at Hanh's house. She was feeding the chickens on the pathway when he came from behind and grabbed her wrist. She cried out and dropped the grain in her hand. His uniform was torn and his toes hung over the ends of his rubber-soled Ho Chi Minh sandals. She remembered his smell, like damp wood from the riverside. There was dark on his uniform, like wet, but it wasn't.

'Where is your father?' the soldier demanded.

'The jungle swallowed him,' Hanh had replied.

The soldier barged inside her home and Hanh had glanced anxiously around the quiet, empty fields before hurrying after him. Inside, his rifle and helmet were on the floor, and her mother was standing with her back to the wall, eyes panicked. 'Go outside, little piglet,' she told her.

The soldier had stayed for supper; they ate soup with peanuts. Afterwards, he sprawled on Hanh's mat, leaned against the wall and stared at her mother. His lip snarled up at one end and his fingers fiddled with the buttons on his shirt.

That night, he slept in his hammock outside, but Hanh could still smell him. She crept to her mother's side and wriggled beneath her arm. 'I don't like him, Mumma.' she whispered.

'He's a soldier, like your father.'

But, he wasn't like Father, she thought. Not at all.

The following day, Hanh had found a little brown bug snuggled up in the bend of her arm. She rushed to the stove, where her mother was cooking. 'Mumma! Look! It's from him. He's dirty!'

'It's just a tick, Hanh. Come here,' said her mother, smiling. She lit a match, let it burn for a second, then blew it out. She held Hanh's hand and pulled her arm straight, then pressed the hot black end on to the body of the insect.

'Ouch!' Hanh yanked her arm from her mother's grip.

Her mother laughed. 'Silly piglet, it didn't hurt. See, it's gone now.' She picked the tick from the floor and it crackled as she threw it into the fire.

Hanh watched her mother's face as she wiped the crease of her arm with a damp cloth, then she glanced outside to the soldier's swaying hammock. 'Why is he here?'

Her mother didn't answer.

Hanh clutched at her skirt, held still by the quiet. 'Mumma?'

The afternoon sun was low in the sky and steam rose from the broth in the stockpot. Hanh saw it lick away from them as her mother exhaled.

'He wants to feel normal,' she said, and she sounded so weary. She rubbed her face with the hem of her blouse, and then took a tin of condensed milk from the basket on the floor. She peeled back the lid and gave it to Hanh. 'Here. Take this to him.'

Hanh frowned. 'But I was going to have that after supper. It's mine.'

Her mother grabbed her roughly by the shoulder and Hanh saw her muscles flex against her bones and stretch so tightly that she thought they would snap if she didn't let go.

'Hanh! This is Vietnam and you are a woman. Nothing is just for you. Not condensed milk, not the sun in the morning, not anything else. Get used to it!'

The memory of the soldier sobered Hanh's excitement. She lit the stove and warmed the old rice without speaking, then filled a bowl and fed her mother. She ate her own share slowly, feeling the thin layer of rice lying warm at the bottom of her stomach. Leaning back, she took the pin from her hair, and let it tumble from her chignon. She slipped her feet from her sandals, stretched her legs and wiggled her toes in the heat that spilled from the stove.

'I thought you were going to see Thuy?' said her mother.

Hanh shook her head. 'I've changed my mind.'

Now she had something just for her. A secret.

FOURTEEN

Phuc came round to the sound of a fly as it murmured above his leaking cheekbone. He lay on the ground in the alley and his vision flickered in shades of faded blue. His mouth tasted of warm blood and gravel and his neck was as stiff as bamboo. There was only one thought in his mind: *Get out of Vietnam.*

As he raced across the city, his thought grew and a plan took shape. He turned it over in his aching head and examined it from every angle. He would get a boat to take his family far away from Saigon. They would sail to Hong Kong or Malaysia and apply for asylum in the United States. They would move to California. He would start a new business and save his money to buy a house. The children would go to good schools. Phuong would be able to sleep at night. Cheung Hu and the Party would be as far away as the cold, white moon.

By the time Phuc reached the Saigon port, he was certain he had found the only solution. The gates were ajar, and he clattered through them and sprinted across the bleak concrete yard before the guard had a chance to lumber up from his seat.

'Hey! That's restricted!' the guard shouted after him.

Phuc kept running, as fast as he could, and he didn't look back. Enormous metal containers were stacked in rows and they towered into the sky; red, blue and sour yellow. He could hear the guard still bellowing, and he ducked down a narrow corridor between the stacks and headed towards to the water that glimmered in the distance. He could see that a ship was docked, but the cranes that hung above his head were eerily quiet and still. His steps rebounded against the walls of the containers. Quick and sharp, their echo was a pressurised drumbeat. Diesel clogged the air, stinging the wound on his face and he could feel his eye being pushed shut by the swelling. He emerged from the end of the corridor on to the open stretch of waterside, and caught his breath in a moment's rest. There were a few men scattered on the tarmac and he quickened his step again, darting between them and scanning their faces. He needed to find Tam.

Tam was the perfect person to help him. They had been friends since childhood. As boys, they had lived on the same street and walked to school together. Each morning, they'd rip sheets of paper from the backs of their notebooks and make vessels to race in the overflowing gutters behind the temple on Bac Street. Tam had been his protector, taller and more wiry and always up for the fight when the older boys stamped on their sailboats. Phuc would pay him back with copied homework, sums and spellings scribbled in pencil for Tam to trace over in dark black ink.

These days, Tam worked for the Government Shipping Company. He had a good job, running the cargo route between

Saigon and Can Tho, and he gave Phuc work whenever he could. Phuong didn't like him much. A scabby sheep, she called him. All sorts of things hidden beneath his fleece. Phuc knew him better than she did, though. Sure, he liked a drink and a girl, and he always had a thin-spun story about his pocketful of money, but his heart was honest and loyal. Most importantly to Phuc today, Tam was the kind of man who knew the men Phuc didn't.

At the far end of the quay, Phuc could see a group of men milling in the open doorway of container. Tam was sitting on a chair in the middle of their circle. He had a clipboard on his knee and was talking to a scrawny deck-hand with rope-brown, tattooed arms.

Phuc tore towards them. 'Tam!'

'Hey, Brother!' Tam shouted back. 'There's no work today.'

Phuc ran nearer, and Tam's expression dropped. All the men had turned and were all staring, and Tam stood up, grabbing Phuc by the elbow and drawing him away from the group, towards the deserted waterside.

'What happened to you? Shit! Clean yourself up.'

He yanked a handkerchief from his pocket and handed it to Phuc. They stood in the shade of a rusting ship. Rubbish knocked against the bow and a slick of black oil meandered across the surface of the water.

'I need your help,' said Phuc as he wiped his face.

'What do you want?'

'Can you get me on one of your boats?'

'There's no work going at the moment, Phuc.'

'No, I mean . . . can you get me *on one of your boats*?'

Tam let go of Phuc's arm and glanced over his shoulder, towards the group of men who were watching them, unabashed. He shook his head. 'I don't do that any more. It's too risky.'

'Don't lie to me, Tam. I need you to help me get out of Vietnam.'

'Shit, Phuc. Shut up! Are you trying to get me arrested?' Tam lowered his voice to a whisper and studied Phuc's swollen eye with suspicion. 'What happened to your face, Brother?'

'It doesn't matter.'

'It matters to me. I bet it will matter to Phuong, too. What happened?'

'I can't tell you.'

'Why not?'

Phuc sniffed and sticky blood surged again at the back of his throat. He looked at the logo on Tam's breast, the little yellow hammer and sickle, and imagined lying on the ground outside his home; he was pinned to the earth by the sickle around his neck and a Party official was bringing the hammer down and smashing his mangled face. He took a deep breath and looked Tam in the eye. 'You know I wouldn't ask unless I was desperate. Just tell me whether you'll help me.'

Tam took two cigarettes from his pocket, lit them both and passed one to Phuc. He sunk a drag and shook his head, again. 'You won't be able to afford it.'

'I'll send you the money when I get to America,' Phuc

cried, snatching hold of Tam's hesitation. 'I'm going to start another business. I'll pay you back.'

'I'd be a fool if I took credit.'

'How long have we known each other, Brother? You can trust me.'

Tam paused. 'Are you sure you have to do this?'

Phuc nodded, and Tam pulled his cap from head. He rubbed his sleeve across his brow, sighing heavily. 'OK. I'll get you a space on the next boat.'

'I need five spaces.'

'No way. You can't take your family. It's too dangerous. Get to America first and send for them later.'

'They have to come with me.'

'Not possible.'

'I'm not going without them.'

Tam slapped his cap angrily against his thigh. 'Listen, Phuc. My boats are old. They were built for the rivers. The South Sea is a demon. If a storm hits, who will you help – your wife or your children? You'll be hungry and thirsty and you'll need your strength to save yourself. And what if the pirates find your boat and Phuong and Kieu are with you? It's madness! You don't know what you're saying, Brother.'

'Why are you telling me this?'

'Because you're my friend. You're a good man. You look after your family.'

Phuc looked away, ashamed. He'd done a really good job of looking after his family this time. 'Please, Tam,' he begged. 'I have no choice.'

Tam puffed out his cheeks and sighed again; it was a long, shuddering sigh, thick with smoke. He knotted his fingers behind his head, tipped his face to the sky and closed his eyes. 'Fine.'

Phuc grabbed Tam's hand and shook it, holding him tightly. 'Thanks, Brother.'

'But you need to get organised.'

'I'll do anything.'

'The boat takes two weeks to get to Malaysia. You'll need enough food and water for the whole journey. Don't bring anything else. There's no room. Once you get to the islands, they'll ask who's sponsoring you in America, so think of someone you know will help. Don't tell the children. Children talk, and if the Party catches you, you're going to prison for sure. You'll have to hide in the cargo crates to start with. There will be inspections before the ship leaves port, so put your head down and keep your boys silent. Don't move until the crew tells you. When you're far enough away from land, another boat will be waiting to take you to Malaysia. There will be about fifty people with you. Watch your back. I'm not happy about this, Phuc. Can you swim?'

'No.'

'Well stay in the fucking boat then.'

'Right. Great. Thanks,' said Phuc, still gripping Tam's hand and trying to take the information in. He was so excited he struggled to concentrate. A sense of relief was spreading over his body, like sunlight.

'We'll probably leave at the start of next month—'

'Next month?'

Phuc's hope fell like a stone to the bottom of a big, dark sea. Cheung Hu would be looking for him in just one week! The Party could come back to his house any day. He had to get out of Vietnam. He needed to go now!

'Sorry, Brother. Next month is the best I can do,' said Tam. 'The pirates have been busy. We've only got two boats at the moment and they're already out. It will be three weeks at least before they get to the islands and back. It depends on the weather too. I won't send the boats if the rains come, so I can't say a day for sure. But I'll let you know as soon as I can. Phuc?'

Phuc let go of Tam's hand and his arms fell limp by his side. The bloodied handkerchief dropped to the ground and a new hit of pain smacked his chest, sudden and crippling. He turned and staggered away from the waterside. The sound of Tam's voice swilled in the air around him and pushed into his ears, but he wasn't listening, and a tear welled up and stung his swollen eye.

FIFTEEN

Alexander walked almost entirely around the lake before he found her. She was sitting on the north shore, in the shade of an Indian oak. She didn't look as calm as she had done yesterday, or as confident. Her shoulders were hunched and she was gnawing her lip.

'Hi, Hanh,' he said, sitting down beside her.

She mumbled a reply at the ground, not meeting his eye.

Alexander positioned himself on the bench, the distance away of an invisible man, and he angled himself just slightly towards her. The canopy of the oak stretched lazily over-head and the bright morning sun shone through the leaves, making them glow citrus-green and yellow. He looked across the blue-green water towards Jade Island. The Ngoc Son Temple was hidden from view by a thick wall of trees, but the gentle red arch of the Huc Bridge rose from the water, like the back of a sleeping dragon. Hanh had certainly picked a beautiful place to meet. He liked her for it.

'What a wonderful day,' he said, and he meant it. 'How are you?'

'I'm fine,' she said, quietly. She was staring forward across the lake, and her forehead was crunched into lines.

Alexander wasn't surprised. He had always known she

would change her mind about showing him around the city. She wasn't ready for long conversations with a rich white man; having to take charge and guide him to places, ignoring the stare of the city on her back. He knew she couldn't cope with it. Not yet. She was far too fresh and unprepared. Still, she had met him, and that was enough. Now, he just needed to keep her here long enough to find out what she was thinking. If he knew her thoughts, he could begin to shape them. If he could shape her thoughts, he could control her. He could fold her up and put her in his pocket and carry her wherever he wished.

'Pineapples! Bananas! Rose apples!'

The distant voice of a fruit vendor was carried across the water by the warm breeze. He came into view, edging around the side of the lake, taking short, quick steps and straining beneath the weight of his baskets.

'Are you hungry?' Alexander asked.

Hanh shook her head.

She was lying. He raised his hand to the fruit-man, who scurried over and dropped down his baskets.

'What can I sell you, Brother?' he said.

'Two oranges.'

The vendor nudged his head towards Alexander and winked in Hanh's direction. 'You like sweet fruit?' he said, with a look of amusement.

Alexander growled as he took the oranges and paid him quickly. The vendor snatched the money, lugged his baskets to his shoulder and shuffled away with a wry smile.

Alexander glanced at Hanh, but she didn't seem to have

noticed the comment. Her eyes were fixed on the fruit that lay on the bench between them. He picked up an orange and dug his nail beneath the skin, peeling it away from the flesh and pushing a segment into his mouth.

'I haven't had any breakfast,' he said, through chews. He lifted the other orange and held it out to Hanh. 'Are you sure you don't want one?'

Hanh hesitated, staring at the fruit with parted lips. For a second, he thought she would refuse, but then her small hand rose from her knee and closed slowly around it. 'Thanks.'

Alexander watched as she pared back the peel. It was as though she were trying to make her movements as small as they could possibly be. She held the fruit in her lap, head bent down and arms still, and only her fingers were moving. Slowly. Carefully. Quietly. She was afraid to be seen, thought Alexander. He let her have her moment of privacy. They ate in silence.

Alexander felt no rush to speak. Patience was one of his greatest strengths – just like the Herder. Moments of quiet like this were as important as anything he could say. Silence put a girl at ease, far better than questions or chatter. Besides, silence was more truthful than words. Girls like Hanh rarely said what they really thought. It was the little details of their bodies that gave them away.

Hanh finished eating and wriggled in her seat. 'I can't show you around,' she said abruptly.

Alexander pretended to look surprised. 'Have I done something wrong?'

'No,' said Hanh. 'I just have to go home. My mother will be waiting for me.'

She was looking into her lap and tugging at the ring on her finger, but she didn't stand to leave. Alexander knew it wouldn't take much to keep hold of her. 'You live with your mother?' he said.

She nodded.

'Does your father work for the Party?'

'He's dead.'

This was a detail too sweet to miss.

'My father is dead too. It's lonely sometimes, isn't it?' said Alexander, wrapping Hanh up and swaddling her in her own reflection. He watched with satisfaction as her shoulders dropped and she sank down into the little thought he had spilled.

'Sometimes,' she mumbled.

'But I'm sure your mother looks after you well.'

'My mother is sick.'

Excellent, thought Alexander. 'I'm sorry,' he said.

'It is what it is,' said Hanh, with a deep, in-breath.

'She must be very proud of you.'

Alexander was careful of the tone in which he spoke. He wanted his words to float through the air as soft as a feather, but land heavy as rock. He knew it had worked. He saw them hit at the moment Hanh blinked, and her pupils shrank in her nut-brown eyes.

'Is it far to your home?' he asked, interrupting her thought.

'A few miles east of the city.'

'That's a dangerous road to travel alone.'

123

'I travel it every day.'

Hanh shrugged and stood up from the bench, but Alexander saw her eyes flitter nervously along the lakeside. They searched through the shadows beneath the trees and paused on the men who loitered and smoked. They swept over the cyclo drivers who dozed in their cabs, and by the children who bickered and teased the cat with the missing eye. She was looking for threats, he thought, with a shiver. As clouds rolled over the blue sky and hid the sun, Alexander felt the peace of the lake dragged down into the darkening water, and Hanh's fear crawled out. She was afraid of what would happen if she stopped looking over her shoulder. She was afraid of being alone. These fears were real and sharp and right beside them.

'Mama!'

A child's scream kicked up beside the bench. A young boy had tripped on the pavement and he bawled for his mother as he lay on the floor. A woman heaved him to standing by his fat little wrist and crouched in front of him. Brushing the dust from his palms and knees, she spoke to him softly and the boy quietened.

Hanh was riveted by them. Her eyes were sad and dewy, like a calf's. The look on her face was all Alexander needed to regain himself.

'I guess we all need family to keep us safe,' he muttered, as though only to himself.

Hanh's stare, which had been locked on the child, snapped back to Alexander, like a snare on a rabbit.

'I agree,' she said, a tiny note of wonder in her voice.

He smiled, and then, quick as a whisper, she had gathered her bag, smiled back and was gone.

Alexander sat for a moment and looked at the empty seat beside him. She really was a pretty one. *Sweet fruit.* The Herder would be pleased. He leaned forward. His leg was twitching. There was something about their meeting that troubled him; a detail he could touch with the tips of his fingers, but not quite grasp, and as he strained, he seemed to nudge it further away. He was sure it was not something they had said or done, but something that hung in the air around them, like the hot threat of a storm. He stood and moved behind the bench, to see if the conversation looked different from there. *It is what it is.*

He left the lake and headed into the Old Quarter. Hanh was still trapped in his head and she flittered like a fly in an upturned glass, knocking against the inside of his skull. He didn't like the way she had glanced around, her head and body deathly still, but her eyes alert and darting. She had the look of a hunted animal. Alexander understood how difficult it was to survive alone, without anyone looking out for you. Vigilance was exhausting. A motorbike tore past him and coughed thick diesel in his face, and he covered his mouth and felt a sudden, urgent need to know her better. How had her father died? In the war? Was he shot by Americans? Alexander blinked and a vision of Hanh's father flashed over him: he was lying face down on the ground in the jungle, his eyes squeezed shut, the sound of his own irregular breath echoing underneath his helmet, little bursts of air popping up through the mud as he gasped, like a carp in a drying pool.

The Old Quarter was as crowded as ever. The pavements were dominated by the overspill of shops, by endless rows of parked bicycles and by shirtless men, clustered in groups, drinking home-brewed wine. Women were huddled in every scrap of shade, rocking their children in their laps and whispering. A bucket of water was thrown from a passageway, and it splashed across his feet and simmered on the tiles.

Alexander had walked this way before; not through the same streets and alleys, but with the same heavy downward pressure on his shoulders and throb of necessity in his chest. It was the morning he had left the US Army base for the last time. He had marched through the streets of Bangkok, chin raised, steps long and decisive, but without any conscious thought to direction. It was only when he had reached the bar in the red-light district that he realised he had been looking for the Herder.

He crossed the teeming street without a look and the bicycles swerved to dodge him. High-pitched bells shrieked in his ears, someone swore, and he ripped around the corner away from them. He looked back, and then at what lay on the pavement ahead, and it was too late to stop when he saw the workman. The man was crouched on a low stool with a pile of metal tools at his feet. Alexander smashed through them, scattering the tyre-pumps, key-cutters and chisels from the kerb to the gutter. The workman glared up and muttered under his breath, dragging his equipment towards him. Alexander thrust a tattered work-belt back with a stub of his toe, and the polished grey of a whet-stone snared his eye. Yes! That was just what he needed. He snatched his knife from his pocket, unfolded the blade and held it out. The workman stared at him. Alexander sniffed. Like he didn't sharpen a million of these. There was a moment like a stand-off, and he felt the workman weighing him up.

'Two dong,' the workman said at last, a hint of a slur in his speech.

Alexander pinched shut an eye, and tipped his chin in agreement. The workman kicked away his slippers and squatted with one bare foot on the end of the whetstone, gripping with his toes to hold it still. He tucked his knees to his chest and began to grind the knife over the small cube. His toes were just an inch from the blade and his fingers were oiled and shining. Alexander watched impatiently, his stare snapping back and forth between the workman and the street. As soon as he had let go of his knife he wanted it back. The workman held the blade to his face, smoothing his fingers along the metal. He raised it up higher, examining it closely and an old military pith-helmet slipped back on his head. It was darkest green and the peak ran all the way around, throwing a band of grey on his face and neck. Alexander hadn't noticed the helmet before – he had been so distracted – but now it made him shudder. The war was following him. He was sure of it.

'Were you a soldier?' he asked. He couldn't help it.

The workman looked at him blankly.

'Did you fight in the war?' Alexander said again, pointing

to the battered helmet. He laced his voice with his strongest Russian accent. He was too aware of himself, the real himself; the disgusting, violent American.

The workman removed his helmet and tapped the side of his head with a fingertip. In the space where his ear should have been, there was a coil of scorched gristle, dry and yellow. The skin around was stretched tight and his hair fled away, like black at the edge of burned paper. The workman went back to the whetstone in silence, his toes whitening as his foot pressed down. Alexander chewed at the shredded flesh inside his cheek and focused on his knife in the soldier's hand. He had seen the North Vietnamese Army in action; they were brave, brutal fighters. If he stabbed me now, Alexander thought, it would be as much as I deserve.

The soldier stopped grinding the knife, rubbed it with his oily fingers and then handed it to Alexander. Alexander paid and strode purposefully away, ramming the soldier to the back of his mind. Holding the knife in his pocket was helpful, but he still had an itch at the back of his throat, a lump of something unpleasant, and he couldn't clear it. He would go and see the Herder, he thought. He didn't feel like being alone.

Outside the brothel, Alexander paused in the shade of the sycamore and looked up at the quiet building with its long shuttered windows and crumbling paint, just drawing in the sense of drowsy contentment. He pushed through the wrought-iron gates, opened the front door and stepped into the cool, tiled corridor. The snap of his heels echoed from the walls and ceiling as he passed the row of sitting girls and climbed the staircase, two steps at a time. He walked along the hallway, his hands folded in the pit of his arms and he stopped at the door to the Herder's room. He went to push it open, but then caught himself and knocked. There was a dull reply and he turned the handle.

'It's only been two days. I haven't got a buyer,' said the Herder, looking up from his table at the window. 'Impatience is a vice, Alexander.'

'I wasn't expecting a buyer.'

Alexander felt suddenly embarrassed and his voice dropped mute. He loitered in the doorway and gripped the wooden frame, waiting for the Herder to offer him a seat. A girl was standing in the corner of the room with her back to them both, and Alexander could hear the rumble of a boiling kettle and the chink of metal on crockery.

The Herder didn't invite him in. 'So how's it going?' he said.

'I'm fine,' Alexander muttered.

'Not you. The girl. You sorted her yet?'

Alexander didn't reply. His head felt thick.

The Herder laughed. 'You're getting slow! Maybe it's your frown she doesn't like. You should try smiling.' He grinned and pointed teeth hung in his mouth, like bats in a cave. Alexander felt himself sag under the weight of a long, awkward pause. The Herder eyed him suspiciously. 'Why are you here, Alexander?'

'I was passing.'

'Passing on your way to where? We're a mile from the

Old Quarter. There are no squat-girls to sweet talk round here.'

'I've been working already today.'

'You must have worked hard, to earn a break by half past nine.'

'I was. I met her at Hoan Kiem, this morning. I bought her fruit. Don't worry.'

There was another weighty pause as the tea-girl brought a cup and a sugar-pot to the table. The Herder heaped a teaspoon of sugar into the brown water and tapped the spoon on the rim. His bored eyes sunk back to the table. 'I reserve my worrying for better things than what you ate for breakfast,' he said as he flicked a glossy page of his magazine.

Alexander caught a flash of naked skin on the fluttering paper and shifted his weight, uncomfortably. Hanh would be back at home by now. She'd be with her sickly mother, and they'd have nothing but the memory of her murdered father to nourish them. He didn't want her to be a whore, like the girls in the photographs.

'What kind of buyer do you think you'll get?' he asked, carefully.

The Herder replied, without looking up. 'A rich one.'

'I didn't mean that.'

'I know what you meant. You agreed no bullshit, Alexander. Remember?'

Alexander nodded and gripped the doorframe tighter to stop the shake of his hand. 'No problem.'

The Herder examined another page of white flesh and

then looked up, glaring. He rested his elbow on the table and held his cup in front of his mouth. 'Are we done?'

'Right. Yes. I'll come back tomorrow.'

'Don't bother. I'm flying to Saigon tonight.'

There was a jump of panic in Alexander's chest. 'You're leaving?'

'I've got business to check on.'

'When will you be back?'

The Herder raised an eyebrow, his cup still suspended by his thick, cracked lips. 'I didn't realise I needed to tell you my travel plans?'

Alexander squirmed and glanced at the floor. 'For the buyer, I meant. That's all.'

The Herder placed his cup on the table and sighed wearily. 'You look stressed, Alexander.' He pointed at the girl who had brought him the drink, now sitting on the floor and leaning against the wall. She was fanning herself with a scrap of card, torn from the box of teabags and her black hair flailed in its gasp. 'Go on, take her. Relax.'

Alexander shook his head.

'Why do you never use my girls, Alexander? What's wrong with you?'

Alexander flinched. 'Nothing's wrong with me.'

'You do like girls, don't you? I can get you a boy, if you'd prefer. A goat? A bullock? A bear! I assure you, I can't be shocked. Tell me what you want.'

'I don't want anything.'

'When was the last time you had a proper hard fuck, Alexander? It'll do you good.' The Herder slapped both palms on the table and threw his chair suddenly back. He seized the girl on the floor by her wrist, pulled her up and wrenched her towards Alexander, like a rag doll. 'I insist,' he said, holding out her arm and smirking.

Alexander released the doorframe and wiped his palm down the legs of his trousers. His eyes grazed over the girl, not her face, but down the length of her neck and over the slopes and points of her tiny body, catching on the needle-point scratches inside her upheld arm. He stepped nervously forward and took the proffered limb. It was limp and impossibly light, bird-like in his fumbled grip. The Herder nodded, pushy and firm, and Alexander nodded back, as much to move himself as in agreement.

He led her to the corridor, and then into a room. His mouth was dry. The girl was tugging at her skirt before he had even pulled the drape across the open doorway, and it dropped to the floor when it reached her knees. Without an instant of thought or ceremony, she pushed her under-wear after it, not bothering to move the little snatch of grey material from where it lay knotted around her ankles. Exposed from the waist down, she stood with her shoulders slumped, her knees turned together and her head a little to the side, and looked at Alexander, flat-lipped and impassive.

Alexander didn't move. He was waiting to feel the heat inside him. He was willing it. He hadn't screwed a girl since he'd come to this country. Not one. He'd wanted to. He'd tried. Not just brothel-girls like this one, either. He'd picked some up in bars and rushed them home, stripping them ravenously down, but when he came to clamber on top of them, he couldn't do a thing. He knew he could do it this time, though. He needed release. The pressure that had built was blistering urgent.

The girl sniffed the dribble of wet from the end of her nose and then lay on the uncovered mattress and stared at the ceiling. Alexander gritted his teeth and wrenched down his trousers, almost running to the bed. He climbed over her and shoved his hand up the front of blouse, grabbing her breast and squeezing roughly, but he still couldn't feel it. He gripped her tighter, rubbing himself between her bare legs and growling in frustration.

She writhed beneath him, tense and unfeeling. 'You like that, baby?'

Alexander ground his hips uselessly harder.

'I make you feel good?'

'Shut up.'

Alexander caught the burning flash of hate in her eyes, then they pinched tightly shut and she turned her face away from him. Her body was rigid, her hands little fists. Alexander felt sick in his stomach. She found him disgusting. She knew what he was. She could tell that he wasn't an important Russian businessman. He was a murderer, the man who killed her father and brothers. He rolled away, breathless and angry. He didn't want to do this. Right now, what he wanted more than anything else was to go back to the café and watch Hanh. She still thought he was a good man. He wanted to sit with her at the lake again, to talk, and find out all about her. He wanted to tell her he understood how lonely and tired and afraid she was.

He collapsed against the wall and shoved the girl's legs away from him, so she fell from the bed and thumped to the floor. He slid down and curled on his side, half-naked and humiliated, and watched as she wriggled back into her skirt and fled barefoot from the room.

SIXTEEN

Hanh bent to the ground and pushed the little tufted seedling of bright green rice into the wet soil. With her trousers rolled to her knees, she inched her way through the paddy. Her ankles were submerged below the water and she could feel the thick mud squirm between her toes. As her hands bobbed beneath the surface of the water, up and down like a bird catching fish, she sank into the satisfying rhythm. A mosquito bounced in the air by her face. She batted it away with a dripping hand and paused to stretch the ache at the bottom of her spine. Wonderful, luminous green stretched out in front of her. Like a sheet of spun silk, it spread across the flat land, all the way to the mountains. Her eyes settled on the jagged rock rising through the haze in the distance, layered in shades of duck-egg blue. She took a breath, drawing the clean air deep into her lungs and feeling the filth of the city being flushed away.

'Hurry up, old tortoise!' shouted Thuy from where she was planting rice just a few feet away. 'I'll have harvested this lot and cooked it for supper before you've finished.'

'Yes, Mother!' Hanh called back, looking up and laughing. She was glad Thuy was with her today. Their chatter distracted her from thinking about Alexander and the lake. She was still angry with herself. Why hadn't she just shown him around the city like she wanted to? She was so weak. She rammed a sprig of rice into the earth, frustrated.

Thuy stood up and plucked her basket from the mud. She balanced it on her hip and began to slosh through the shallow water towards Hanh. 'You're quiet today,' she said.

'Just thinking,' Hanh replied.

'It's a wonder your hair hasn't turned white, all the thinking you do. What are you thinking about?'

Hanh shrugged. 'I don't know. The whole world.'

'Don't think about that. You'll never get a husband with white hair,' Thuy grinned. She grabbed Hanh's wrist and dragged her to the ridge at the edge of the paddy. 'Come on. I'm thirsty. Let's have a rest.'

Hanh dried her hands on her trousers and sat beside Thuy. She pulled her feet from the water and the mud on her skin began to crisp in the hot sun.

Thuy rummaged in her basket and pulled out a bottle of water. 'So tell me what's really bothering you. I won't tell anyone. You know I won't. We're sisters.' She took a swig and passed the bottle to Hanh.

Hanh sipped slowly. This was her secret, wasn't it? She had wanted to keep it just for her, but what did it matter anyway? 'I went to the lake with a man,' she whispered.

Thuy's face broke into a wide smile and she squealed in excitement. 'You have a boyfriend!'

'No I don't, Thuy.'

'Ha ha! Hey, buffalo, hey, birds! Hanh's got a boyfriend!' she teased, scrabbling to her feet and bellowing to the empty paddy. 'Have you married him yet, in your dreams? I bet you have!'

'No, I haven't.'

'What are your sons called?'

'Thuy! Stop it!'

Thuy collapsed on the ground, giggling. 'So why do you look like a miserable old mule?'

'I made a fool of myself. I was nervous and I didn't even say anything.'

'That's not a problem. Men don't like women who talk. What's he like, then?'

Hanh dug her fingertips into the soggy ground, pausing. 'I think he's from Russia.'

'Russia?' Thuy sat up and looked at Hanh. Her face was screwed into a puzzle. 'Why is he in Hanoi?'

'I don't know.'

'Does he work for the Party?'

Hanh shrugged. 'Probably.'

Thuy was quiet and Hanh could see she was thinking. 'Have you told your mother?'

'Of course not,' Hanh frowned. She knew what her mother would say if she told her about Alexander. Good girls didn't meet with men they didn't know. They especially didn't meet foreign men. Good girls came home to their mothers to cook and clean and sweep and stitch. She ripped a clump of weed-grass from the paddy and chucked it behind her.

'I think it's a bit strange,' said Thuy, after a while. 'Why would a Russian want to talk to you?'

'Thanks, Thuy.'

'You know what I mean. It's not normal.'

'Russians go out with Viet girls sometimes, don't they? You've heard the stories.'

Thuy crumpled her face, tighter. 'I've heard the stories about wealthy city women and Party men's daughters, Hanh. Not squat-girls.'

Hanh sniffed, tearing up another clump of stubborn grass. She knew Thuy was right, but she couldn't help feeling offended. 'Maybe,' she shrugged.

'Are you going to see him again?'

'I doubt it. I only met him in the first place so Dinh would see. I thought it might scare him into paying my wages if he saw me with a Russian.'

'You need to be careful playing games like that, Hanh. If the Russian really is a Party man, he'll twist what you say and sell you upriver for a bowl of stew. You'll end up in a deeper mess than you started.'

'I know,' Hanh nodded. 'I didn't tell him anything important. He might be a businessman, anyway. He didn't seem very . . . *official*.'

'Was he wearing a uniform?'

'No.'

Thuy downed the last drips of her drink and laughed. 'Well that makes even less sense! He's got no reason at all to talk to you if he's a businessman. You're a nobody!'

Hanh sulked. 'He's nice,' she said, defensively.

'A fair face can hide a foul heart,' Thuy chirped.

'I never said he was handsome.'

'You don't know anything else about him, so he must be. Where did you meet him?'

'At work. I gave him directions and he asked me to show him around the city.'

'So you took him to the lake?'

'No. Well . . . sort of. Are you laughing at me?' Hanh looked away, aware of the irritation prickling through her voice.

Thuy shuffled close and leaned her head affectionately on Hanh's shoulder. 'Yes. I always laugh at you. You do silly things. Why do you find it so difficult to stay out of trouble?'

'This isn't trouble.'

Thuy tipped her head to the side and gave Hanh a soft, knowing smile. 'We should get back to work,' she said, holding out her hands to Hanh. 'Help me up.'

Hanh forced herself to smile and pulled her friend to standing. As the girls waded back into the middle of the paddy Thuy paused and picked a feather from the surface of the water. She wiped it dry with her fingers.

'Here. Your Russian may like it,' she said, tucking the feather into Hanh's hair and smiling. 'Just be careful. If you stick your head above the grass, you might get shot, little duck.'

SEVENTEEN

Phuc sat back in his chair and took another deep swig from the bottle of rice wine. It tore down his throat like a flame. Kieu stood over him, carefully threading a needle through the split in his brow. Through a heavy cloud of alcoholic numbness, he felt the flesh above his eye lift and drag. She pulled at his skin and his vision blurred, little bright spots dancing like fireflies before his eyes. He felt a tug as the eye of the needle resisted and held his breath as the fishing wire squeaked slowly through his skin.

Phuc had taken his family fishing, once. They had all gone to the coast together – him, Kieu, Phuong and the boys. Phuc showed them his boats bobbing merrily in the harbour. He introduced them to his fishermen, who shook Phuong's hand and told her what a good man he was to work for. They met the woman who untangled the nets, her fingers scuttling like spiders across a web of pearly white wire. They ate red mullet for lunch. They sailed a boat out into the East Sea and watched the land sink behind the horizon and Phuc bellowed to the wide blue ocean: *Welcome to my office!* His family had laughed. He remembered lifting Kieu on to his shoulders so that she could see the turtle that flapped alongside the boat, and how she held on to his hair as the boat swayed softly in the waves. The memory pierced his groggy mind, more painful than the needle. He swigged again from the bottle of wine.

Phuc's eyes crossed on the silvery thread that hung down from his brow. Kieu snipped the thread and it fell to the floor like a thick, grey hair. She took a damp cloth and dabbed it over the gash on his cheekbone. The water was warm and fragrant and the soothing musk of lavender rose above the sour alcohol. He watched her rethread the needle, breathing deeply. She pushed the metal back into his skin.

Phuong had chosen their daughter's name. Kieu was the most famous heroine in all of Vietnamese literature and Phuong liked the poem that told her story very much. Kieu was beautiful, intelligent, loyal, brave and dignified. She was the best of every woman in Vietnam. She sold herself into a life of misery to save her stricken father. His daughter's name had become too fitting; it wrapped around her and squeezed like bindings on little girls' feet. Phuc groaned as alcohol swilled the poem up the sides of his mind, like waves on the bow of a little boat, aimless and melancholy, lost at sea.

A hundred years – in this lifespan on earth, talent and destiny are apt to feud. You must go through a play of ebb and flow and watch such things as make you sick at heart. Is it so strange that losses balance gains? Blue heaven's wont to strike a rose from spite.

What had Phuc done in his life to provoke the heavens? That day, when he took his family to see his fishing boats, had he been bragging? Did he deserve this for his arrogance?

And when the soldiers had stormed his home and he hid his savings on little Kieu and her silence had saved him, what did he do with the money? He bribed his way out of the army, out of the battles that raged on the Cambodian border, out of the re-education camps. Every dong that Kieu had hidden was spent on buying his freedom. He told himself that his family would starve without him, that they would be miserable. Had he been wrong? Maybe they would have been better without him. Maybe he was a coward and a traitor, just like the Party said he was. This was his punishment.

Beautiful Kieu. Talented, devoted Kieu. She who suffers so terribly for her father. This was not Phuc's punishment, it was hers. He thought of the girl in the room behind the tobacco store, counting bullets with her painted red nails. He pictured Kieu in her place, sitting beside Cheung Hu as he smoked his cigar, the man in the suit watching from the corner as he wiped Phuc's blood from his knuckles.

Phuc felt faint. A dull thud of blood throbbed against the shell of his body. He touched his hand to his cheek and felt the needle sticking into him, like a harpoon. Kieu batted his hand away and scolded him. Her voice came as though from under water. The needle slipped through his skin and he took another swig from his bottle of rice wine. It soothed him, calmed him. It helped him see the situation clearly. Tam had been right. Escape was too dangerous. Cheung Hu would never be merciful. The Party would always come back. Phuc needed to be cleverer. There would be a way to fix this – he just had to find it.

He felt his wound close slowly together and he closed his eyes to think.

Phuc woke from sleep with a dry tongue, raw eyes and aching limbs. He turned stiffly in the bed, dragging his knees to his chest along the polished wooden platform, and a hangover rolled across his body like a tank. The smell of rich, buttery yam crept through the gap beneath the kitchen door and saliva burst suddenly into his mouth. He coughed, swallowed and pulled the cotton sheet above his head, cramming his fist between his lips to smother the sound.

The door to the bedroom opened and Phuc hissed a curse between his teeth.

'Phuc?' said Phuong's voice from the doorway.

Phuc lay still, his breath hot and damp beneath the shelter of his sheet.

'I know you're awake, Phuc.'

Phuong sat on the edge of the bed and rapped her fingers against the wood.

Phuc eased on to his back and stretched his arm above his head, as though he were slowly waking. He smiled and reached out to touch Phuong's hand. 'What time is it?'

'Breakfast,' she said, scowling.

'Ah! Is that sweet potato? It smells delicious.'

'You won't be getting a spoonful. You missed a whole day's work.'

'It was only one day,' said Phuc. 'I'll make it up. Don't worry.'

'Don't tell me not to worry,' Phuong bit back. 'Those

boys of yours eat like gorillas and I can only spin the rations so thin. This week was the best chance of work you've had in months. Who knows when the Russians will be back at the port? We need the money, Phuc. What were you thinking?'

Phuc dragged himself to sitting and the room spun through his vision. 'I wasn't thinking,' he said seriously, rubbing the back of his hand against his clammy brow.

Phuong's lips puckered and she shook her head. 'Too much wine to go to work! That's a great example to set for your sons. And your face is a fright. What happened?'

'I fell. I was drunk.'

'I know you were drunk. The whole of Saigon knows you were drunk. Standing in the gutter outside and wailing for me to let you in, like a Chinese banshee.'

Phuc cringed. His street had prying, pitiless eyes.

Phuong unravelled her arms and let her hands slip to her lap. She flexed her fingers nervously, and looked at him. 'You were talking in your sleep, you know.'

Phuc's mind cracked rigid. 'Was I?'

'Yes.'

'What about?'

'The Party mostly.'

'The Party?' He strained to hold the panic back from his voice and brought his hand back to his forehead to hide his eyes. 'What did I say?'

Phuong shrugged. 'I don't know. You weren't making sense. You were tossing for hours, though. You'd wound yourself tight as a spring, all that wriggling. You were talking about Tam, too, and the port.' She slid along the bed, until her leg was pressed against his side, then dipped towards him and lowered her voice. Her face was scored with worry. 'Phuc? Tell me what's going on. Why were you drunk? What happened to your face?'

Phuc took a deep, steadying breath. 'I argued with Tam,' he lied. 'He promised me work, so I went to the port, but he'd given the job to someone else. I shouted at him, and he hit me.'

Phuong launched herself from the bed, clicking her tongue like an angry gecko. '*Troi oi!* That man pretends to be your friend, but he's trouble. I knew it!' She threw her hands in the air and steamed into the kitchen, furious. 'What did I tell you about him? There's no ivory in the mouth of a dog!'

Phuc dragged himself up and staggered after her. He slumped into a chair at the table and his head fell heavily into his hand. 'I'm sorry, Phuong,' he mumbled, but Phuong wasn't listening.

She was cursing Tam beneath her breath and clattering through the cooking pots and crockery that were stacked at the stove. She snatched a bowl and ladled it through the stockpot, then dragged a chair to sit beside Phuc, grabbing his head and jerking it towards her.

'Ouch, Phuong!' Phuc flinched away as she splashed a cloth into the bowl and smeared it roughly across the wound on his cheek.

Thao kneeled on his stool, propping himself up with his elbow on the table and stretching forward to examine his father's face. 'What happened, Dad?'

'Nothing.' Phuc grumbled as the cloth snagged on his fresh stitches.

'Why did you have a fight with Uncle Tam?'

'Thao!' scolded Phuong. 'What have I told you about spying?'

'Did you win?'

'Of course he won,' said Quan, climbing on to the table too.

'Boys!'

'Well, if Dad won't tell us what happened, we'll have to ask Uncle Tam.'

Phuong smacked the edge of the table and pointed at them, sharply. 'You're not to speak to that man. I mean it! You're to cross the road if you see him in the street! Do you hear me?'

The boys rolled their eyes and crawled down from the table. Phuong grabbed Phuc's head again and dunked the cloth into the water, but he batted her hand away before she could touch him.

'I'm going out,' he said, pushing his chair from the table. He needed to be away from the house. He would never be able to think like this; not with the guilt, the fuss and the relentless chatter. Tam was a good friend; he shouldn't have blamed him. It scared him, too, how easily he'd lied. The words had fallen out from his mouth before his mind had a chance to check them. Gambling. Drinking. Lying. What sort of a man had he become?

Phuong jumped up, wringing the cloth anxiously in her hands. 'Where are you going?' she asked. 'Don't go to the port, Phuc. Don't apologise to him. I know you. You're too kind. He doesn't deserve it. That scabby sheep won't ruin my flock!'

'I'm not going to the port,' Phuc replied wearily, stepping outside.

He shut the door and Phuong's screeching dropped from his ears. At once, he knew where he was headed; the alley was drawing him back. He put his head down as he walked, and his fingertips ground at the dust in the pit of his pockets. The thought of seeing Cheung Hu or his thugs was terrifying, but there would be answers there, clues to look for. *To catch a fish, remember where you cast your net.* Something in Fán T'án Alley would trigger a thought in his tired mind, and he'd trap it there and fix all the trouble that wretched place had caused him. He was sure of it.

Cholon was seething as Phuc weaved through. Bicycle bells chirruped like birds and the slosh-boys yelled as they moved between cafés, collecting waste from the kitchens to sell as pigswill.

The alley, however, was unnervingly still, and he stopped at the entrance and loitered, uncertain. The doors were all shut, and some had been bolted, but he knew the games still simmered behind. From one sunken archway he could see just the pointed white tips of a doorman's shoes. A beggar was lying on the ground in another, asleep and shirtless, and the arch of his backbone rounded out like a chine of meat. He peered into the gloom and concentrated hard, as if he expected to see the solution glaring back, like cats' eyes.

Suddenly, there was movement. A door flung open and a flash of green broke Phuc's stare. What was that? A silk shirt? Cheung Hu was here! He threw himself to the side of the alley, out of view, and his feet faltered over the uneven pavement. He scrambled up, glancing back over his shoulder as a body turned from the corner of the alley. He groped for the door handle on the wall beside him, ramming it open and crashing through before Cheung Hu had a chance to see him. He slammed the door shut and slumped against it, drum-and-cymbal panic crashing through his chest and head.

'Are you OK?'

A girl looked at Phuc from behind the bar, a tumbler in her hand and concern on her face. She untwisted a rag from the glass and hooked it into the loop of her belt, watching him.

Phuc kept his back pressed to the door, holding it shut. The room before him was long and thin, hardly wider than the bar itself, and concrete walls led up to a dark, distant ceiling. Deep-red paint had been spread on the walls, but abandoned in a wavering line six foot or so above his head, where bare grey won over, like a smoggy horizon. There were tables at the back of the room, all quiet and empty. Bulbs with splaying metal shades hung over them and were throwing light down in small circles that barely stretched beyond the edge of the benches. The dimness made Phuc feel safe. Hidden. He looked back to the girl as she tucked the tumbler into a crate on the bar, and his eyes wandered along the line of the gleaming liquor bottles on the shelf behind her.

'Give me one of those,' he said, peeling his back away from the door and nodding towards the brown, labelless bottles in the fridge. 'How much?'

'We're not open,' said the girl apologetically.

Phuc collapsed on to a barstool and his coins echoed as they fell on the polished countertop. The girl paused, and then slid the money over the edge of the bar into her palm. She took a bottle from the fridge, chipped the cap and placed it in front of him.

Phuc nursed his beer slowly, swilling the cold, sour liquid in his mouth before swallowing it down. The girl sat on the end of the bar, swinging her legs, waiting for him. Her feet tapped gently against the crate of empty glasses and they chimed like the toll of a bell tower in the bare room. Another girl came into the bar and squeezed herself through the narrow gap between Phuc's stool and the wall, passing him with a gust of musky perfume. She spoke to the bargirl briefly, then she went through a door at the back. Phuc heard the crack of high-heeled footsteps on hollow stairs. They faded away and the room was silent.

As the alcohol seeped into him Phuc began to regain his composure. It could have been anyone in the green silk shirt. The chance of Cheung Hu being here at this time of the morning was as slim as a snake, and even if it had been him Phuc felt sure he'd escaped unseen. The figure had been walking away from the alley too. He'd be far gone by now, in his hidden office at the tobacco store probably, a dozen streets away. He wouldn't come back until the games picked up again this evening. For now,

Phuc was safe. He would finish his beer, he thought, and then go outside to think of a plan. He gave his bottle a twist, to see how much he had left inside, and a little beige froth hissed up at his movement. He tilted the bottle and watched the bubbles slip down the side of the glass. When he heard the front door open again, he didn't bother to look up.

The stool beside Phuc dragged across the floor and a man thumped heavily down. Phuc took him in, through the side of his eye. He had a wide, Western face and coarse black stubble pricked his skin. Strings of lank hair clung to his cheek, and he smeared them aside with an enormous hand and folded them behind his purple ear. The metal seat groaned beneath his weight.

Perfect, thought Phuc. There are six barstools to choose from, and he sits next to me. He shifted his body, attempting to nudge his stool away. He wanted to be alone. He was busy thinking.

The man rapped his knuckles on the counter. 'Vodka,' he barked, in a deep Russian accent.

The bar-girl leapt from her perch, scurrying to the liquor bottles and hurriedly pouring a measure of liquid into a cloudy tumbler. She scraped the tumbler towards the man, tucked the bottle beneath the counter, and then retreated to the end of the bar. Phuc pinched his lips. Even better, he thought. Some fat Russian – a friend of the Party, no doubt – getting drunk beside him.

The Russian sipped his drink. 'How's the beer?'

'Fine,' replied Phuc, not looking up.

'Good. I don't want to hear about monkey-piss beer in my establishment.'

Phuc grimaced. The Russian owned the bar. He would definitely be a friend of the Party, and probably of Cheung Hu, as well.

'It's fine. The beer's fine,' he said again.

The Russian smirked. 'You're almost done. Have another.'

'No thanks.'

'Go on. It's on the house.' He leaned back on his barstool and rested against the wall, blocking Phuc's exit. He waved a swollen finger at the cowering bar-girl. 'She brews it. She's a talented girl,' he said, with a wink.

'It's very good beer.' Phuc nodded as he swigged the last dregs from the bottle. He looked at the bar-girl; she had retreated to the farthest corner of the room and was briskly polishing tables, reaching forward and whipping her rag over the wood, in and out of the scattered spotlights. She was glancing at the bar with a nervous frown, but when she caught Phuc looking at her, she quickly turned away.

The Russian had caught Phuc looking too. 'You like her?'

'She's nice enough,' said Phuc, without thinking.

'I can give you a good price.'

'What? No!'

Phuc rammed his stool back from the bar, horrified. Of all the places to hide, he'd picked a whorehouse, and now the Russian owner was trying to cut him a deal! He quickly corrected himself. 'No thanks, Brother,' he said, and shook his head, impulsively.

The Russian slipped a wry grin across the bar. 'I under-stand. It's a little early in the morning to be . . . *amorous*. But then again, it's a little early for drinking too.' He raised his glass and chinked it against the neck of Phuc's bottle.

Phuc winced and slid awkwardly down from his stool.

The Russian stayed pinned to the back wall. 'You're not leaving me to drink alone, are you?'

Phuc shook his head. 'I have to go.'

'What's the rush?'

'I've got things to do, Brother.'

'Such urgent things you can stop for a drink before breakfast?' The Russian laughed and stretched over the bar, seizing the bottle of vodka and pouring himself another greedy measure.

Phuc clenched his teeth and pushed through the brief gap that appeared behind him. He headed for the door, and the Russian's deep, rumbling voice chased after him.

'If you change your mind, come back any time. I'm in the city for a few days; just ask for the Herder. A wife, a maid, a mistress – it doesn't matter to me. I can get you a girl for whatever you want.'

At that moment, an idea shot into Phuc's mind, fully formed and firm and beautiful. It rooted him to the spot. He took his hand from the doorknob and spun back to face the Herder.

'Can you get me a daughter?' he said.

EIGHTEEN

Alexander sat forward and rested his elbows on the table. On an ordinary day he would never have sat with his back to the street, but today was different. Hanh was sitting opposite him and she was more important. He needed her to have the view. That way, when there was a pause in their conversation, she would look up, out of the café and across the street and she would see the squat. This was his plan: show her a little of a new world, then throw her back to the old.

There had not been any pauses yet, though. Alexander had not seen Hanh look at the squat, even once. She was still being wary – these girls had been raised on caution for too long to let go. Yet despite her carefully chosen words and the spark of vigilance in her eye, he knew he was making progress. She had fixed her stare firmly on him, and he could tell by the tumbling rhythm of her voice that she was excited. She picked up her coffee, then put it down again without drinking, and fiddled the spoon about clumsily beneath her fingers. She was asking him question after question, and her shoulders seemed to relax, just a little softer, each time he answered.

Alexander couldn't help but smile. So far it had been a

good day. When he had asked Hanh to come for a drink with him, he didn't expect her to say yes so quickly or with such determination in her voice. It was just what he needed to pick himself up. He reckoned he had a week at best before the Herder returned to Hanoi. It would be nice to have her all wrapped up and ready by then – for her sake as much as for his own. He felt glad she was making it easy.

It was the middle of the morning, neither breakfast nor lunch, and the café had only a few seats taken. Beside them, a fan was spinning. Alexander watched as it swept over Hanh's shoulders, fluttering the sleeves that cupped her brown shoulders and teasing wisps of hair from her ponytail. The strands danced around her cheekbone.

'Why are you in Vietnam?' she asked him.

'I'm working,' Alexander replied.

She paused. 'Do you work for the government?'

The girls always asked if he worked for the government. She had probably been wanting to know since the moment they'd met. Russians who worked for the government were almost the only foreign men in the whole of Vietnam, and the girls didn't want to talk to government workers. Spies were everywhere. He gave what he thought was his warmest smile, to reassure her. 'No. I have my own business.'

'What do you do?' said Hanh, a ripple of awe obvious in the rise of her voice.

Alexander slowly pushed the handle of his cup with his finger until it was perfectly lined up with the edge of the table. He nodded his head seriously, like an important businessman considering a big deal. 'I'm a trader.'

'Like a market trader?'

'In a way.'

'Do you spend lots of time in Hanoi?'

'I travel all over the country.'

'Have you been in an aeroplane?'

'Of course.'

'Were you scared?'

'Not at all. You wouldn't believe how peaceful the world seems when you look from the clouds.'

'Do you like Hanoi?'

'I'm usually so busy when I'm here, I've never really had a chance to see the city.'

Hanh stopped her questions abruptly and glanced down into her drink. Good, Alexander thought. She was thinking about how she had refused to show him around, about how she owed him. He deserved an apologetic silence. He sat quietly and left her to simmer in her guilt. As he waited, he winched his eyes sideways as far as he could. He wanted to grab a check of the street behind him, but all he could see was the bleary black arm of his glasses, and the strain of it made his head ache.

A plate clicked down on the table and called Alexander's wandering eyes back, like the snap of a thumb. He hadn't noticed the café owner move, but now he was standing at the side of the table. He gave Alexander a sly grin and scraped the plate – and the little French pastry – towards Hanh.

'For Madame,' he said.

Hanh's face broke into a sudden, nervous smile and she looked at Alexander for approval. Alexander gave her a nod and tried not to scowl. He hadn't asked for the pastry, but he knew he would pay for it. It wasn't the money that bothered him, but the principle. It irked him when men took advantage; if they saw he was with a girl and knew he wouldn't argue. Hanh twisted the plate, savouring her treat with her eyes, before pulling at the edge and slipping a tiny piece into her mouth. He bared his teeth, not sure if it would look like a smile or a grimace. Still, the pastry had a morsel of value, if it kept her happy.

'*Bon appétit*,' he said.

Hanh's smile stretched wider. 'You speak French too?' she said, with her mouth full. 'Say something else.'

Alexander shrugged. 'That's all I know. "*Bon appétit*" and "*bon voyage*".' He used an overblown French accent and rolled an enormous, imaginary moustache between his fingers.

She laughed. 'You are much better at Vietnamese.'

'I spend more time speaking Vietnamese than French.'

'How did you learn?'

'A friend taught me.'

'A Vietnamese friend?'

'A Russian friend.'

'Does your friend work with you?'

The Herder slunk into Alexander's head. He was tapping his spoon on the rim of his teacup with a sneering grin. *What's wrong with you?* he whispered. Alexander's hand gave a twitch on the table. There was nothing wrong with him. When he left the brothel yesterday he hadn't gone to find Hanh straight away, as he wanted to. He knew she would be embarrassed after her shyness at the lake, and she needed time to recover. He had taken the effort to calm himself too. He wanted to win Hanh properly. That *proved* there was nothing wrong with him. He would show the Herder just how well he could do.

'Sometimes,' he said bitterly.

Hanh licked her fingertip and dabbed it against the crumbs that had spilled from her plate. 'What's your home like?'

'I have a flat in Saigon, by the river,' Alexander lied, without thinking. He hadn't called anywhere home for years. It was bad for business to settle. The Herder hadn't let him.

Hanh shook her head. 'No. Tell me about your real home.'

Alexander frowned into his coffee. In America, his mother had asked what was wrong with him too; when he came home from school and she gripped his face in her rough hands, and he had to tell her he hadn't been *good*. 'My real home?' he said, off-guard.

'Yes,' Hanh nodded, expectant. 'Is Russia a paradise?'

Alexander caught himself and looked sharply up. Of course she meant Russia. He dragged a smile back up to his lips. 'It's the coldest paradise on earth.'

'Do you have a big house?'

'I have a cabin in the countryside, just north of Moscow. It sits in a valley with a lake at the base, and the water is as green as jade. The hills are more like mountains, covered in thick forest trees, and I cut them down for firewood when winter comes.'

He leaned across the table and described the picture he had seen on the back of the crate of Roskamov in the kitchen at the brothel. He always described the same house, by the same lake, with the same roaring log fire. The girls loved it. They were so predictable. She would ask if it snowed next.

'Does it snow?'

Alexander smiled. 'We have snow so deep it could bury a bear.'

'I love the cold,' she said, cramming the last of the pastry into her mouth. Then she paused and dipped her face coyly. Her voice was quieter. 'Do you have a family in Russia?'

Alexander put down his coffee cup. The girls always asked about Russia, but they were rarely so bold as to get personal. 'No,' he replied, bluntly.

'You don't have children?'

'No.'

'Or a wife?'

'No.'

'Do you have a girlfriend?'

Shit, she was forward. He thought of the girls he had had in America. He thought of fifteen-year-old Bess Truitt, her bright white skin and the crisp tan-line around her arm when she took off her blouse behind the old oak in the spinney at Mr Greene's wheat field. He thought about pinching the little white, spiky tips that poked from the pillows at Pattie Smith's house, pulling out the feathers that scratched his face. He thought about that blonde with the lazy eye that Eugene Arnold-Lovett fucked before him. Were they girlfriends? They were closer to girlfriends than any hateful judging bar- or brothel-girl that had ended up on his mattress since. Some other man would probably have them now though – not that it mattered. An old marching cadence sounded off in his head, like an air-horn. *Ain't no use in goin' home, Jody's got your girl and gone. She wouldn' want you anyway, you've changed since you been far away* . . .

'No girlfriend,' said Alexander, and the tremble in his voice made him wince. He closed his eyes for an instant longer than a blink and steadied his thinking. He'd had enough of this. It wasn't how it should be. He was wasting time. They needed to be talking about Hanh, not him. He downed a large, hot gulp of his coffee, set the cup firmly on the table and gritted his teeth.

'How's your mother?' he asked.

Hanh's smile disappeared. 'Strong as a bear, so she says.'

'She's getting better?'

'I don't know.'

'What's the matter with her?'

Hanh sighed heavily and her dark eyes glazed, slipping away from him. 'Weak nerves and ill winds,' she shrugged. 'She hasn't been well for months.'

Alexander scraped his chair to the table, lowering his head beneath the wandering line of her sight. 'She's lucky to have you to look after her. You work very hard, Hanh. You must be tired.'

Hanh snatched her hands away from the table and hid them quickly in her lap. He knew she worked in the fields, as well as at the squat; her short, dirty fingernails gave her away. He scratched the stubble at the corner of his mouth to hide his flickering grin. This was more like it. Now he'd gotten a hold on her.

'Who was the girl I saw you with, when you were here before?' he asked, casually pushing.

'That's Thuy,' said Hanh.

'Is she your sister?'

Hanh nodded.

'I'm glad your mother has two good women to look after her. It must help, having someone to share the responsibility with.'

Hanh fidgeted. 'Thuy doesn't live with me,' she said, quiet and awkward.

'She's married?'

'No.'

'Where does she live then?'

Another squirm, and hesitation. 'She lives across the paddies . . . with her own mother.'

Alexander smiled invisibly. Perfect. 'She's not your real sister?'

'No,' Hanh muttered. The fan beside the table turned and swept hot air across her back, throwing the strands of her loose hair in front of her eyes. She fumbled to push them behind her ears. 'Thuy is very kind to me. She treats me like I'm family.'

'There's no family like blood,' said Alexander. He took another long, slow sip of his drink and watched Hanh frown and slip down in her chair. He tucked his own seat even closer to the table and leaned forward, smiling. 'I knew you couldn't be related,' he whispered. 'You're far prettier than

160

she is. I bet she's jealous of all the attention you get.'

Hanh laughed. It was the kind of laugh where breath escapes in a rush, like when the balloon-sellers outside the cathedrals released a dash of air, after blowing the rubber up too tight. He watched with satisfaction as she took a deep breath, picked up her cup of coffee and sipped through a bright-hot, blushing smile.

Alexander sat in the dark on the edge of his bed. He tried the light switch, but there was still no power. He hated the blackouts. They came almost daily, wherever he was in Vietnam, sweeping across the cities like a velvet cape. There was never enough power to share between the private houses, but tonight the streetlights were stubbed out too, and they left the sky coal-black and endless.

It was hot tonight – as hot as anything he had felt since he'd been in Hanoi. On a rooftop balcony, blue torchlight flickered. Alexander had seen a mother there earlier, spreading blankets on the ground and laying her children down to sleep. The air in the buildings was near unbearable without a fan to churn and cool it and he'd seen whole families sleeping outside like bandits. He would rather be inside, though, with the door locked and bolted, to keep him safe.

The blackouts bought silence with them, also. Snide, bottomless silence. When the power was on, there was always the spit of loudspeakers – the voice of the Party letting him know that he wasn't alone – or the rumble of an air conditioner. Now, he heard nothing but the ringing in his ears. With the dark, the heat, the quiet and the leaden unease in his gut, the night became as suffocating as the jungle. He flicked the switch again. On off. On off. His leg jittered on the floor and the wooden headboard knocked against the wall like a heartbeat.

He couldn't sleep for thinking of Hanh. He had been caught unready when she asked about his family. The girls never normally asked him anything so personal. His thoughts had been adrift, and he didn't have an answer ready. That was careless. He should have seen it coming. When she asked about his business too, it had thrown him. For an instant, he considered telling the truth – what harm could it do? He wiped away the sweat that had pooled above his lip with a shaking finger and went to the windowsill and turned the jar, so his baby faced him. He sat, lowering his head to her eye-line, and he tapped on the glass as though she might wake.

Alexander had been in such perfect control of Hanh at the lake, when she watched the crying child and his mother so intently. What the fuck had he found so difficult this time? He lifted the jar, tipped it in his lap and cradled it. His baby slid back through the fluid and lay against the glass. He slipped his hand around the jar until it rested beneath her head. 'I've helped you, haven't I?' he whispered. 'I've looked after you?'

When he had found his baby at the market, lost and alone in the midst of a table piled high with batteries, lighter fluid, guns and grenades, he had felt such dreadful pity. Agent Orange, the vendor had said, the defoliant sprayed from American planes to strip the jungles bare. It poisoned the wombs of a generation. Alexander had picked her up and taken her home. It eased his guilty conscience.

He looked down at the sleeping face, the wisps of downy black hair that floated from her head and the lines of loose, wrinkled skin that covered her body. 'Don't worry,' he said and ran his finger over the glass above her brow, as if to smooth it.

But it was not his baby's worries that troubled him really. It was Hanh. He cursed himself for letting their conversation slip from his grip so often, for letting his guard down. He was supposed to be asking the questions. He was supposed to be in control, not her. He put his baby back on the windowsill and she bobbed in the formaldehyde, her tiny clenched fist knocking soundlessly against the glass. Anger itched in his belly. This baby belonged to him entirely. She wasn't like the other girls – the ones who used him, who passed him by on their way to a better life. His hand twitched on the lid of the jar. Just briefly, he thought he might open it.

'You don't ask questions, do you, baby? You know who's in charge.'

NINETEEN

'It's time to go to bed, little Hanha.'

In her dream, Hanh lay on the porch and dusk speckled the sky, falling down around her like cool, grey ash. The door to her house was open and it rapped against its frame in the swirling wind. Her father's voice blew out from the darkness beyond.

'It's time to go to sleep.'

'I want to go to the river,' said Hanh. She rested her hands by her sides, running her fingers over the low ridges of the bamboo flooring. They felt like ripples of water, frozen to ice. She pushed her hands back and forth over the silk-smooth wood, harder and faster, until it felt as if the water were real, and moving, and carrying her. She squinted up at the pointed tips of the thatched leaves that made the roof, and they hung like palms at the riverbank.

'Come inside. It's safe inside,' her father called to her.

'It's safe at the river,' Hanh whispered back. She moved to the edge of the porch and rested her foot on the top rung of the ladder. The bamboo creaked beneath her. As she looked out across the paddies the darkness deepened. She could hear the flow of the river gushing below the wind.

'Listen to me.'

As she left the porch and crept inside, she could see the curled, black bulks of her parents sleeping. She lay on her mat beside them and slid her knees to her breast.

'Did you pull up the ladder, little Hanha? You have to pull up the ladder at night, or tigers will creep in while we're sleeping.'

Her father's voice came from all around her. She closed her eyes and sank down into sleep, like a stone through oil.

'Did you pull up the ladder, Hanh? Are we safe?'

'Yes, Father.'

Below the sounds of the rolling river and the howling wind Hanh thought she heard the creak of bamboo and a dull thud, like the beat of a fist on a soft hide drum. She tried to think, but couldn't remember if she had moved the ladder or not.

'You're a good girl,' said her father, but his voice sounded different. The words were deep and foreign. They were short metallic drips; water falling heavily from a leaking tap.

'Good girl.'

He spoke again and the drip sounded thicker, as if it hit the ground but never splashed, or stayed in a ball, a neat little droplet of thick red blood.

'Good girl.'

There's no family like blood.

'Good girl, good girl.'

But it wasn't a drip. Hanh hauled herself up to the surface

of her deep sleep. The noise was real! What was it? Her eyes shot open and her body tensed. She looked urgently around the room, afraid to move. The sound was the pluck of chicken-mesh away from the frame of her window, of staples being pulled carefully from wood. She heard the creak of diamonds of wire, twisted and moved, one by one.

'Mother!' Hanh screamed. She scrabbled to the wall, away from the gaping hole in the wire and the shadow of the man who was clambering in through her window.

'Give me your money,' the shadow growled as he thumped to the floor. Hanh pushed herself against the wall, terrified. He said it again, slower and louder. 'Give me your money!'

'We don't have any money.'

'You're a liar!'

Hanh heard herself mewl like a kitten. The man was facing her, his silhouette solidly black against the grey night sky. There was an animal hunch to his spine as though he were ready to pounce and attack. His chest and shoulders jerked with the rapidness of his breath.

'I'm not lying,' she whimpered.

'Where are your ration books?'

Hanh bit her lip. She couldn't give him the ration books – they'd be left with nothing – but she couldn't think of anything to say to throw him. Her mind was limping. Words swung uselessly in her head.

'*Where are they?*' The man shouted this time, and Hanh's hands flew impulsively to her face to shield herself.

Her mother's ragged voice grated through the air. 'Tell him, Hanh.'

Hanh shook her head. 'No. We need them.'

'Tell him where the books are!' Her mother strained and let out a violent, hacking cough.

'Shut up!' The man lurched across the floor towards Hanh's mother.

'Stop!' cried Hanh. She pointed to the wicker basket at the entrance to the back porch. 'By the door! The ration books are by the door!'

The man twisted and lumbered towards the basket, bouldering into the cooking pots stacked beside the door. At the bottom of the basket, he found the paper booklets, and he opened them, leafing quickly through the pages before stuffing them into his pocket.

Hanh grabbed her breath and watched as his hand darted back into the basket. Please leave, she begged in her head. Please leave. Please leave. *Don't find it!* The tapioca roots thudded and rolled on the floor, and he picked them up and crammed them in his pockets too. He upturned the basket, shaking it empty, and Hanh stared in horror as the vial of her mother's medicine skittered across the wooden floor and hit his foot.

He paused, lifting it up to the window and examining it in the dismal moonlight. When he spoke, his voice was softer. 'What's this?'

Hanh waved her hand at him. 'It's nothing.'

'A tiny bottle of golden nothing, hidden at the bottom of a well.'

'Please put it back.'

'Why do you care what I do, if it's nothing?'

The man slipped the vial beneath his toe and held it there, staring at Hanh. She looked at the fragile glass pressed under the tip of his rubber sandal. One bump of his foot and it would shatter, for sure.

'Please don't,' she moaned.

'Is it drugs?'

'Please give it back. It's medicine. My mother needs it. It's no use to you.'

The man plucked the vial from the floor and squeezed it happily in his fist. 'You're wrong, little girl. Medicine is drugs. Drugs are money.' He tucked it into his pocket and turned to Hanh. 'What else have you got for me?'

'Nothing,' she said quickly.

'A real nothing or a liar's nothing?'

Hanh summoned her strongest, bravest voice. 'Honestly. We have nothing left.'

A dog barked suddenly somewhere in the hamlet, not far away, and the man jumped. 'Fucking peasants,' he said, spitting on the floor.

He slunk back to the window, heaved himself through the hole in the wire and disappeared into the night.

Hanh kept her breath tightly held, straining to hear his steps on the creaking bamboo above the noise of her thundering heart. She waited until there was nothing but the sounds of the normal night around her, of the hissed breeze through the thatch, and the river in the distance.

'Mumma?' she whispered, her voice quivering.

'It's OK, little piglet.'

Hanh crawled to the window. She didn't dare stand up.

What if he were still outside in the paddies? What if there were others too? She didn't want to know. Reaching above her head, she tried to bend the wire back across the hole, but her hands were shaking and she couldn't see what she was doing.

'Come here, Hanh,' said her mother.

'I need to fix the window. I can't leave it open.'

'It's fine. He won't come back.'

'You don't know that!'

'He's gone, Hanh,' said her mother, softly.

Hanh's arms fell to the floor. She slid across the floor towards her mother's mat and tears began to dribble down her cheeks. 'I'm sorry, Mumma. I'm so sorry.'

'What are you sorry for?'

'I told him where our ration books were,' she sobbed.

'There was nothing else you could do.'

'I tried to stop him.'

'We can tell the Party tomorrow. We can get new ration books.'

'The Party won't believe us. They'll think we're trying to get more food. They don't care about us.' She wiped her nose with the back of her hand and sniffed. 'And he took your medicine.'

Her mother flicked her hand, dismissively. 'There was hardly a drop left.'

'How will we afford any more?'

'I don't need medicine. I'm almost better.'

'Don't say that, Mumma. You need it. You know you do.'

Hanh's mother took her head in her arms, pulling her

to her chest and rocking her like a baby. 'Shhh, child. It's not your fault. It will be OK.'

Hanh pushed her mother away, suddenly angry. 'How will it be OK? You don't understand!'

'I do,' said her mother, calmly.

'No. You don't!' cried Hanh. 'You think if I'm quiet and polite and I work hard and smile at officials and pray to Father's mouldy photograph we'll be rich and well fed and safe.'

'Don't talk nonsense, Hanh. That's not what I think.'

'That's all you ever tell me to do. *Be a good girl.*'

'Being good is important.'

'Being good doesn't protect us at night or put food in our bellies. You've been stuck in this house so long that you don't know the world outside any more.'

'The world is the same as it's always been, Hanh. Do you think that you are the first person to suffer? Life is cruel for a woman alone. I don't want you to suffer the shame and loneliness that I have. Being good will find you a husband.'

'I don't want a husband.'

'You need a man to look after you.'

'No, I don't.'

'Every woman does! What will you do when I'm gone? Hanh, look at me. How will my spirit rest if I don't know you're safe? Promise you'll be good and find a husband when I die.'

'Mother, don't talk about dying. I can't stand it,' said Hanh, and the tears began again to run down her face.

She pushed herself as close as she could to her mother and pleaded.

'Promise me, Hanh,' said her mother, firmly.

Hanh squeezed her eyes tightly shut and clung to her mother's chest. She could feel her mother's breastbone pushing through her rough skin and into her cheek. Her heart was a weak, stammering whisper.

'I promise, Mumma,' she whispered back.

TWENTY

'Tam!'

Phuc ran across the shipyard, waving frantically at the figure on the quay. An enormous ship was docked in the harbour and he could barely hear himself shout above the commotion of men and machinery. Cranes twisted and creaked as they hauled containers from the ship's deck and ditched them on to the concrete. The thumping roar of electricity generators beat against the high walls of metal, and the earth beneath his feet vibrated. He shoved his way through the throngs of people.

'Tam!' he bellowed again, as loud as his breathless lungs would let him.

The figure turned and waved his clipboard above his head. 'Hi, Phuc!'

Phuc reared up at Tam's side. The muscles in his calves were burning and he slouched forward and propped himself up with his hands on his thighs. 'I've searched half of Saigon for you,' he said, looking up and panting heavily.

'Should have searched here first,' grinned Tam, but his eyes gave Phuc a skittish once-over. 'Someone's fixed you up nicely, Brother. You look much smarter than the last time I saw you.'

Phuc cringed. He hadn't thrown a thought at how he'd left their last meeting – staggering away in a daze as Tam yelled after him. 'Sorry about the other day,' he said, embarrassed.

'Don't worry about it,' replied Tam, with an easy shrug. He paused and eyed Phuc closer. 'Are you OK?'

'Can we talk?'

'Go ahead.'

'In private?'

Tam flicked his pen at the ship in the harbour, and then tapped the clipboard. 'I'm a bit busy now, Brother. This girl's just arrived from Can Tho and I've got to unload and check the cargo before it gets up and scampers away. The Party doesn't take kindly to scampering containers.' He winked and tipped his cap.

'It'll only take a few minutes,' said Phuc. 'Please?'

Tam leaned in and waved his finger at Phuc's stitched, swollen face. 'Is it about this?' Phuc nodded, and Tam nodded too. 'Sure we can, Brother.'

Tam swung his arm around Phuc's shoulder and guided him away from the quayside. Phuc swallowed, gathering himself and he wiped his dripping face on his sleeve as he caught his breath. They ducked into a narrow corridor of large red containers where they were hidden from view.

'So what's the problem?'

'I need money,' said Phuc, abruptly. He knew his approach was direct, but he didn't care.' I'll pay you back.'

Tam frowned and hit his clipboard against the container beside him. It gave an angry, hollow trill. 'Come on, Phuc.

This is hardly talking. What's going on? How did your face end up like a butcher's scrap-bag?'

Phuc rubbed his chin and spat an impatient breath into his clenched fist. A broken face was the very smallest thing he had to worry about. 'I just need to buy myself out of a couple of mistakes.'

'How much do you need?'

'How much can you lend me?'

'What makes you think I have anything spare?'

'You always have cash.'

'How much, Phuc?' said Tam sternly.

Phuc hesitated and glanced at the thin snatch of clear blue heaven above him. 'Three thousand dong.'

Tam's eyes widened. 'That's a lot of money, Brother! It's more than I earn in six months at the port.'

Phuc stepped forward and clutched Tam's forearm in his sweating hands. 'But you have other income, don't you?'

'Not that much, Brother. The Party's been hawk-eyed lately.'

'How long have we been friends?' said Phuc, squeezing tighter. 'My father loaned your father money all the time. He loaned him rice too.'

'Don't chuck that swill at me,' said Tam, tearing his arm free from Phuc's grip. 'You know my father never asked for six months' wages.'

Tam was right. Phuc had no right to demand money like this, and he deserved an explanation. His eyes fell to his feet, ashamed. 'I'm sorry, Brother.' He took a deep breath and steeled himself. 'I went to Fán T'án Alley. I owe Cheung Hu.'

As soon as he forced his confession out, he felt like a weight had been craned away. He heaved a sigh and looked to Tam for reassurance, but there was not a hint of comfort in his friend's expression. Tam was staring at him, open-mouthed and disbelieving.

'Since when do you gamble?'

'I thought I could pay the Party to leave me alone. They came to my house and I promised them money, but I didn't have it. They threatened to kill me! They said they'd take my family to the camps. I didn't know what to do.'

'Shit! I knew it was bad when you asked about the boats, but Cheung Hu is dangerous. You have to pay him.'

'I know. That's why I need the money.'

'You owe him three thousand dong?'

A gasp burst from Phuc's lips before he could stop it. 'I owe him Kieu!'

Tam stepped back, his face horrified. He turned away and began striding furiously back towards the harbour.

Phuc sprinted after him. 'It was Cheung Hu's idea. I couldn't say no! You should have seen my bad fortune, Brother. No man has ever been so unlucky!' He pulled at Tam's arm. He needed his friend to tell him that it wasn't as bad as he thought – that he wasn't to blame. 'Please say something!' he pleaded.

Tam spun around and pushed Phuc, hard. His spine and the back of his skull slammed against a container, and the metal roared as he slumped to the ground.

'You're an idiot. A fucking idiot!' Tam shouted. 'What were you thinking? Do you know what Cheung Hu will do to Kieu if he gets her? And I was worried about the South Sea pirates! They're fucking washerwomen compared to him!'

'I won't let him have her,' Phuc mumbled, his head spinning.

'Well, you're dead if you don't! Heavens, Phuc. It's a wonder Phuong hasn't killed you already.'

'She doesn't know.'

'She'll find out.'

'Not if you help me,' said Phuc, scrambling to his feet. 'Lend me the money, Tam.'

'What use is money? Cheung Hu will never negotiate.'

'I know, but I can fix this. I met a Russian. He says he can sell me a girl, and I'll give her to Cheung Hu in Kieu's place. I just need to pay him.'

Tam shook his head. He looked at Phuc as if he were looking at a stranger, cool and distrusting. 'It'll never work.'

'It will,' cried Phuc. 'Cheung Hu doesn't know what Kieu looks like. I could give him any wilting flower and pass her off as my own.'

'Why would a girl play along? She's got nothing to gain. She'll give you away.'

Phuc threw up his hands, frustrated. 'I don't know. I'll pay her to keep quiet. She'll be sold anyway, so what difference would it make? I'll threaten her if I have to,' he said, and he saw Tam wince.

'And what if Cheung Hu has spies at your house?'

Phuc's memory searched urgently through the faces of the men he had passed on his street this morning. There was smug Thinh with his black boots, the children and the limping dog, the beggar who reeked of gin . . . but who else? Was the guard-boy watching? 'There were no spies,' he said, loudly and firmly, to reassure himself.

Tam was still shaking his head. 'Even if this works – even if you do fool Cheung Hu – what will you do next? Will you keep Kieu hidden forever? Saigon is not as big as the ocean, Brother.'

'We'll have to leave Saigon,' said Phuc, the realisation dawning upon him for the first time as he said it. 'We could go to the Delta. Or North. I'll tell Phuong I'm looking for work.'

He felt suddenly weary: the barrage of questions, the diesel-thick air, the soreness in his head. He collapsed into a crouch and looked up at Tam. He wanted to say how sorry he was; to tell Tam that he was the only friend he had, but, like a bubble of air in an outboard motor, the quiver in his throat stopped him. He let out a shuddering sigh. 'Please, Brother. Help me. What else can I do?'

For a moment, Tam was silent. He looked down at Phuc, took his cap from his head and wiped the sweat from his brow with his handkerchief. Then, he crouched beside him. 'OK, Brother,' he said, placing his hand on Phuc's shoulder. 'I'll help you.'

'You can get me the money?' asked Phuc, relieved.

'No,' said Tam. 'I can get you a job.'

TWENTY-ONE

Hanh sat on her blue plastic chair at the entrance of the squat passageway. A bead of sweat dribbled uncomfortably between her breasts and she pressed her blouse to her skin to absorb it. The heat had arrived with the dawn this morning, creeping in through the window of her house and falling heavily to the floor, just like the robber had done. Now, it was hotter than it had been for months; an overbearing, breezeless heat, trapped between the tall buildings, thick as sour milk.

The Old Quarter seemed to slip by in slow motion. No one ever walked fast in Hanoi, but now they moved as slow as a dream through the tree-lined streets. Sandals shirked along the concrete, the steps of their owners sluggish and dull as they snagged on the heat. Bicycles leaned in lines along the pavement. An old guard-woman tore apart a cardboard box and weaved her way between the bikes in her care, spreading the fragments over their seats to stop the black from sucking in the sun. She muttered to herself, another fragment held above her head as shelter. A man stood shirtless in the gutter at the side of the road, sloshed a red flannel into a bucket and wiped beneath his arms. He was deathly thin and his spine seemed to curve and strain, like the bamboo cross of a kite in high wind. He kept one foot and one bullet-hole eye on his bicycle pump. Other men around him dozed in shaded shop-fronts. Leaning back in their chairs, their bodies slipped down and the soles of their feet faced Hanh, black as ink. Sly cats, she thought, their sleep is a trick.

Dinh was sprawled in his own chair on the opposite side of the passageway, not near enough that Hanh could touch him, but she could smell the stale alcohol seeping through his skin. She watched him grumble and stir. As he stretched, a thin, wet curve of sweat grinned at her from where his shirt had been pinched in the fat folds of his belly. He reached to the ground and took a handful of longan berries from a dish beneath his chair, piercing the skin of one with his nail and squeezing it between his grubby fingers. It split and the fruit slid out, like an eyeball. He threw the empty shell to the floor and pushed the longan into his mouth.

Hanh ground her teeth together and watched Dinh's cheeks heave and then dimple as he sucked on the fruit. She had been waiting for more than an hour for him to wake up, but now that he had, she didn't know what to say.

'Uncle Dinh?' she whispered. He didn't respond.

A man in the street shouted as he caught a sack of shallots, dropped to his shoulder from the back of a truck. Flakes of onion-skin escaped through the red netting and fluttered like moths in the sunlight.

'Uncle Dinh,' Hanh said, again. She tried to make her voice sound light and casual, as though she were talking spontaneously, as though she had not agonised all morning about what she would say. Dinh peeled open one eye and twisted it towards her. 'I need you to pay me, Uncle Dinh.'

'We talked about this,' he said, easing his eye back shut.

'I know,' said Hanh, 'but I can't wait any longer. I need my money today. It's important.'

Dinh growled, clearly irritated. 'Use your rations, greedy girl.'

'I can't. A man came into our house last night and stole our ration books.'

Dinh perked suddenly, opening both eyes and scraping his chair across the pavement towards her. He leaned on his knee and examined her face. 'You were robbed?'

'Yes,' said Hanh, blinking back the hot tears that stung in her eyes.

'What happened?'

'He broke in through the window in the middle of the night.' She swallowed a tremble from her throat and closed a fist around the deep gash in the palm of her hand. She had tried again to bend the chicken-wire back this morning, but it had twisted, snapped and sprung in her hand, spearing her.

'He took your books?'

'Yes, and our food. And my mother's medicine.'

Dinh's eyes narrowed to a scored line, but then he sat sharply back and sniffed. 'Sorry,' he said glibly. 'I can't give you what I haven't got.'

Hanh squeezed her fist tighter until she winced with the pain of her torn palm. 'I know you have it,' she said firmly. 'You're a liar.'

'Rude bitch!'

Dinh burst up from his chair and leapt towards her. Hanh tensed rigid and threw her back against the wall – ready to scream or shout or run – but instead, Dinh paused and flicked his eyes aside into the street. When he brought his stare heavily back, it felt different. He flattened his greasy hair over his scalp, licked his lips so they shone and looked at her with bloodshot, lecherous eyes.

'How much do you want that money?' he said, lowering his voice. He gripped Hanh by the elbow. His hand was warm and tight and slippery. She cast her eyes sideways too, looking for a friend, or support, or a witness. The street carried on, disinterested.

'Let go of me,' Hanh murmured, but Dinh squeezed harder.

'I'll give you your wages if you come to my house,' he whispered, dipping close to her face. The purple veins on his cheeks slipped from her focus.

She shook her head. 'I don't want to.'

'You've already offered to come to my house, little whore.'

'I didn't,' Hanh said. She tried to pull her arm away.

'It's the only way you'll get your money.'

A shudder ripped through Hanh's body and she let out a weak, pitiful moan. What else could she do? Behind her, a generator roared into life, the wall of sound walloping her like guilt. What would her mother think of her? She would be as bad as any common pavement girl. She looked at the ground and the flash of bright, sluttish pink on her painted toenails made her feel sick. She felt her limbs slacken in Dinh's grip, numbness spreading through her, her fate seeping in and she lifted her head to look at him.

But Dinh wasn't looking at Hanh any more. He was staring past her, over her shoulder, down the street. His face was puckered by angry surprise.

'I think you should give Hanh her money,' said a deep, strong voice.

'Who the fuck are you?' Dinh spat the words from his mouth as though they were a cluster of rancid berries. He let go of Hanh and her arm fell by her side. She turned around and looked up at Alexander with astonished, watery eyes.

'I'm a friend of Hanh,' he said. 'I think you should give her the money you owe.'

'Get lost,' Dinh snarled.

Alexander clicked his heels together and straightened his back. 'What's your name, Comrade?'

'What's yours? Comrade Fuckov!' Dinh snorted a laugh, but there was a sudden flicker in his eye. It was doubt, flaring like a match. Standing tall, with his face straight, Alexander looked like a Party man. Hanh watched Dinh shift and glance along the street, then he dropped his shoulders. 'Nguyen Tra Dinh,' he mumbled.

Alexander stared at him. 'Speak up.'

Dinh stiffened to attention, like a soldier. 'My name is Nguyen Tra Dinh.'

'How much does he owe you, Hanh?'

Hanh could feel herself trembling and she knotted her arms together to steady them. This was the chance she'd been waiting for. Alexander could help her! 'He owes me twelve weeks' wages,' she stammered weakly.

'Pay her,' Alexander barked.

Dinh shook his head. 'She's lying. It's never that much.'

'It's true!' Hanh cried. Her arms whipped free from their knot and she looked at Alexander, desperate.

Alexander locked his elbows by his side, scowling. 'You need to pay her for twelve weeks' work,' he said to Dinh. 'Not a day less.'

Dinh's face crumpled. 'Comrade! Be reasonable.'

'It's reasonable to pay what you owe.'

'Life is never that simple, Brother.'

'I'm not your brother.'

Dinh stepped backwards. 'I'm sorry, Comrade,' he said, lifting his palms. 'But surely you understand that there are complications? This is Vietnam!'

Alexander flicked a threatening shot of his eyes towards the squat. 'Perhaps the Party would like to hear about your complications?'

'All right!' cried Dinh. 'I'll pay her tomorrow.' He threw his hands in the air and lowered his head in surrender, but his gaze crept slyly upwards, checking for Alexander's reaction.

Alexander gave him nothing. 'Pay her now.'

'I can't. I don't have the money with me.'

'Go home and fetch it.'

'I don't live in the city, Comrade. It would take me two hours, or longer. You don't want to wait here all that time, do you?'

Alexander hesitated and glanced at Hanh. She stared back, shocked and silent. Her heart was hammering in her chest.

'Fine,' Alexander said, looking back to Dinh. 'You can pay her tomorrow, but I'll be coming back to check, so you'd better be an honest man.'

'Honest as Buddha, Comrade,' said Dinh. He bowed low, and then he edged backwards before spinning around and scampering away without another word.

Alexander turned to Hanh. 'Are you OK?' he asked her gently.

Hanh nodded, her mouth pouting. She didn't feel OK. She felt exhausted.

'You look tired,' he said.

'I didn't sleep last night.'

'Is your mother sick?'

'No. We were robbed. A man came into our house while we were sleeping.'

Hanh screwed her face up tightly and a thin dribble of tears escaped down her cheek. She smeared them quickly away with her fingers and gave a wet, childish sniff. 'He took my mother's medicine and our ration books. That's why I needed my money.'

Alexander paused and studied her, not speaking. He slipped his hand into his pocket and took out his wallet. Flicking it open, he pulled out a wedge of banknotes, folded them in half with his thumb and held them out to Hanh. 'Take this.'

Hanh squirmed away and shook her head. 'I can't take your money.'

'It's OK,' he said, stepping after her. 'We're friends.'

'No. Really, I can't.' She twisted her hands into her armpits and puckered her lips, tighter.

'Your mother needs medicine, doesn't she?'

Hanh's head flicked a sharp, painful nod.

'You can give it back to me tomorrow after you've been paid.'

She shook her head again, more vigorously. 'Dinh still won't pay me.'

'I'll make sure he gives you everything he owes,' said Alexander, calmly. 'Please, Hanh. Take the money.'

Hanh's eyes sunk down to Alexander's outstretched hand and he grabbed her wrist, pushing the banknotes against her rigid fingers. She flinched, but he wrapped his hand around hers, holding hers firmly. She stared at the money in his strong white hand. This was what she had wanted, wasn't it – protection? She took a deep breath and felt her muscles slacken, and slowly her hand began to close.

TWENTY-TWO

The man in the boat with Phuc looked as much like a skinny brown rat from Saigon's gutter as any man could. He was crouched on the empty deck, sitting back on his haunches. His eyes flashed along the shore, scanning the length of the government shipyard. Lifting his face to the sky, his nose gave a twitch in the cool night air. Then he turned to Phuc and growled, 'Put the light out.'

Phuc reached obediently across the deck. He twisted the dial on the lantern and the flame coughed and shrank into darkness. As he moved, his stomach rolled. The water in the harbour was as flat as sheet-ice, so he knew it was dread that pitched his balance over. He swallowed and blinked, his vision adjusting to the moonlight. They were lucky tonight – the clouds had shown mercy. Soft, forgiving silver seeped down from behind a thin veil; enough to light their mischief, enough to keep them hidden.

'What are we waiting for?' Phuc whispered to the gutter-rat and wrung his hands together.

The gutter-rat held his finger up, like a warning. He didn't look at Phuc. His eyes were still scouring the shore. 'Shhh,' he whispered back. 'We have to wait for the guard to leave.'

Phuc crawled to the side of the boat and peered carefully over the rim. Covered by the dark slick of night, the shipyard looked bigger than it did in the day. Containers were stacked along the waterside and they stretched for a hundred yards or more. They were bleak and impassibly tall, like the walls of a fortress. Phuc hadn't seen the guard earlier, but now he found just a smear of slightly darker black, inching along the concrete at the brink of the water, the light of a torch swinging weakly by his side. He ducked back down and scrabbled anxiously across the deck. 'You said there weren't going to be any guards tonight?'

'Calm down, little girl,' said the gutter-rat. 'He'll be gone soon.' He pointed to the fence at the east end of the shipyard and Phuc's stare followed the line of his long, bony finger. 'See those containers at the end of the quay? Once he moves past them, he'll have finished a round of the yard and he'll go to the office for a whisky and a nap. He won't be back for more than an hour.'

'I know this shipyard,' said Phuc, trying to suppress his rising panic. 'The guard station is right by the pier. He'll hear us.'

The gutter-rat rubbed his thumb and forefinger together. He gave a stringy, buck-toothed grin. 'The guard's a deep sleeper,' he said.

'Look!' Phuc scrambled to his knees as the torchlight reached the end of the quay, changed direction and disappeared from sight. 'He's gone!'

The gutter-rat sprang instantly up and darted to the back of the boat. He wrenched the cord of the outboard motor and Phuc's heart jumped as the sound of the engine exploded into the quiet night. The gutter-rat forced the tiller hard towards him and the boat spun to face the shore, rolling so steeply sideways that Phuc thumped to his tailbone and sprawled on the floor. They ripped through the water, rearing up against the quay in just a few seconds.

As suddenly as it had started, the engine cut out, but Phuc could still feel the bass pounding through his chest. He clambered to his feet and placed his hand on the cold, concrete wall at his side, as much to steady himself as from the sway of the boat. Looking up, he could see the side of the fuel pipe running along the land, eight feet or so above him. It was a broad curve of dark, heavy metal. It looked impenetrable. How were they supposed to steal diesel from here? He rammed his shirt nervously down into the waist of his trouser and dragged his hand across the nape of his neck. 'What's the plan?'

The gutter-rat turned away and dropped to the floor, rummaging through a crate on the deck. 'Here,' he said, standing up and thrusting a huge, battery-powered drill into Phuc's hand. He jerked his head to the top of the wall. 'Go on. Get up there.'

'We're going to drill into the fuel pipe?' cried Phuc aghast.

'*You're* going to drill into the fuel pipe.'

'Why me?'

'You need the cash.'

'No,' said Phuc, shaking his head. 'It's far too dangerous.'

The gutter-rat eyed him, a twitch of amusement on his thin lips. 'What did you expect? We're paying you a mighty sum of money, Brother. You were always going to earn it. We can pick our own flowers.'

'But I don't know what I'm doing!' Phuc protested.

The gutter-rat shrugged. 'You don't need to be an engineer. Just find a spot on the bottom of the pipe and start drilling. What's the problem with that? The metal's about an inch thick – give or take – so just be careful not to drill too far. You don't want to go all the way through; you'll cause a spark and then . . . *bang!*' He grinned and threw his arms wide open.

'Bang,' muttered Phuc, staring down at the drill in his hand.

The gutter-rat stooped back to the crate and pulled out a satchel. He slung it roughly over Phuc's head, gripping his shoulder and staring into his eyes. 'There's a mallet and nail in the bag. When you've almost drilled though the metal, you tap away the last part with those. They're rubber, so no sparks,' he said. 'Understand?'

Phuc gave a meek nod. He couldn't believe it had come to this.

'There's a valve in the bag too. Once you've made a hole, the pressure in the pipes will make the diesel flow like the Mekong in a monsoon. You need to get that valve fitted and closed as quickly as you can. The whole thing shouldn't take you more than fifteen minutes. Then you give me the nod and I'll throw up the hose. We'll fix it up to the barrels and we're laughing.'

The gutter-rat let go of Phuc's shoulder and stepped back. He hauled open the trapdoor at his feet. Phuc peered down at the cluster of oil drums that were squeezed beneath the small deck. He didn't feel like laughing. 'There's only five barrels,' he said, with despair. 'I'm risking my life for five barrels of diesel?'

'Do you know what five barrels is worth today?' said the gutter-rat, jabbing Phuc sharply on the arm. 'With the blackouts, five barrels of diesel is five barrels of gold. The entire country is desperate for fuel. We send these barrels over to the boss, he'll water them down with cooking oil or animal fat, and then he'll have ten barrels. He'll sell them right back to the Party. It's top-quality stuff we're pinching, here, Brother. The purest fuel in the country! Even diluted, it'll fetch a mean price. I heard he inspected fuel from every port in the South before he picked this one – tried it all on the tip of his tongue! I took him a fistful of samples myself last week,' said the gutter-rat proudly.

'The boss?' asked Phuc, though the lurch in his gut had already told him the answer.

'Cheung Hu!' cried the gutter-rat. 'He's the boss of all that shines in Saigon. Doesn't every man know that? He's setting up a new enterprise. We're only taking five barrels today because someone will notice if we take any more, but once the valve is in place we can come back any time we like. We'll be back every night like this, I reckon. That's why this job is paying so well – it's an investment. Cheung Hu is a clever man.'

'Clever as a cobra,' Phuc murmured, with a grimace. Of course Cheung Hu was behind this. What other man in Saigon would have such gall as to steal from the Party? His memory spat back to the tobacco store, to the little shallow dish on the desk with the vials of glittering, liquid gold. He hadn't given them a thought at the time, but now they made sense. The reminder of that terrible room was all that was needed to steel him. He crammed the drill into the satchel, hitched it up on his shoulder and looked at the gutter-rat. 'We're wasting time.'

The gutter-rat squatted down, linking his fingers together. Phuc stepped into his hands. Snatching a last, quick check for the guard, he hooked his arm over the top of the wall and heaved himself up. He flattened his body to the ground and slid beneath the pipe, wriggling into the shadowy gap between the duct and the row of containers behind.

Running his hand along the belly of the pipe, Phuc searched blindly for a spot he could own. He didn't know what he was looking for. He had hoped to feel a shred of control, but the metal was smooth and coolly uniform. It gave him nothing. He pulled the drill from the satchel and pressed his finger on to the trigger to test it. The drill-bit spun into frantic action and he let go again, startled. He kicked his shoes from his feet and wrapped his bare soles around the pipe, pushing backwards and bracing his spine against the containers. He glanced at the sky and muttered a prayer, then lowered the drill to the metal.

The noise was deafening. In the quiet dead of the Saigon night, metal forcing into metal felt like the loudest sound Phuc had ever heard. It spat through his arm and into his jawbone, echoing across the surface of the slumbering harbour. He clenched his teeth and counted the seconds through his mind, two heartbeats for each, and he concentrated hard on steadying the juddering tool in his hand. A line of sweat dribbled down his forehead and into his eye and he flinched at the sting, but he kept his hands securely ahead. He wanted this over. Even if he didn't drill too far and cause a spark, even if all his body parts stayed firmly together, with a roaring bellow like this it would only be a matter of time before someone from the Party came running and caught him.

He paused and took his finger from the trigger, and the night fell back to silence. He took the drill away from the pipe and slid his hand beneath it. His finger caught in a small, warm indentation. Was it ready so quickly? He didn't dare to chance his luck any more, so he tucked the drill back into the gutter-rat's satchel and pulled out the nail and mallet. As he ran the nail along the underbelly of the pipe, it snagged in the drill-dent. He held it there with a trembling hand, picked up the mallet and gave a soft, upwards tap. Just gently. Tap-tap. A dull chime rang out across the water. Then, he hit the nail harder. Tap-tap, he went. TAP-TAP.

The pipe gave way beneath the nail and the smell of diesel was instant and choking.

'Shit!' Phuc hissed, falling backwards and grabbing urgently into the satchel, searching for the valve. He wasn't ready! Diesel glugged from the hole in the pipe and spilled over the concrete, pouring from the wall to the sea in surges and gasps.

'What are you doing?' the gutter-rat shouted from the boat. 'Get the valve!'

'I'm trying!'

Phuc threw the contents of the satchel on to the floor and scrabbled for the valve. He crammed it under the pipe and groped for the hole, his hands fumbling in the flow of slippery diesel. As he rammed the nozzle upwards, as hard as he could, he felt the torrents over his hands and arms ebb and then cease. He reached for the mallet and gave the valve a sharp crack just to be certain, then slumped back against the containers, panting. From head to toe, he was covered in diesel, and stinking, and his mouth was foul with the taste of fuel. He coughed and spat a thick syrup of spittle on to the ground.

'Throw me the hose,' he called over the edge of the wall, still coughing.

The gutter-rat scurried to the trapdoor and uncoiled a length of clear plastic tubing. He spun one end of it into the air like a lasso and Phuc took a grab, pulling it underneath the fuel pipe and twisting it tightly on to the neck of the valve. He wiped his hands pointlessly over his smothered trousers, then carefully tugged at the turnkey. The tube gave a whiplash crack with the force of the pressure and Phuc saw the orangey liquid begin to flow through. He leaned over the wall again and looked at the boat. The gutter-rat peered back, all eyes and teeth in the moonlight, and held up his thumb.

Phuc fell back against the wall of containers and slid to the slippery ground. The reek of the fuel was making him dizzy and his eyes were blistering-raw. His tongue felt as though it had been greased by hot, bitter oil, but still, he could taste something fragrant. Cheung Hu sidled into his mind; he was hunched over a barrel, his sleeves rolled to his elbows and dirty smears of diesel on his shimmering silk shirt. In his hand, there were chunks of fluffy, white pig-fat and he dropped them in and stirred until they melted. He was completely oblivious to the man who had stolen this bounty for him. Cheung Hu was paying for Phuc to trick him. What sweetness!

Phuc reached to his side and curled his fingers around the dripping handle of the mallet. He'd give the turnkey a proper hard thwack when he left, to break it. He'd ruin Cheung Hu's new enterprise before it began. As the diesel began to fall into the barrels below with a dead metallic patter, Phuc exhaled and allowed himself just the smallest of smiles.

TWENTY-THREE

Hanh lifted her hat from her head and wiped the damp strands of hair from her brow. She lay back along the ridge between the paddies. The sky above her was brilliant; flawless blue silk drifted to the earth with heavenly calm. The light had a rare crispness today. Hot sun had seared through the haze and the fields were glowing yellow and green, not as a shimmer or a fade, but all at once, like fresh lime peel spread out across the land. The gentle, cleansing wind fussed about her and she let out a deep, comforted sigh. She felt so relieved to have told Thuy about the robber, and Dinh, and Alexander.

Thuy was sitting on the ridge beside her. She pulled her knees to her chest and wrapped her arms around them, tapping her empty water bottle on the top of her foot. 'Hanh, this doesn't feel right to me.'

'I know,' Hanh replied bitterly. 'Dinh's a fat pig.' She held her hands up to the sky and fanned the silhouette of her fingers against the luminous blue.

Thuy shook her head. 'No, not Dinh. The Russian.'

Hanh's hands dropped and she pushed herself up. She looked at Thuy, confused. 'Alexander helped me.'

'Are you sure?'

'Of course I'm sure. Weren't you listening? Imagine what Dinh would have done to me if Alexander hadn't arrived.' She flinched at the thought of Dinh's slimy skin and his dirty fingers clamped around her quivering arm.

Thuy paused and took a small breath. 'That's just it, though, isn't it, Hanh?' she said, carefully. 'Don't you think it's a bit strange how he came along at exactly the right time? It's like he knew.'

'Knew what? That I needed help? I work at the squat, Thuy. I think he knows my father isn't a Mandarin.'

'Yes, but *right then*? He knew you were desperate. It was like he'd been watching.'

'It was good fortune, that's all.'

'You think?'

'Maybe it was fate.' Hanh grinned and the frown lines in Thuy's nose deepened.

'Since when do you listen to Princess Fate?'

Hanh shrugged. 'I don't know. Since she smiled at me at last.'

A creak like a rusting hinge pierced through the quiet paddy and a loudspeaker started to sizzle out a stern bulletin. It was slung from a pole at the corner of the field nearest the road, and the hollow tin voice cut in with something about the Land Reform, and a court case and a smuggler from China who'd been caught at the border and sentenced to death. Thuy stared at her feet and scraped the drying mud from her toes with the bottom of her water bottle.

'I think you should forget about the Russian, little duck,'

she said, when the voice of the Party fell back into ominous silence. 'Just go back to normal.'

Hanh screwed up her face. Normal made her bones ache. 'That's easy for you to say. Your life is easy.'

'My life's just the same as yours,' said Thuy.

'No, it's not. You have your family to look after you. What do I have?'

Thuy chipped a chunk of mud from her fingertip and flicked it into the paddy. 'You have me,' she chirruped.

Hanh remembered standing on Thuy's doorstep yesterday morning, tears pouring over her cheeks, and nothing but the echo of a wooden knock answering her. Alexander had been right; blood was what mattered – the little droplets of all her history and future that flowed through her, and came together in powerful red rivers and kept her alive. A girl was nothing without a real family. She moved to the edge of the ridge, away from Thuy, and shoved her feet down into the stodgy earth. She tugged a wiry blade of weed-grass up from the water and began to tear it into threads, tossing them back into the paddy.

Thuy shuffled after her. She picked Hanh's hat from the ridge of the paddy and balanced it carefully on her down-turned head. 'I wish you hadn't taken his money,' she said quietly.

'What was I supposed to do?' she said. 'Let my mother go without medicine and food?'

'You could have borrowed money from me.'

'Don't be stupid. Your mother already has enough mouths to feed.'

'Everyone would have spared something for you.'

'Not enough for medicine.'

'We would have tried. You shouldn't have taken it.'

'I couldn't refuse. He just pushed it into my hand.'

Thuy looked at Hanh, shocked. 'He touched you?'

Hanh stared back. She couldn't understand why Thuy was being so negative, dredging the riverbed for slippery eels that just weren't there. 'Yes,' she said, frustrated.

'On the street?'

'Yes.'

'Were people watching?'

'Heavens, Thuy! I don't know. Why does it matter?' Hanh threw away the last thread of grass and ripped another up from the muddy water.

Thuy was still watching her, her head tipped to the side, like a nosy bird. 'What does he want in return?'

'He doesn't want anything. I'm going to pay him back.'

'He'll want something more than money.'

'He doesn't.'

'Don't be a fool, Hanh. Men don't do good deeds.'

'Why can't you just be happy for me?'

'Happy about what?' said Thuy.

Hanh gulped the air. She didn't know how to answer. What was it that she felt happy about, exactly? She shook her head free of Thuy's question and rammed her feet deeper into the mud. 'What harm am I doing? You told me I needed a man to look after me.'

'He gave you money, Hanh. That's not looking after you. Dinh's got a hot temper. He won't forget this. What do you think he will do when your Russian has gone?'

'I don't know.'

'You'll never find a Vietnamese husband if you let a Russian man ruin you first.'

Hanh spat at the ground, disgusted. 'I won't let him *ruin* me. We're just friends.'

'Have you ever heard of a rich man making friends with a squat-girl?'

'This is different.'

'How do you know?'

'Because I've seen enough men at the squat to recognise a dirty stare when I see one. Alexander's not like that.'

'Why's he bothering to talk to you then?'

'I don't know. To be honest, Thuy, I don't care. You know I'm always careful, and I haven't promised him anything at all, so why shouldn't I let him hang around if he wants to watch my back and teach Dinh a lesson? I've got nothing to lose.' She paused and shrugged crossly. 'Besides, I don't want a Vietnamese husband.'

Thuy laughed. 'Do you think the Russian is going to marry you, Hanh?'

Hanh frowned. 'Of course I don't.'

'Good, because he's not. He's going to go back to his home and leave you here.' Thuy shunted herself across the ridge and put her arm gently around Hanh's shoulder. 'Stop dreaming,' she whispered.

Hanh pushed Thuy away, standing up and sloshing backwards into the paddy. 'I'm not dreaming,' she stammered, suddenly furious. She realised then that she had been, though.

Over the past few days, her thoughts had found their way to Alexander more than often. She had seen herself in a cabin by a lake, in a snowy Russian paradise. The squat, the paddies, Dinh, the robber, her worry and her hunger had already begun to loosen their grip and fade away. She glared at Thuy. 'Why are you being so cruel?'

'I'm not being cruel. You need to be realistic. Girls are like raindrops. Some fall on palaces, some fall on rice fields. Look where you are. Your ankles are under the water. Your spine is bent. The back of your neck is burned by the sun. You're in the rice fields, Hanh. Accept it.'

Hanh didn't know what she was going to say until the words exploded out of her. 'You're jealous!' she cried.

Thuy looked up, her eyes wide and disbelieving. 'Don't talk swill.'

'You are!' Hanh stamped her foot and the paddy-water spat around her. She raised her voice, even louder. She couldn't help it. 'You can't bear the thought that I'll end up with a better life than you!'

'How can you say that, Hanh?'

'It's true!'

'I'm your sister.'

'No you're not.'

'*Hanh!*'

Hanh saw the hurt pinch Thuy's face. Thuy was shaking her head, and her bottom lip shivered as though she was going to cry, but Hanh didn't care. She couldn't stop herself. It felt great to be shouting, letting go. 'You're not my blood!' she screamed.

Thuy burst into tears. Hanh stood in the paddy, listening to the race of her heart in her ears and watching Thuy's hands scramble to collect her gloves, hat and water bottle and cram them into her basket.

Thuy bundled the wicker basket on to her hip and wiped her streaming nose with the ball of her hand. 'Don't come crying to me when you end up as his whore!' she spluttered, and she hurried away along the paddy ridge towards her home.

Hanh stood alone in the field, her feet in the mud, the sun on her neck and her body shaking, waiting for Thuy to turn and look back. She never did.

TWENTY-FOUR

Phuc liked Cholon less and less every time he returned. It was different from the rest of Saigon; the streets and alleyways tangled together as an unfamiliar and unknowable world. Snatches of curt, clucked Cantonese speech walled him apart from the people he passed, and he felt himself studied by pale-moon faces and slithery eyes. From the crested rooftops, spike-backed dragons snarled menacingly down and he quickened his walk past lines of shops selling garish gold offerings for the Chinese gods, not bothering to look up at their unreadable signs. Ducks had been lynched in a window and they hung in a row, a hook through each neck. Whiskered fish flittered in tanks below them, their tails thrashing against grime-green glass. From the restaurants, the smell of sickly, perfumed sausage and sizzling grease leaked into the street's stagnant air. It mixed with the fumes of diesel, still thick in his lungs, and made him feel nauseous.

He had the sense too, that unfriendly Chinese weren't all who watched him. He seemed to pass a temple with every second step, glimpsing the sombre, vacant faces of plump deities peering at him like porcelain dolls. How many gods did the Chinese need to protect them? The talismans scared

Phuc also. Little piles of pebbles guarded every shuttered doorway, as though a hundred bad spirits flew loose in this part of the town. He strode on unhindered, at an urgent pace; the pavement was almost empty. The Chinese never sat outside, drinking tea and talking, like the Vietnamese did. Perhaps they felt watched too, he wondered.

He darted quickly past the entrance to Fán T'án Alley, not daring to sneak a sideways glance, and reached the bar and barged open the door, without hesitation. Inside, the room's emptiness, its dull light and cool concrete walls, gave him a morsel of relief. No spirits were loose in here, for sure.

'We're not open,' said the bar-girl. Her eyes scanned him warily.

She was a different girl to the one who had been here before. Her skin was darker and her teeth were chipped and askew. She looked older and less forgiving.

Phuc leaned across the bar, his elbows on the cold polished countertop. 'I'm here to see the Herder.'

The girl paused, frowned and then nodded. She pulled the cloth from her shoulder and wiped her hands before throwing it into a bucket on the floor and ducking beneath the bar. She walked to the far end of the galley-thin room, glancing back at Phuc and disappearing through the door in the wall. Phuc listened to her footsteps echoing in a slow plodding climb up the staircase. They ended and he held his breath, his ears straining to listen.

The footsteps returned as a tumbling gallop, rushing from sky to earth as though they were fleeing. The girl charged back through the door and slammed it behind her. She gathered herself with a smooth of her hair and slipped back under the countertop without looking at Phuc. He watched her guiltily. There was a slight, frightened heave to her breast. It did nothing to settle his nerves.

'Good to see you again, Brother,' said the Herder suddenly. 'You're lucky you caught me. I'm not often in Saigon at this time of year.'

Phuc leapt from his stool, startled. How had this enormous Russian wolf been able to sneak up on him? His exhausted mind was faltering.

'I've got your money,' he said, pulling the block of banknotes from his pocket and holding them out clumsily.

The Herder stared at the money and then at Phuc, his lips pulled slightly to the side by amusement. He pushed past Phuc and sat down at the bar. 'Have a drink.'

Phuc shook his head. 'No thanks.'

The Herder ignored him and snapped his thick fingers at the bar-girl. 'Two bottles of Saigon 333.'

'I don't want a drink,' said Phuc, hovering nervously. 'I just want to settle our deal.'

The Herder pulled a barstool close beside him. 'Only dull deals are made with dry veins,' he said, and he slapped the seat's plastic top. 'Sit down.'

Phuc lowered himself reluctantly on to the stool and crammed the money back into his pocket. The Herder was so huge that he didn't feel brave enough to do anything else. The bar-girl took two beers from the fridge, chipped their caps on the edge of the bar and placed them down.

The Herder gulped back a swig of his drink and gave a long, satisfied sigh. Phuc pinched the rim of his bottle between his fingers and waited for the Herder to say something. The Herder stared quietly ahead, scratching his chin and drinking.

'So, you can get me a girl?' said Phuc at last, when he couldn't stand the hush any longer.

'Of course,' the Herder replied. He held his drink to his lips and his breath sang across the neck of the bottle. 'Do you live with your mother?'

'No,' Phuc frowned. He didn't understand.

'Good. I've got a sexy one in mind for you. Mothers don't like the sexy ones.' The Herder nudged Phuc's arm and winked. 'She's got a real pretty face. Nice figure. One hundred per cent virgin, guaranteed. She's a village girl, not a city girl. Village girls are purer. They work harder. You're getting a real bargain from me, Brother. It breaks my heart to see her go so cheaply.'

The Herder looked down at the bar and shook his head, falsely solemn. His speech had a well-buffed, unnerving pallor.

'Remember she needs to be fifteen years old,' said Phuc, wriggling on his seat. 'I won't take her unless she's fifteen.'

'Sure. She's fifteen. No problem.' The Herder clapped his hands together, like a deal had been done. 'I promise you a real good time, Brother.'

'She's not for me,' Phuc murmured at the bar.

The Herder's eyes shrank into thin, wry lines and a grin bled across his face. 'Ah, yes. I remember. You're settling debts.'

Phuc winced and clutched his drink, tighter. He wished he had never told the Herder what he needed the girl for, but the thrill of the plan had just overspilled when he thought of it. 'It's not as bad as it sounds,' he lied.

'The refrain of a true gambling man.'

'I'm not a gambler.'

'And I'm not your wife, so I don't give a monkey's ass what you are. It's a shame, though. Like I said, she's a good one. Cheung Hu is a lucky bastard.'

The barstool gave a creak as Phuc squirmed. He glanced anxiously at the Herder. 'Do you know Cheung Hu?'

'Every man in Cholon knows Cheung Hu.'

'No,' he faltered. 'I mean, do you know him *personally*.'

The Herder paused and looked Phuc over. He reached out and coiled his heavy arm around Phuc's sagging shoulders, pulling him in. His breath stank of beer and damp tobacco. 'Don't worry,' he whispered, still grinning. 'I won't get paid if I tell him, will I?'

Phuc shook his head.

The Herder lifted his arm away and went back to his drink. 'Anyway, it's none of my business what you do with your girl,' he shrugged.

An image of Cheung Hu shuddered through Phuc's mind. He wanted to ask the Herder what he knew about him. He wanted to ask what he'd do to a girl and how he would treat her, but ignorance made a softer bed than honesty.

'So what do I need to do now?' he said, stuffing his hand into his pocket and restlessly flicking at the banknotes.

'You don't do anything.'

'How do I get the girl?'

'I'll sort it.'

'When?'

'The next few days. I'll get in touch with my associate. He'll get in touch with you. You meet him. You pay him. She's all yours.' The Herder held his beer bottle by the neck and tilted it at Phuc. 'I don't allow returns. If you don't want her you'll have to get rid of her yourself.'

Phuc nodded, limply. He couldn't bring himself to speak any more. This was one of his problems solved, but hardly a celebration, and the thought of the sentence he'd handed this girl was brutally shrill. He dropped his chin to his chest, closed his eyes and breathed deeply. The Herder placed a hot hand on his shoulder and gave him a slow, sarcastic pat.

'Normally, I'd offer you a replacement if she runs away within a year, but I don't suppose you give a shit about that, do you? If this one escapes you'll have far bigger things to worry about.' He leaned back against the wall and belched an enormous belly laugh. It kicked a hollow bounce about the empty room. 'Oh, Brother, I don't envy you! Your little brown bollocks must be made of pure granite. I've never known a man to bet bigger!'

Phuc took a gulp of beer. 'It was a mistake,' he muttered angrily. 'I told you.'

'No.' The Herder shook his head, but his grin was stretching wider. 'Not the bet you've already made; the one you're about to. You're placing your trust in a stranger.'

'You'll keep your word,' said Phuc. 'It's business.'

The Herder laughed, even louder than before. 'Flattered though I am that you think I'm honest, I was talking about the girl. You're trusting her with a lifetime of silence. It's a brave move.'

At the pit of Phuc's stomach, fear pinched him suddenly. I'm not brave, he thought. I'm *foolish*. When Tam had suggested the girl might talk, he had been quick to dismiss him. Now, in the quiet calm of the bar, the flaws in his plan seemed to grow and blacken. 'I've thought it through,' he murmured, as much to defend himself from his own doubt as the Herder's.

'I hope you have!' the Herder boomed back. 'I don't want that Cheung Hu on my doorstep either. If I were you, I'd hope he hates you enough to kill the little whore quickly before she has the chance to give us both away. I respect initiative, Brother. I like a man who fights for his life. That dragon won't be so forgiving.' The Herder shunted his chair towards Phuc's, leaning in and lowering his head to find Phuc's eyes with his own amused, watery stare. 'You know the Viet barber from the market square? He lost barely a hundred dong in the alley, but couldn't pay it back. He promised Cheung Hu a year of personal service but disappeared into the Zones before he'd snipped a whisker. He was gone for months before Cheung Hu tracked him down and had him scalped with his own rusty razor. If he'll go to lengths like that for a haircut imagine what he'll do for an insult like yours.'

'He won't find out what I've done,' said Phuc through

his rising sickness. He gripped the edge of the bar to steady himself, but the Herder grabbed his wrist and yanked him closer. He held him vice-tight and peered down at Phuc's glistening palm.

'I see a future of nothing but rice and stress, my friend,' he laughed, dragging a heavy finger along a crease of Phuc's skin like a fortune teller. 'I predict you'll never shit again!'

'Let go!'

Phuc snatched back his hand, but the fear in his voice was as clear as a thunderclap. He could barely breathe. For more than a week, he hadn't sat still, and he felt exhausted. Not a single moment of lucid thought had passed through his head since he first went to Fán T'án Alley. He'd raced across the city, tripping from one misshapen plan to another as they flew from his panicked mind and dropped at his feet. How different he was now, from his youth; how shameful! He should have known better. He'd built his business – his family's lives – with care, taking his time and planning each success through thought and reason. When it mattered most, though, he'd done everything wrong. Errors chipped at his insides like sharp-beaked birds. The Party were still leeched to his ankles, and he didn't know how to prise them off, and even if his girl-swap worked and he saved Kieu now, he knew he'd still doomed his family. The Herder was right; one day, Cheung Hu would be back again. He had hoped that now the slats of his plan were all in their place he would see how they fitted together and feel such relief! He had wanted to know for certain that the plan would work, but the

TWENTY-FIVE

Hanh woke with the dawn. She was curled on her side, her arms folded neatly into the softness of her breast. Bright yellow shone through the broken window and lit a square on the wall in front of her. There were noises on the breeze outside: distant, muffled voices of women in the hamlet, birds chattering in the trees, a barking dog. Inside, the room was silent. Hanh held her breath and listened. She could not hear her mother's wheeze.

She rolled slowly on to her back, the bamboo mat clicking dryly beneath her. She blinked and exhaled as quietly as she could. Dust glittered above her, scattering through the air. There was still no sound. She didn't dare move. She lay rigid and shifted her eyes into every inch of the room they could reach, struggling to calm the rising pace of her panicking heart. Through the corner of her vision, she saw the painted toenails of her mother's pale, motionless feet.

'Mumma?' she said quietly. Then louder, 'Mumma?'

Hanh bit her teeth into her bottom lip and dragged herself up. She crawled across the floor, her arms weak and trembling. Her mother was flat on her back. Her legs were spread a little apart and her feet lolled outwards. One frail hand was hooked over her breast. The other was loose at her side, with palm upturned. Her face was as though she slept, eyes closed and parted lips. The colour of her cheeks was different, though. It was thinner.

'Are you sleeping, Mumma?' Hanh whispered.

She stared down and waited, her body shaking, but there wasn't one flicker of movement from the mat below. She raised her hand and lightly touched her fingers to her mother's wrist. It was resting in the sun and her skin was warm, but the warmth felt thin and deceitful, as though it sat on the surface. She flinched away, a moan of air slipping out through her lips. Her mother was dead.

Pushing her knuckles roughly into her cheeks, Hanh blinked hot, stinging tears back from the rims of her eyes. She pulled herself across the floor, towards the family altar, and her pyjamas snagged on the splintered floorboards. Her father's photograph stared at her blankly. His eyes were cool and directionless, and his tight lips did nothing to assure her of the comfort of death. Hanh opened her mouth to speak, but she didn't know what to say to him. She wanted to ask for his help. She wanted to say something meaningful, like her mother would have done, about what a good man he was or how he had protected them, and how grateful she was to be his blood, but suddenly she couldn't remember anything about him. Her memories of him were bound so tightly to her mother. They had always played in her head in her mother's voice, and now they circled up into the air, like dead leaves, and Hanh wasn't sure she had ever known him at all. She fumbled to light a stub of incense, but the match scraped uselessly against the worn side of the box and she dropped it to the ground. Her focus slipped from her father's face to the shadow across the mirror-like glass and the reflection of her mother's body sprawled out on the floor.

She hauled herself up and stumbled to the back door, throwing it open and bursting on to the porch. Soft spots of pastel colour rippled through her vision and she fell from the ladder before she reached the bottom rung. She scrambled up and crossed the path to the paddy and sharp spikes of gravel stuck to the balls of her bare feet, but she didn't care. She could see the figures of women bending down in the fields around her. They didn't bother to look at her. On the other side of the paddy, a clean, white smoke rose above Thuy's house, like a benevolent spirit. She thought of Thuy's mother, crouched at her stove cooking breakfast, and of Thuy sitting peacefully beside her. She turned away bitterly and began to run.

Hanh sprinted along the paddy ridges, towards the river. Her eyes were blurring with tears and her feet faltered over the rocks and the weeds and the wet mud, and she thought of all the mornings she had walked this way before, with her mother holding tight to her hand. Her mind was already at the riverside. It had sunk back to the times that her mother had beaten wet laundry on the rocks, and Hanh had crouched in the grass with a bar of slippery white soap in her hand. She remembered her father too, now; he was with them. He was threading silkworms on to his fishing hook with strong, calloused fingers. She remembered his line, tossed into the water, and how the crystal light spun down the wire like a wish before the current snatched it away. She remembered the feeling of the three of them together, like water beneath her, and it left her breathless. Now, there was nobody who remembered these things but her.

She reached the river, staggered down the bank and she let her body slump into the shallow water. Air bubbled up through her pyjamas and the faded blue-green pattern billowed like waves. She slapped her hands down on the swollen material and the water whistled and kissed back in her face, and she closed her eyes and let the cool river hold her.

TWENTY-SIX

Alexander sat at the window in the guesthouse. He leaned forward in his chair and drummed his fingertips on the low windowsill, his gaze skittering along the rooftops of the untidy Hanoi skyline.

Ever since Dinh had slunk away from the squat, Alexander's skin had tingled. No. It was more than a tingle. It was a real, electric buzz. The hairs on his arms were pricked to attention. He couldn't keep from twitching his fingers and toes. Toying with Dinh was the best fun he'd had in ages. He'd been in total control. That man was a helpless mouse, batted back and forth between his powerful paws. *Yes, Comrade. No, Comrade. Whatever you want, Comrade. Let me rub your feet, Comrade.* He knotted his fingers behind his head and a laugh jerked from his lungs. He wished the Herder had been there to see how well he'd done. He would have laughed too.

The sound of a fist knocking on the door made Alexander start. His head snapped round and he stared at the rattling bolt. 'Who is it?'

'Mr Alexander?' The high-pitched voice of the proprietor's son squawked eagerly back from the corridor.

'I'm busy.'

The knock came again, a frantic cluster of little rapped knuckles. Alexander swore and dragged himself from his chair. He grabbed two shirts from the open wardrobe – one to cover his naked back and one to cover his baby – then opened the door. The proprietor's son beamed up at him.

'Good afternoon, Mr Alexander,' he said, wiggling his toes on the tiled floor and peering shamelessly into the room. 'How are you today?'

Alexander glowered down and spread his hands out to the doorframe, blocking the boy's view. 'What do you want?'

'Telephone call, Mr Alexander.'

Alexander's heart stiffened. He touched his thigh to check for the key in his pocket, then slammed the door shut and tore down the staircase. Only one person would be on the line. He didn't want to keep him waiting. The boy scampered after Alexander, clutching the rail to keep his balance and still grinning expectantly. In the lobby, the proprietor was idling back in his chair, his shoeless feet splayed across the reception desk. He weeviled a toothpick between his teeth and stared as brazenly as his son had done, but with none of the smile. The boy clambered on to the counter-top, a flurry of scrawny arms and legs, and grabbed the receiver and held it out. Alexander snatched it and wiped the earpiece with the ball of his hand. He turned his back to the desk and took a deep, excited breath. 'Hello?'

'Why are you at the Salute in the middle of the day?' The Herder's voice was smug and authoritative. 'You should be working.'

Alexander let slip a slight smile. 'I've been working hard all week,' he said.

'You better have been. I don't expect to crack my nuts while you're sipping jackfruit cocktails and fondling that little runt who answered the phone.'

'Don't worry,' said Alexander, with a flick of his head. He swapped the receiver from one ear to the other and straightened his shoulders. 'I'm taking care of it. I went to the squat and the girl's boss was there, and they were arguing because she hadn't been paid—'

'I didn't ask for a dossier, Alexander.'

'Right, of course not.'

'What's the headline?'

'Brilliant. It's going brilliant.'

'Good. I need you to put the cow in the truck and bring her to market.'

Alexander swallowed a sudden lump from his throat. All morning, he'd thought about the Herder and how pleased he would make him. He'd been thinking of Hanh too. She had looked at him with such genuine admiration that it made him blush. Not that he didn't deserve it; he'd already done so much for her. He hadn't stopped to think about what happened next, though – about where she was going. 'You've found a buyer?' he asked, deflated.

'Damn right.'

'In Saigon?'

'No. In Washington DC. It's Nixon. He's had time on his hands, since Watergate. Asked me to find him a hobby.'

Alexander didn't answer. He gripped the receiver tightly

217

in his hot hand and felt the Herder measuring his pause.

'You do have her ready, don't you?' the Herder asked suspiciously.

'Yes,' Alexander lied.

'Good. The buyer's on a deadline.'

Alexander hesitated, again. He twisted the telephone wire around his wrist. The loops of the plastic cord stretched and creaked. He glanced at the desk, at the dozing proprietor and his gap-toothed, gawping son, then edged away and lowered his voice. 'What's he like?'

'Nixon?'

'The buyer.'

There was a sharp hiss of breath down the line. 'He's a fucking saint.'

'I want to meet him.'

'Just get the girl down here.'

'Do you know what he wants her for?'

'Shut up, Alexander.'

Alexander snatched the receiver from his face. He hated it when the Herder scolded him. The man's jaws were crocodile-strong. He let a long, jitterish sigh escape, then wiped its dregs from his mouth and brought the telephone back to his ear. 'When do you need her?' he said, levelling his voice.

'Yesterday.'

'What do you want me to do?'

'Get the fuck down here.'

'Is that all?'

'Call him. The name's Phuc.'

'What's the number?'

Alexander snapped his fingers at the boy on the counter and pointed to the notepad beneath his father's feet. The boy ripped the paper out and rooted for a pen, and he leaned against Alexander's arm as the Herder reeled off a telephone number and Alexander scrawled it quickly down.

'OK,' he said when he'd finished scribbling. 'I'll get it done.'

The Herder growled. 'Just do the job. Nothing else. Don't start asking him any of your questions.'

'I won't.'

'I mean it, Alexander.' The Herder's voice was stern. 'What he does with the girl is his business. Don't fuck this up.'

Alexander closed his eyes and scrabbled for an answer, but the line had already clicked dead. He pressed his finger to cut off his own call and held it pushed down on the telephone. What kind of a buyer had a deadline? It sounded so brutally final. Alexander didn't like him already. The Herder was not as good at choosing buyers as he was. He lifted his finger, waited for the tone and then dialled. The telephone gave a shrill bleat.

'Saigon Port,' said a distant, wary voice. 'Shipping Arrivals office.'

'Mr Phuc?'

'Yes?'

'My name is Alexander. I believe we have a deal to arrange.'

'That's right.'

'When do you want her?'

'By Friday.'

Alexander pushed his fingers into his brow and squeezed his eyelids hard together. Friday! Just four fucking days to find a girl and ship her a thousand miles south! He wished he hadn't told the Herder that Hanh was ready. It hadn't left him any time to prise her gently away from her life in Hanoi; she would need to be wrenched. Alexander never enjoyed wrenching. It left a rancid taste in his mouth. What the fuck was he going to tell her to get her to leave? It would have to be something dramatic, something he couldn't think of right now. He knew what the Herder would say. He would tell him to force her, to slip a ring through her nose and give it a yank. Alexander cringed at the thought of it.

'Friday's too soon,' he said, rubbing the throb in the side of his head. 'I need more time.'

Phuc snapped instantly back: 'That's not acceptable.'

Alexander scowled down the telephone. 'You are not buying a watermelon, Mr Phuc. Sometimes procurement of women can take longer than you'd like.'

'The Herder promised me a girl by Friday.'

'I'll do my best.'

'I need a guarantee.'

'Not possible.'

'Then I'm going back to the Herder. We made a deal.'

The telephone dropped into uneasy silence. The Herder would be furious if he knew Alexander had lied. 'Fine,' he spat. 'You have my guarantee.'

There was quiet on the line again, but for an ominous crackle, like oil and water in a hot pan.

'There's another thing we need to discuss,' said Phuc.

'You pay me at the handover.'

'No.' His voice sounded hushed and suddenly cagey. 'This is about the girl.'

Alexander sniffed. 'What about her?'

'I'm going to give her to someone else – someone who must believe she is my daughter. She needs to call me Father. If anyone asks her questions, she needs to lie. If you can't get her to do this, I won't buy her.'

Alexander sucked a breath suspiciously inwards. This was a new one. 'Why does she need to call you Father?'

'The Herder said you wouldn't ask questions.'

'The Herder was wrong. Who are you giving her to?'

'That's my business.'

'Since the girl is currently under my care it's my business too.'

Phuc hesitated and Alexander could hear the weight of his breath. The tremble gave him no scrap of reassurance. He left the pause open, to menace him. It worked.

'I'm giving her to a man called Cheung Hu,' Phuc mumbled at last.

Alexander's heart skipped. 'Chinese Cheung Hu?'

'Yes.'

'You expect me to tell her this?'

'Yes.'

'And to get her to behave?'

'Yes.'

'And what if I say that's your problem?'

'Then our deal is cancelled.'

Phuc slammed down the receiver before Alexander had a chance to reply and for the second time in just a few minutes, he was left with only the dry hum of a broken line in his spinning head. He snarled and dropped the telephone. This was a real thick fucking mess! Cheung Hu was a serpent, as cold and slippery as any beast from the depths of the sea, and Alexander didn't feel happy about sending Hanh with him, but what choice did he have? The Herder's voice tolled deep in his head. *Don't fuck this up.* Alexander shuddered. He didn't feel braced to withstand a lashing.

He dug his hands to the bottom of his pockets and barged outside into the oppressive Hanoi heat. Whatever fate he feared for Hanh, the threat of the Herder's rage was more urgent. As he marched through the heaving Old Quarter streets, the restless tin voice of the loudspeakers vibrated in the air. Perhaps it wouldn't be as bad as he thought. The Party would never go troubling her if she worked for Cheung Hu. He might want to keep her for himself too. She wasn't a bad little thing. Who wouldn't want to keep her? He was rich, so she'd never be hungry, and nobody would dare to touch Cheung Hu's woman. Yes. That was it. It would probably be fine for them both, in the end. He just needed to find her.

Hanh was not at the squat when he got there. Instead, Dinh was sitting at the entrance of the passageway, lounging back in his chair, his face as angry as a thundering sky. Alexander ran towards him, crossing the road without a look or a thought.

'Comrade!' he barked, standing stiffly in front of Dinh, his shoulders back.

Dinh jumped sharply up. 'Listen, I'll pay her as soon as she gives me the chance.'

Alexander frowned. 'What do you mean?'

'I mean, I'm not going to look for her.'

'She's not been at work?'

'Not since you played the hero.' Dinh paused and tilted his head, studying him. A smirk crept over him. 'I was wondering what you had done with her,' he said.

Alexander's stomach tightened. The look in Dinh's eye made him feel queasy. It was all too knowing; like he'd sussed who he was and what he was up to. He shook his head. 'I haven't done anything.'

Dinh shrugged. 'I wouldn't care if you had.'

'Where can I find her?'

Dinh lowered himself back to his chair, folding his arms and resting them on the ball of his belly. He slouched calmly back, still grinning. 'I'm surprised you don't already know, since you two are such good friends.'

Alexander glared at him. 'Tell me.'

'Twenty dong.'

Alexander ripped his wallet from his pocket and tore out a banknote, thrusting it into Dinh's greedy, outstretched hand. Dinh folded the note neatly and tucked it into the breast of his shirt.

'She lives in a hamlet off the East Highway,' he said, 'about fifteen miles outside the city. It's the first clump of shitty peasant houses beyond the old French cemetery.'

223

Alexander was already striding away, but Dinh was shouting after him.

'Check the ditches at the side of the highway! She's a yappy little dog! I wouldn't be surprised if someone has slapped her around and thrown her away,' he called along the crowded street. 'Whatever has happened to her, you can be sure she deserves it!'

Alexander did check the ditches, though the thought wasn't conscious. The Herder's threats were still in his ears and he just didn't want to miss anything out. He clung to the back of the motorcycle as the driver sped from the east rim of the city and on to the highway. They raced along the simmering tarmac, whipping by sharp-boned buffalo in the roadside scrub, overtaking a row of stout-nosed government trucks with shining eyes and glinting rifles peering out from the canopied backs, and he counted the weathered stone road-markers one by one, with increasing impatience. They passed the shattered headstones of the cemetery, and the driver swerved abruptly and skidded to a halt in the red-orange soil at the side of the road.

'Why have you stopped?' shouted Alexander, raising his voice above the noise of the idling engine.

The road stretched out for as far as he could see in both directions, but this couldn't be it. There weren't any houses here, just a wall of dense bamboo trees.

'The hamlet's down there,' said the driver. He pointed to the trees and Alexander saw the narrowest cut of a track. An elderly woman was sitting on a log-pile at the entrance.

She stared at them, her bright, betel-stained lips slobbered around a cob of pale yellow corn.

Alexander looked up; the sun was scorching and he didn't have time for pissing around. 'How far is it?'

The driver shrugged. 'A mile.'

'Can't you get any nearer?'

'No, Brother.' He waved his hand and his head dismissively. 'The path's too bad. All rubble and dirt.'

Alexander scowled and lifted himself from the back of the motorbike. He told the driver to wait and cast a look down the shaded track. The old woman dragged herself from the log and tapped lightly on his arm. She made some inaudible, toothless muttering and held out a begging hand. Alexander ignored her and stepped beneath the canopy. He heard a sudden spin of tyres on loose earth and the sound of the motorbike accelerating into the distance. He spat a curse beneath his breath and walked ahead. Bamboo began to merge into palm. Enormous, tattered leaves sagged limply down from bowing spines and sunlight mottled the ground below him.

The trees that flanked the path stopped suddenly and the landscape plunged into squares of flat green paddy. Alexander raised his hand, shielding his eyes from the blasting bright light. His view was littered by ten houses or more: wooden-box shanties clinging to the side of the snaking path and poised above the land on perilously leaning, strain-bowed stilts. He chewed his lip and rubbed the bridge of his nose beneath his spectacles. How the fuck would he find her? From the field, a woman spied him. She uncoiled her bent spine and stared with barefaced suspicion. He hated that look. He'd felt it before, time and again, when he'd walked the exposed gangways of paddy-ridges, with black-green paint smeared on his face, a M16 clutched to his chest and blood on his hands. He slipped from her view, behind the first house he could, throwing apart a cluster of shrieking chickens at his feet. Then – with a flood of cool relief – he saw her.

Hanh was sitting on a porch above him, knees hugged to her chest. Her eyes were fixed on some point in the distance and her hair was piled on top of her head, a nest of straggly, tangled mess. Alexander waved and walked towards her. 'Hanh?'

Hanh snapped out of her stare and looked at him, panicked. She sprung to her hands and knees, like an animal. 'I wasn't stealing!'

'Stealing what?' said Alexander, taken aback by her sudden-ness.

'Your money!' she cried. She drew her body back to the wall of the house, but kept her huge black eyes on Alexander. Her voice was pure, rasped grit. 'I wasn't going to steal it. I would have found you. I would have paid you back!'

Alexander opened his palms and raised them beside his shoulders. 'It's OK, Hanh,' he said, gently. 'That's not why I'm here.'

She looked at him and tipped her head to the side, pouting. Her fingers scratched through her hair and the heap shook and knotted more wildly. She clasped her hands together and glanced nervously around.

Alexander took a cautious step forward. He felt the risk she would bolt and flee. 'Dinh said you haven't been at work. Is everything all right?'

'I'm fine.'

He took another careful, light-footed step and climbed on to the ladder. She didn't look fine. She looked exhausted. Inky purple crescents sagged beneath her eyes and there was an untouched bowl of rice on the floor beside her. 'Are you sure?'

She paused. 'My mother died.'

Alexander took a long, thin breath and swallowed hard. This was the very best news he'd had all day. Slowly, he moved to the top of the ladder and eased himself on to the porch. The bamboo floor creaked beneath him.

'I'm sorry, Hanh,' he said, and he shot a furtive look to the path. There was nobody around, but he felt a pressing need for privacy.

Get her inside.

Get her packed.

Get her out.

This was his chance. There wouldn't be a better one. He slid along the porch, a little closer. 'Why are you sitting in the hot sun, Hanh? You'll make yourself sick. Come inside.'

Hanh pinched at the skin on the back of her hand. 'My mother's inside.'

Alexander looked at the door and scratched his nose, impulsively. He had seen what the ruthless heat could do to dead bodies. He flicked a shiver from his tightening shoulders. 'How long has she been there?'

227

'A day,' Hanh whispered.

'It's hot, Hanh. She can't stay here.'

'I know.'

'When's the funeral?'

Hanh wrinkled her nose.

'You haven't arranged anything?'

She shook her head.

'Is there anyone who can help you?'

Silence.

Alexander slipped along the floor, until he had put himself right at her side. He placed his hand gently on top of hers, and his white skin covered her brown flesh completely, like a drift of snow over scorched earth. She looked at him with pleading eyes.

'Don't worry,' he said. 'I'll help you.'

Alexander stood beside the grave at the edge of the paddy, staring down at the mound of freshly turned earth. Hanh had tried to cover it with jasmine flowers and frangipani, but dirty brown rubble still peeped through the petals. It looked like nothing more than roadside debris.

Hanh stared down too, and sniffed thickly. Her neighbours were already leaving, bowing their heads to her and then turning away and walking towards her home. Alexander had arranged for a cook to prepare the funeral supper, and three heaving bench-tables were laid out and waiting with meat and wine. Hanh had said it was more food than she'd seen at any feast in the hamlet and the neighbours couldn't scurry away fast enough, but even as they slipped away from the fresh grave to gorge themselves, Alexander could see them glance back at him, whispering. They didn't give two shits about Hanh's mother. He felt a little sad for her, but mostly relieved for himself.

'Are you ready to go?' he asked her, gently.

Hanh shook her head.

Alexander leaned back against the trunk of the banyan. Mud was drying grey on the legs of his trousers, and it cracked and flaked away as he dug into his pocket and pulled out a packet of cigarettes. He tugged one free from the box and lit it, cupping the spark in his dusty hands, then he took a drag and tilted his face towards the sun. He didn't feel the rush to leave like he had done yesterday. With her mother dead and buried, there was no doubt in his mind he could tease Hanh away from here in time for Phuc's deadline. He'd slept well last night, feeling sure of it. In a certain way too, he found that her misery had helped him relax. Now, she was really alone. She needed him, and wherever he took her – Cheung Hu or not – was better than this.

The last of the neighbours wandered away and Hanh gave a deep, weary sigh. She sat on the grass at the side of the grave, pulling her knees to her chest and staring across the paddy. She rubbed the back of her hand over her wet nose and wiped it down her *áo dài*. 'The neighbours think I'm a beggar,' she said.

Alexander blew a line of smoke above him and shook his head. 'You're not a beggar.'

Hanh looked up at him, still holding her knees. 'They know I haven't paid for the feast.'

'Does it matter?'

'It matters to them.'

'You would have paid, if you could have. That's what matters.' Alexander pinched his cigarette between his finger and thumb and jabbed it crossly in the air for effect, before planting it back between his lips. 'If Dinh had given you the money he owed you'd have paid every for every grain of rice and glass of wine on those tables.'

Hanh blushed. 'Perhaps,' she mumbled, and she fiddled with the petals on the ground.

Alexander crouched beside her. 'Your neighbours know how hard you work, Hanh. They see you in the fields and cycling to the city every day. They can't possibly think you're a beggar.'

Hanh shrugged. 'They see you here too, and that's enough.'

'What difference do I make? I'm a friend.'

'Girls like me don't have friends like you. They're afraid of you.'

'Are you afraid of me?'

Hanh laid her cheek on her shoulder and smiled sadly. 'No. I think you're a good man.'

Alexander felt a real smile too; he liked being called a good man. He looked deeply into her dark, soft eyes and his stomach gave a kick. 'I'm going back to Saigon tomorrow, Hanh.'

Hanh's eyes slipped suddenly rounder, flickering with fear. 'You're leaving?'

'I have to. It's business.'

'Can't you stay a bit longer?'

Alexander shook his head. 'I was only ever going to be in Hanoi for a few days and I've already stayed longer than I should.' He paused and licked the inside of his teeth. 'Why don't you come with me?'

Hanh wrinkled her nose and looked away. 'I can't leave my mother.'

'Your mother wouldn't want you to stay here.'

'She would,' said Hanh, plucking at the petals beside her and squirming nervously. 'She was very traditional. A family's home is sacred.'

'But your home isn't safe.'

'I'll be OK.'

Alexander edged along the ground, a little closer. 'Will you?' he said. 'What if Dinh doesn't pay you? Or the robber comes back? You're alone, Hanh. Your mother wouldn't want you to be in danger, would she?'

The lines in Hanh's nose deepened and she stared at the ground, pale and mute. White tears glimmered in the nub of her eye. Alexander lifted his hand and placed softly it on the back of her neck, feeling her powerful shiver. He stubbed his cigarette out on the grass and leaned in.

She shook her head again, but weakly.

'I'll look after you,' he whispered.

TWENTY-SEVEN

Alexander sat on the motionless train in Hanoi Station. It was dusk, but the platform was crudely lit and crawling with activity. Men, women and children crowded through the high iron gates that blocked the station from the city and a young Party official battled to check their tickets and identification documents before they shoved hurriedly by and flooded across the platform. Bicycles and rickshaws pushed through the gates too. Crates were unstrapped from their backs and loaded somewhere beyond Alexander's view, then they disappeared back through the straining city threshold. Vendor-women scurried alongside the train, tapping on the windows, touting baguettes and bags of yellowy popcorn carried in their upturned *nón lá* hats. A beggar limped through the crowds and tugged on shirts, bedraggled.

Inside the train, the streak of people moving through the carriage was unceasing. Hanh was sitting opposite Alexander, her ticket clutched tight in her hand. She had angled her head slightly down, but Alexander could see she was studying the other passengers carefully. They barged along the aisle, scrutinising tickets and seat numbers, impatiently passing sacks, bags and boxes over heads and climbing on to seats to cram their belongings into creaking storage racks, chattering like chickens at market. They paused only to gawp at Hanh and whisper. He could see it was making her nervous. It made him nervous too. There weren't many reasons a girl like her – with her young face, farm-worker's fingernails and cheap silk *áo dài* – would be sitting with a white man like him. They thought she was his whore and weren't trying to hide it. Hanh must have known what their stares meant too, and the more they smirked and scowled, the greater his risk. She might start to doubt him also. She might even run. He needed the train to start moving.

'Ignore them,' he said, sitting forward. He said it as much to himself as to her. He didn't like the truth being shoved at him either. Pulling a handkerchief from his pocket, he wiped his mouth. The heat was stifling, full of the stink of bodies and spent tobacco sweated out through dirty skin. He reached up and opened the sash window just a slit. The vendors swarmed to his side, screeching as they tried to force their hands and goods through the narrow gap. 'Do you want something to eat?' he said, to distract her.

She shook her head shyly.

'Nothing at all?'

'No, thanks.'

Alexander shrugged. Hanh had barely said anything all day. Prising words from her lips was wearing thin, but he couldn't stand the frowns and the silence. Frowns and silence left too much space for them both to think. There was a rumble of engine, a jolt, relief, and the train was off, and

Hanh shuffled to the edge of her seat and peered out through the window. A small table jutted from the wall, between them; blue Formica trimmed in scuffed, sticky metal, and she clutched the edge with both twitching hands. Alexander searched her face for any signs of a smile, but he couldn't find one. It made him feel worse.

'Have you been to Saigon before?' he asked her.

Hanh shook her head. 'I've never been further south than Hoang Mai.'

Alexander wiped his mouth, again. Shit. He'd have said that Hoang Mai was still in Hanoi. She'd never been any-where! She'd be pulled apart by those tough-skinned, worldly Saigon women, let alone the men. 'You'll like it,' he said, and he tried to sound convincing.

Hanh gripped the table tighter. 'Where are we going to stay, when we get there?'

Alexander sniffed. Accommodation had caused him a fucking headache. Phuc didn't want Hanh later than Friday, but he wouldn't take her earlier either. It wasn't an easy task, finding a place to stash a girl who didn't know she was being stashed. In the end, the Herder had bailed him out, though he'd made a right scene of it.

'My friend has a villa on the edge of Saigon,' he said bitterly. 'We're going to stay there.'

Hanh looked surprised. 'We're not going to your house?'

'No. I live in the city. It's better if we go somewhere quiet for a few days until you're feeling better.'

'But I thought you had to work?'

'It can wait.'

'I don't want to cause any trouble.'

'It's not trouble.'

'Will your friend be there too?'

'No. It's just us.' Alexander shook his head. The Herder was staying elsewhere so as not to spook Hanh. 'Evicted from my own home by a slut!' he had bellowed as he cursed Alexander's poor planning. Alexander scowled harder. The Herder owned at least three flats in the city – plus his bar – so it didn't matter one bit to him. He just liked to scold and embarrass.

Hanh sucked on her lip. She looked even more anxious. 'What's it like . . . your friend's house?'

Alexander paused. 'It's peaceful,' he said. *It's isolated*, he thought, guiltily. 'No one will bother you.' *There's nowhere for you to escape.*

Hanh nodded awkwardly and looked back at the window as the last traces of daylight abandoned the sky and Hanoi slipped from view. Alexander rubbed his palms on his legs and left her to it. If the train ran on time, it would be forty hours before they reached Ga Saigon, and then he had another full day of this. Maybe the silence was better, after all. He had never spent so much time with one of his girls – or with any girl, for that matter. He would need to think of new things to talk about. Another complete day and night of uninterrupted pretending; he felt tired before it had even begun. He stared outside at the boundary of the city. Spotlights from the checkpoint booths splintered into stars as the train pushed past. A soldier with a rifle was illuminated. His stoic expression blazed for a moment at a booth's door, and then he was gone and there was just Alexander's own dry face staring stubbornly back. A conductor marched through the carriage, throwing out blankets, tossing them into each passenger's lap with a soundless scowl. Alexander watched Hanh slip her sandals from her feet, curl her legs to her chest and fold her limbs all tightly into her little space of train, then spread the blanket over herself and tuck in her arms so only her head peeked out. She closed her big, worried eyes and Alexander wrapped his own blanket over his body too, ramming it tightly down the sides of the chair.

The train was gathering speed. The noise of the wheels on the track was deafening and the loose-springed seat bounced and creaked beneath him. There was a slight smell of oil and hot metal, like a gun. Travelling sitting backwards made him feel sick. He shunted up in his chair and straightened his legs. As the train jerked, the knees of the man beside him jarred into his and he shifted his body towards the window. His rucksack was on the floor in front of him, and he linked his foot through the strap and felt his shin rub against the thick heavy glass of his baby's jar. He wished he could have slept in a cabin, all alone with the door shut and locked, but it had been such short notice they were already booked. He clenched his leg against his jar, to soothe himself. It was going to be a long night.

After restless sleep on the Hanoi train, the cool Saigon air felt wonderful. As the rickshaw sped further away from the downtown station, the roads became dustier, wider and more

236

empty. The traffic thinned and the towers of crowded bedsits shortened. Their density eased and trees began to rise in their place. The sky – slashed apart by tangled electricity wires – cleared into broad, bright grey, and in minutes there was nothing but a few stilt-shacks teetering along the tarmac's crumbling rim. The rickshaw crossed the river-bridge like a threshold, and Alexander pressed his hands to his knees and listened to the rippling thud of an outboard motor. In the folds and swells of the water, white bubbles pricked up and the flick of fishtails broke the gloss-smooth surface. He glanced at Hanh, sitting beside him. She stared ahead in the cab, not watching where they were going. A linen rice-sack slouched against her ankles. It was less than half full with the meagre possessions she had scrabbled to collect from her hamlet. She worried the hem of the sack through her trembling fingers.

The road curved sluggishly towards the sun and Alexander held his hand to his eyes, shielding them from the bright-ness. Ahead, where the trees were clustering as dense as jungle, a ring of brick-stone pushed suddenly up. He peered forward, unable to see the house behind the high, white walls, but he knew it was there. He could feel it. He tapped the driver on the shoulder and pointed.

'Over there!' he shouted, but the sound of the rickshaw's engine was so loud that only the rumble in his throat let him know he'd made any sound.

The driver nodded and raised his thumb, veering side-ways and braking, and a huge wooden gate slid into view.

Hanh's fingers linked softly through Alexander's as she

stepped from the cab; her smile was shy and her rice-sack swung in her hand. The rickshaw disappeared and the air settled quiet. Heaving open the heavy gate, Alexander heard Hanh gasp. An old French building was revealed to them; an enormous, colonial villa of grey-white stone, with dark amber roof tiles and a solid, wooden door. Resting in a dip of land in the centre of the garden, it was just one storey high, and enclosed on all sides by soaring trees and thick-leafed shrubbery. Iron-fretwork windows peeped out from behind half-open shutters and a pillared veranda hugged the villa's brim. The veranda was topped with vast rolling archways and edged by a low stone buttress, engraved with the faces of elephants and fearsome tigers, and with just a hint of creeping moss. The hairs on the back of Alexander's neck prickled. They were only a few kilometres outside the centre of the city, but he felt a sense of deep, unnerving seclusion. Behind the villa's walls, they were truly alone. He didn't know if the itch in his gut was fear or freedom.

'It's beautiful,' said Hanh, with an astonished smile.

'I thought you'd like it,' Alexander replied, though he didn't agree with her. To him, the house looked arrogant and cruel. He had been here only once before, when he was summoned to explain why he'd let the buck-toothed girl from Sapa go. He hadn't enjoyed it. Now, he felt the violent sense of the Herder closing in.

He charged down the path, bending his neck to avoid the low branches and the cuffing of dewed leaves. Dangled, ringlet vines dribbled down from the canopy, and he thrust them aside with his hand and threw open the front door. Hanh followed after him.

Inside, the main room was as overbearing as he remembered. Despite the whitewashed walls, it was gloomy, and strong columns stretched up to a dark, painted ceiling. Crosses had been carved into the stone above the windows and light spat through in a desperate glow, spilling on to the polished dark wood floor. The chairs and tables were black lacquered wood and they dominated the room with an ominous, masculine presence. There wasn't a photograph anywhere, nor a painting, nor a book. There wasn't anything that gave away that the house was lived in. Nothing that told you the Herder was real. When they first met, the Herder made sure he knew every detail about Alexander's life – his family, his war, his dreams and nightmares – but Alexander had always known nothing of him. He'd asked, in the past, but was met with blunt silence. This house was just one more menacing secret. He felt the sudden need for air. There were double-doors on the back wall, long and thin like shutters, and he opened them too, striding out to a kitchen stove, two wrought-iron chairs and a table, breathing deeply.

Alexander stood at the top of the veranda steps, tension climbing inside him. He looked across the courtyard: a square of uneven, red-orange tiles, trimmed with jackfruit trees and wild, overgrown garden. Beyond that, a snaking trail led back to a small, brick bathhouse. The Herder's boots were on the tiles beside him; worn leather and loose laces, tipped on their sides and caked in grey Southern mud. He flinched at the sight of them. It was as though the Herder had only just been here. It was as though he were here now, as though he were hiding and could step out at any time and creep up on him. Alexander wanted to look around more. He wanted to search through the house and the garden, and get his bearings and steady himself, and check he was wrong. *Alone.* His glance crept back over his shoulder. Hanh was still standing at the threshold of the front doorway, the rice-sack clutched to her breast.

'It was a long journey,' said Alexander, pacing back into the house and snapping his fingers at her. 'You must want to take a shower.'

Hanh jumped at the sound and looked at him, awkwardly. 'A shower?'

'Yes,' he nodded. 'In the bathhouse.'

She didn't move.

He pointed impatiently across the main room, out through the open doors at the back of the house, across the square of sheltered courtyard. 'It's the building at the end of the pathway.'

Nothing.

'Do you want me to show you?'

Hanh shook her head, but she still didn't shift. What the fuck was her problem? What was she doing, just standing there like an idiot? He pursed his lips and hit his knuckles against his leg, then he realised. She wanted a room. He went to one of the doors in the side wall, slung it open and snatched a hasty look inside. Small. Sparse, Single bed.

Perfect, he thought. 'This can be your room,' he said, and he clicked his fingers at her again.

She padded over and stood beside him, her shoulders knotted about her neck. At the door, she stopped and peered inside, then gave an uneasy nod and looked at Alexander. He stared back, widening his eyes and waiting for a look that could be his permission to leave. There wasn't anything else she could possibly need. Why didn't she move?

'You really should have a shower before it gets dark,' he said, pushing her. 'There won't be any lights in the bath-house.'

At last she seemed to understand, and she took a few tiny steps back from the door. He grabbed the handle and slammed it shut, just to seal the deal for her. She turned away, carrying her sack outside and glancing back at the top of the veranda stairs. Alexander nodded, still guarding her door, and she slipped away across the courtyard and slunk from his sight.

Alexander exhaled, slowly. At once, exhaustion fell over him. In his limbs, he felt the persistent weight of antici-pation. He didn't want to be mean to Hanh, but he just couldn't help it. This was the Herder's house and his pres-sure was everywhere. He stepped to the edge of the veranda and slipped his feet inside the Herder's boots. He flexed and bent his toes, splintering the mud on the boot-caps, and thick, round raindrops began to splatter on the court-yard tiles. He dragged himself to the kitchen stove and picked a half-full bottle from the shelf above. He uncorked it, sniffed and swigged. Vodka. Of course. He wandered back into the house, plucking his rucksack from the floor and a deck of cards from the table and swinging the vodka bottle by his side.

He found the other bedroom; it was next to Hanh's. Again, it was bare and coldly faceless, but he knew it belonged to the Herder. It was obvious. Big room. Big dresser. Big wardrobe. The biggest bed he had ever seen. A giant silk robe on the back of the door. He pulled it down and slipped it over his shirt and trousers, tying the rope at his navel with a tight-seized knot. He placed his rucksack carefully down with a dull glass thud on the floor, crouched and unzipped it. Pulling the bag open, he eased out his baby, picking her up, placing her on the dresser and twisting the jar so she faced him. He stood with his hands on his hips and looked at her, and then he looked back over his shoulder and frowned; she was opposite the door. He picked her up again and slid her underneath the edge of the bed, tucked against the wall by the headboard so that Hanh wouldn't see if she came nosing in.

Alexander sat on the Herder's bed, his baby by his feet, and wrapped his hands around the edge of the mattress. If he closed his eyes and tried really hard, he might be able to push out the pressure. He might be able to forget what he was doing just for a little while. He could pretend he really was an important Russian businessman. This was his mansion and Hanh was his guest. He sucked on his cheeks. Yes, he could do that. Muggy air shoved in through the open fretwork windows; wet and deeply organic, damp earth and leaves. He could hear the spray of the shower in the distance, water pattering down on a tiled floor, the irregular rhythm as it tumbled like a waterfall and rico-cheted over Hanh's naked body. He took a vast gulp of sour vodka, squeezed shut his eyes and forced himself to imagine.

TWENTY-EIGHT

Hanh stood on the cool white tiles in the bathhouse cubicle and water spluttered thinly over her body. She was still wearing her sarong. Before, she had only ever washed at the river and it would have felt wrong being naked as a baby in the light of day. The sodden material clung to her breasts and thighs and she hitched it up and tightened the knot at her side. There was no roof above her head, just a small square of open air, and she glanced up and saw trees towering higher than the walls on every side. Layers of green leaves, slicked dark by rainwater, blustered against a gloomy white sky. She took the bar of soap from the ledge and held it under the flow of the shower until it became slippery. As she smoothed it over her arms, the scent that rose up was wonderfully fruity. Thin suds fell at her feet and she wriggled her toes in the fragrant white foam. Then she looked up at the bathhouse door – the unfamiliar, lock-less, door. She hoped Alexander was still in the house. As she moved her hand beneath the swag of her sarong, sliding the soap across her stomach, she kept her eyes fixed firmly on the door handle.

She had done the right thing – hadn't she? – coming here with him. When the train had pulled out from Hanoi last night, she had told herself to be brave and stay sure. The turn of the wheels had drawn her away from her misery like a loose thread from a ball of string. The city had unravelled and shrunk behind her, until there was nothing left. It had felt like escape. This morning, however, the cool, Southern air had doused her. The moment of rising into wakefulness, of opening her eyes and not remembering where she was had panicked her. All night, her mother's voice had spun in her dreams: 'How will I rest if I don't know you're safe?' The thought of her spirit wandering the earth, never sleeping peacefully, made Hanh feel sick. It had to be better for them both if she was here. If she was a good girl like her mother had taught her, perhaps Alexander would let her stay for a while. She would wash his clothes and sweep the house and cook for him, every day. Perhaps he would never send her home if she did everything that he asked.

What *would* he ask her to do though? She only had to think of Disgusting Dinh and his hot pincer fingers to know that the things Thuy said about men were true, sometimes. She ran the soap over her stomach and made a list of the things she knew for certain. She wouldn't be hungry. She would sleep in a bed. He would keep her safe. These were the things that were important. Alexander was a good man; she knew he was. He had proved she could trust him. She didn't need to know the details. Whatever he asked her to do would be worth it. If it made her a whore like Thuy said, she didn't care. Anything was better than what she had left behind.

Back in the room that Alexander had given her Hanh perched carefully on the edge of the bed, sinking a little into the downy mattress. She stretched the tips of her toes to the cool, polished floor and tapped them nervously on the wood. She felt better to have washed and be wearing fresh clothes. It made her feel more ready to face whatever came next. She brushed her hand across the soft, quilted diamonds on the bedspread and squeezed the last drips from her damp hair. This room was a corner of heaven, she thought. It was shaded and cool, and not so big as to be overwhelming. She had her own dresser and a mirror on the wall, and she could peep at a glimpse of the sky through the trees from her latticed window. The whole villa was magical. It was a world so far removed from anything she had ever touched before that she could barely believe it existed.

She slid from the bed and picked her wet sarong from where it was heaped on the floor, draping it over the rail at the end of the bed. Then she felt a frown begin to crawl across her face. The threadbare cotton looked so horribly wrong, slung against the expensive furniture. She tugged it flat and tried to arrange it more smartly, but it just wouldn't fit. Flowers and fluttering birds decorated the bedstead; the shimmering mother-of-pearl images seemed to glow against the lacquered blackness of the wood. She ran her fingers over them – they were as smooth as glass – and a sigh escaped from between her lips. Everything of hers would look out of place in this beautiful room. She ripped the old sarong back down again, bundled it into her rice-sack and pushed it under the bed.

'Hello?'

Hanh's chest leapt. 'Hold on!' she cried, checking her reflection in the mirror and rushing to neaten her hair. She opened the door and Alexander was standing right in front of her.

'Are you hungry?' he asked.

'I can cook,' said Hanh. 'I'm good at cooking.' There was a glaze to his eyes that made her uneasy, but she wanted to make herself useful right from the start. If she made herself useful, he would like her better. He would want her to stay. She slipped through the bedroom door, pulling it shut behind her with a dull clunk, then squeezed past Alexander and padded on her tiptoes towards the kitchen veranda. Alexander followed after.

For a house so impressive, the kitchen was simple. The orange clay stove was the same as the one she had at home, only bigger, and it sat on a bowed wooden countertop held up by a stack of dusty, cut bricks. On the ground, chopped wood was arranged in a pyramid. She picked a few pieces from the top of the pile and pushed them into the belly of the stove.

As it warmed, Hanh reached up and pulled down the jars from the shelf one by one, unscrewing the lids and peering inside. There were lots of things she didn't even recognise, harsh-smelling alcoholic drinks and jars with pickled meat, but there were fresh vegetables too, and *nuoc mam* and a bag of beef and fish that Alexander had bought in the market outside Ga Saigon. With the rations, Hanh had never had much choice of what food to prepare and her mother had always said she could spin a feast from a pig's trotter, but she didn't know what to make. She wanted to please him. She stared up at the shelf and chewed on the skin at the base of her fingernail, then glanced anxiously back at Alexander. He was sitting on the table behind her and he poured himself a drink and leaned back in his chair, watching her closely. He fanned a deck of cards in his hand. She stretched up again, reaching right back, and her hand nudged against a cardboard box. She lifted it down and looked at the unfamiliar, foreign lettering.

'Is this Russian food?' she asked, raising the box so Alexander could see.

He glanced at it briefly, and then looked straight back to his cards. 'Yes,' he nodded, flicking his head.

Hanh carried the box to the table. 'What is it?'

Alexander didn't answer. He placed his cards reluctantly down and took the box, turning it over in his hand and examining it. His face seemed suddenly, oddly concerned.

Hanh shifted on her feet. 'I can cook it for you, if you tell me how.'

'No.' He sucked a breath and shook his head.

'Why not?'

'You won't be able to.'

'I could try?'

'You wouldn't like it.'

'I might do.'

'No!' Alexander raised his voice and made Hanh flinch. He scraped his chair abruptly back from the table, almost pushing her aside as he strode across the veranda, then grabbed the basket of food from the market and thrust it at her, slumping back to his drink and his cards at the table. 'Just cook what I bought you.'

Hanh's fingers fumbled into the wicker basket and found a packet of yellowy egg noodles and she tipped them into a pan, quick and embarrassed. Alexander thought she was a simple rice girl. She didn't have sophisticated tastes like he did. He would rather eat poor Vietnamese food, than let her cook his Russian food wrong! As she filled the pan from the tap and placed it over the stove, she kept her back to Alexander so he wouldn't see her blush.

The water began to bubble. Alexander rapped his knuckles on the table and Hanh spun round. 'Sit down,' he said. 'Have a drink with me.'

Hanh looked at the empty glass on the table in front of him. She would never have drunk with a man in Hanoi. She wouldn't have drunk at all, except maybe at Tet. This was different though. It would be rude to refuse him. It might make him cross again and she didn't want that. She lowered herself cautiously into the chair opposite Alexander, watching him pour an inch of clear liquid into the glass and scrape it across the table towards her.

'*Za Vas!*' he said, raising his drink in the air. 'To you!'

Hanh felt herself blush, though this time it wasn't in shame. She was glad of the fading evening light to hide her. Sipping her drink, her head instantly swam. She swallowed the foul surge of saliva from her mouth and stared down at the red floor tiles, tracing her eyes along the wide, brown seams and gathering her breath. She looked up at him guiltily and tucked her hands between her thighs. 'I promise I'll cook you a good supper,' she said.

She waited for a reply, but Alexander wasn't paying attention. He picked up his deck of cards, rubbed his finger through the corners, then dealt them on to the table – not to Hanh, but to the empty spaces on either side of her. As the cards spun across the surface, he seemed to stare at them just a little too intently. She wondered if he was drunk, or if she was.

Then he spoke. 'Do you like it here?'

'I think that this is the most beautiful place I have ever seen,' Hanh replied truthfully. 'Your friend must be very rich to have a house like this.'

'He is,' Alexander nodded, still looking down. 'He's a clever man.'

Hanh paused. 'You must be a clever man too . . . working with him.'

Alexander leaned slowly back. He appeared to give the slightest of nods. The rain had stopped, and the mosquitoes were starting to swarm. They flocked to the candle on the table and twitched in the air, their tiny black wings and bodies bouncing soundlessly around the unsteady flame. Alexander flinched and swatted his hand above the table.

'You don't like the insects?' said Hanh.

Alexander frowned. 'No. Don't they bother you?'

'Not much. They like white skin,' she smiled.

She stood up and took an empty bottle from the shelf above the stove. She uncorked the cap, filled the clear glass with water and put the lid back on again, then dragged her chair to the doorway, climbed up and balanced the bottle above the thin ledge of the door.

'What are you doing?'

'I'm rescuing you,' she said. 'When the insects fly past the door, they'll see their reflection in the glass. They'll think it's a monster and they'll fly away scared.'

Alexander laughed. It was the first time that Hanh had heard him laugh out loud; a proper laugh, not just a smile. It sounded as though it came from the bottom of his chest.

'Tomorrow, I'll look in the garden and see if there is any lemongrass,' she said, stepping down from the chair and pulling it back to the table. 'If you rub the leaves on your skin it keeps the mosquitoes away.'

Alexander stared at her with his head cocked to the side, his eyes narrowed and a curious smile on his lips. 'What a useful girl you are to have around,' he said quietly.

Hanh tucked her seat back close to the table and looked down. She lifted her glass, smiling, and took another burning sip of her drink.

Alexander looked at the spread of food on the table in front of him. He licked his lips impulsively. There was a golden, crisp-skinned fish, propped up on a bed of soft, sticky rice. Its tail was shredded to ribbons, its mouth an open oval of surprise. There were deep-fried spring rolls, folded tight and pinched sharp at the corners. Hot grease dribbled out from underneath them and shone yellow on the plate. There was salad, bright with every colour he could imagine, piled high and overspilling from bowls made of purple teardrop leaves. There were fried shallots and juicy beef in pinkish slivers, and black-brown fish sauce and flakes of dry red chilli, and slippery vermicelli and a dozen different fresh green herbs that he didn't even recognise, and Hanh looking perfect, stood next to it all. She topped up his drink and the oily liquid swirled into the tumbler with appealing glitter. He rubbed his hands down his legs in anticipation.

The more the evening hours had passed – the more he'd drunk – the better he felt. He'd got good at pretending. He'd shoved the Herder and the job to the back of his head, and now his spirits were soaring. Though the food was great and he crammed his belly full, he knew there was more to like about this than the meal alone. It was different from being at the café, or the lake, or anywhere else. He had found an intimate, private place. Here, he could say and do whatever he wanted, without anyone to watch or judge him. He could be exactly whomever he pleased. In this house on the brim of Saigon city, with the red-tiled courtyard and the iron-lace windows, he really was an important Russian businessman.

Hanh believed it too. He loved the way she scurried around him, so shamelessly desperate to please. He took another slug of his drink and looked her over, smiling. The Herder would have called her a lusty little thing. Slender waist, tight young breasts and lips plum-ripe. Alexander could see it too, just a glimpse. She was attractive, in the way of porcelain on a shelf: delicate and ornamental. When he spoke she sat quietly and listened, like she should. She would do anything for him if he asked her to. It was just the same as if she were his wife.

Alexander swallowed a last lukewarm mouthful of fluffy white fish, licked the length of his chopsticks, and laid them across the rim of his empty bowl. He leaned back in his chair and ran his hand across the hard swell of his stuffed stomach.

'I can make you something else?' said Hanh, skipping eagerly up.

He shook his head and she dropped back to her seat looking disappointed. He gave her a smile. 'It was an excellent meal, Hanh.'

Her cheeks flushed. 'I wanted to thank you for helping me,' she said shyly.

A rush of pride flooded through Alexander. He had always known that he helped his girls, but Hanh was the first to thank him. The feeling quivered in his chest.

'When we first met,' she said, 'I knew that you were different from other men. I could see that you were kind and fair and honest.'

Alexander laughed. 'You can tell all that from a man's face?'

'From his face,' she shrugged. 'From the way he holds his shoulders.'

Alexander hitched himself up in his chair and uncurled his spine into a stiff, upright line. Hanh was right. Russian businessmen, *good men*, sat straight and tall.

Hanh folded her hair behind her ears. 'What does your name mean, Alexander?'

Alexander tapped his foot on the floor and thought for a moment. 'I don't know.'

'Don't you? I thought every man knew what his name meant!' Hanh blinked, held her finger to her lip, and then opened her eyes, smiling. She picked up the liquor bottle, pulled out the cork and topped up his drink. 'I think Alexander must mean the honourable Russian hero! Alexander the Saviour!' she giggled.

'I like it,' Alexander grinned. He took a proud sip from the tumbler. The drink was warm and comforting inside him. It was an uplifting, honest warmth, like the glow of a hearth fire, by a lake in the Russian wintertime. 'What does your name mean?'

'Hanh means "Faith". Even when the sun looked as pale as the moon at night, I stayed true to my name. I always kept faith that things would get better.' She paused and looked suddenly down at the table. 'Do you miss your home?'

Home. Alexander blinked away an image of a ripe Kansas wheatfield, of his mother at the window with her wilting beehive hairdo. He blinked away his lonely hammock, creaking in the bows of the dark night jungle. He blinked away his beloved flat in Bangkok that the Herder had found him with the blue-painted shutters, where – for the very first time in his life – he had felt calm and free. He swept them aside and replaced them all with his Russian log cabin. 'I don't think about home often.'

Hanh wriggled in her chair. 'I miss my home.'

Alexander took another drink. A long one. Hanh's squirm

and the dart of her eyes were making him nervous. 'It will pass,' he said coolly. 'You've only been away a day.'

'No.' She shook her head. 'It's been years since I had a home. In Vietnam, a girl without a father is like a house without a roof.'

Alexander pushed his teeth against the lip of his glass. He didn't want to hear about her father. Not now. He was enjoying himself.

Hanh didn't stop, though. She stared at him and kept talking. 'I used to have nightmares,' she said. 'I would dream an American soldier was asleep in my house and I rattled the window and begged him to let me in, but he never woke up. It wasn't my home. It was his home. He had taken it. I haven't had a home since my father was killed. I've lived outside and suffered through hot sun and cold rain with nobody to shelter me.'

Alexander inched his chair back from the table and glanced across the courtyard. Where the fuck was this coming from? She was spilling herself all over the table, laying out her ugliness for him to see. He wanted to force her to stop. He didn't want to talk about American soldiers. 'It doesn't do any good to think about the past,' he said, and he heard the shake in his voice.

'I know,' said Hanh. She was staring at him now, her hand clutching the edge of the table. 'I like it here, Alexander. I want to stay. I can't bear to think what would have happened to me if I hadn't met you. Really, anything could have happened. The streets of Hanoi are brutal. People take advantage of girls like me.'

Alexander took another big gulp of his drink, draining the glass of every last drop, and his head began to throb and swirl. Shut up, he wanted to say. *Shut up.* He didn't want to be tugged back to reality, back to the war, back to sweltering, suffocating Hanoi. He wanted to stay here, drunk and pretending. His mind starting hobbling again, from his hammock, to the steaming barrel of his rifle, to brown-skinned bodies in the mud, to the scowling face of the Herder, to his baby asleep in her jar. *Murderer.* The word rustled through the leaves and the candle on the table shuddered. He grabbed the bottle and refilled his glass. It wasn't him. It wasn't.

Hanh scraped her chair away from the table. 'I want you to know how grateful I am, Alexander. I want to say thank you.'

She stood up, slowly, and he saw that her hands were trembling. She looked at him, slipping her fingers around the hem of her blouse and gripping it for a moment before lifting it above her head. She reached her hands up and unknotted the ribbon at the back of her neck. As she let go, the sheath of material that covered her breasts slipped down and dropped at her feet. The candlelight caught the curve of her ribs and they shone like ivory. Alexander was pinned to his chair, shocked. She stood there, looking at the ground, not moving. He didn't speak. Thoughts were spiralling through his head and he swung for them, but he couldn't catch them. Hanh's mouth was open, her lips moist and smooth, and he could see the tip of her tongue between her teeth. He could feel his heart quickening and a warm, heavy weight in his lap. Hanh glanced nervously aside, and then she stepped towards him. He let her lift his hand from the table and place it over her breast. He felt her flinch when he touched her, but she held him there and through her soft flesh he could feel the frantic flutter of her heart, like a bird panicking in a cage.

Alexander's hand slipped from Hanh's breast up to her shoulder. She felt his fingers flex against her skin, then he tightened his grip. She took a breath, trying to relax, trying to make herself ready for whatever he wanted. But then, something changed. Alexander's eyes hardened. He hooked his lips up over his gums and Hanh could see that his teeth were gritted. In the next moment, the back of her head cracked against the tiled veranda floor as he pushed her to the ground. He held her there, one hand pressed heavily on her breastbone, the other snatching her trousers from her legs. She tried to drag her knees upwards to hide her nakedness, but he clambered over her and forced her flat. The pain was sudden, like a knife between her legs. Hanh bit her lip to stop herself from crying out as a blunt pressure thrust against the pit of her belly. The sound he made was harsh and guttural like a wounded animal and his crushing weight pinned her down. The stink of his sweat and the supper she had cooked and stale alcohol filled her nose and mouth and she gasped for air. She squeezed her eyes shut and tried to keep the tears inside. It felt as though he were breaking her.

Alexander heaved a final alcoholic groan and rolled on

to the floor beside her. She forced her eyes to open. His face was red and scowling.

'Put your clothes on,' he said without looking at her.

Hanh didn't move. She couldn't. Her limbs were numb with shock and terror.

Alexander glared at her for a moment, then spat on the tiles by her head. She flinched and he stood up, fumbling to close the button of his trousers. He grabbed her clothes from where they were strewn and threw them down at her. 'Put your clothes on!' he yelled, and he stormed inside the house.

Hanh scrambled across the veranda and pulled on her trousers and blouse, as quick as her shaking hands and stumbling legs would let her. She grabbed her torn underwear and staggered to the bedroom, slamming shut the door and dropping to the floor. She crawled hurriedly beneath the bed, pushing herself against the back wall and bracing every muscle in her body. She lay there, hiding and listening, thick tears streaming down her cheeks. There was a burning sting between her legs and she could feel sticky blood on the inside of her thigh. Her stomach ached. She blinked uselessly in the dark, staring beneath the bed and watching the bottom few inches of the door, terrified and hawkish. Speckled grey moonlight ran below the black wood, as if the dark had been slit by a knife.

She couldn't understand what had made Alexander so angry! She'd been trying to say thank you, to let him know she was in his debt! She thought she had given him what he would want. It was what Dinh had wanted. She must have done something wrong. Their conversation rebounded through her head like an echo, and she winced each time she was hit by her words. She had humiliated herself. How arrogant of her to think a man like him would ever want a girl like her. She wasn't rich or clever or beautiful. Her skin was dark and ugly. He could have any white-skinned Russian girl he pleased. He probably already had one. Of course he found her disgusting. Thuy was right! She really was a cheap whore.

She pushed her fist into her chest, trying to ease the pressurised gallop of her heart and feeling a shortness of breath, as though he were still on top of her. She pressed down harder, trying to force her heart to calm. When he had touched her, she felt dizzy, as though someone had spun her up in the air and shaken her around. His hands had been cold and limp. They didn't feel like hands were supposed to. A shadow swept suddenly over the crack of light below the door and her hand shot to her mouth to smother her terrified sob. Alexander was outside! She held her breath and listened to the drum of her heart. Though the change in the dark was subtle, she was sure he was there! Her ears strained for the noise of a footstep or a laboured breath, but there was nothing except the thunderous panic inside her. She lay still, her hand clamped over her mouth and her eyes fixed on the line of trembling light.

TWENTY-NINE

It was early morning and Phuc's family were still asleep. He sat at the kitchen table and pinched his tired eyes between his thumb and fingers. The ache in his head was as deep as a mine. The lantern had burned all night and was dimming, and its flame shuddered and gave a hiccup of black smoke as he twisted the dial. He poured himself another cup of tea, hooking the loose flakes of leaf from the cup with his finger, and then went to the window and peered at the sky. Rain was falling hard – it struck his metal roof like handfuls of gravel – but he could see the first suggestions of light straining through and softening the rooftops with a line of mottled grey. Dawn was coming. At last it was time.

He cracked open the bedroom door and crept carefully into the darkness, grateful for the noise of the rain and wind to smother his steps. The shadow of Phuong lay with her back to him. The boys had wriggled and chucked their blanket on the floor, and he stepped across it and crouched by the chest at the end of Kieu's bed. He reached inside and fumbled for a skirt and blouse, then picked up her sandals. He bundled them beneath his arm and then stood beside her and gripped her wrist. She woke suddenly.

'Dad?'

Phuc pressed his finger to his lips, shook his head and pointed at the kitchen. Kieu frowned and hauled herself up, climbing from the bed and following after him.

'Sit down, Kieu,' said Phuc as she pulled the door shut behind her.

She knew at once there was something wrong. 'What's the matter?'

'I need to talk to you,' said Phuc. 'Please. Sit down.'

Kieu didn't move. Instead, she hovered at the doorway, worry beginning to crease around her eyes. Phuc took her hands, pulling her to the table and into the seat opposite him. Reaching across the wood, he kept firmly hold of her. He could feel the tension in her body and his own nervous shake. She stared at him. A look of deep confusion was spread across her face.

'I've done a terrible thing to you, Kieu,' said Phuc, staring back. His heart was hammering. He had to say it quickly or he wouldn't say it at all.

The worry in Kieu's brow thickened. 'What do you mean?'

'I mean that I'm sorry. I need you to know that I love you, and that I'll go through a hundred holes of hell to pay my debt before I'll ever be reborn as a man.'

Kieu tried to tug her hands away. 'You're scaring me,' she said, but Phuc held her tighter, leaning forward and dipping his head below the line of her skittering sight.

'Do you know that I love you, Kieu?' he said slowly and gently.

At the rims of her eyes, thin tears were brewing. 'Tell me what's going on, Daddy. Please.'

'The Party came to our house last week,' Phuc whispered. Kieu's face tightened in horror. 'Dad! Why didn't you say?'

'Shhhh! You're mother mustn't hear us! I didn't want any of you to worry. An official found my file again. He was calling me a traitor and demanding money. I thought if I offered him more than he asked for I could get the Party to leave us alone. We made a deal. He agreed to destroy my records and make sure that nobody bothered us.'

'But we don't have any money, Dad.'

'I thought I could get some. I gambled my wages, but I lost, Kieu. I lost and I made the most horrible mess of things, and I now I need you to help me pay the man that I owe.'

'Why can't Mum help you?'

Phuc paused. 'Because I promised him you.'

Kieu's eyes shot open, as wide as caverns. They were nothing but enormous, wet-black pupils, fixed on Phuc and disbelieving. She was breathing so deeply that her whole body rocked and in her yellow pyjamas, with her long, messy hair, she looked so young and fragile. She shook her head at him. 'I don't understand.'

Phuc took in an unsteady breath and blinked away the tears that stung in his vision. 'I told the man who runs Fán T'án Alley he could take you as payment.'

Kieu's skin flared a furious, panicking pink. '*How could you?!*' she cried.

Phuc clutched desperately at his daughter's hands as she

recoiled in her chair, her body twisted away from him, her delicate face streaked by tears and terrified. He wanted so badly to hold her, to bundle her up in his arms and protect her. It made him ache. He scraped his chair around the table and gathered her into him. 'I know! I made a mistake. I'm so sorry!'

'How could you?' she moaned again, trying to shove him away from her.

'I did this for you, Kieu,' he pleaded. 'I did this for our family. I know I've let you down, but you have to help me.'

'No! I won't go!'

'There's nothing else we can do.'

'Please don't make me!' she sobbed breathlessly.

Phuc didn't reply. He felt her fighting ebb and he struggled to hold back his tears as he saw her expression drop in resignation.

'Listen to me, bear cub,' he said, holding her by the shoulders and searching her face. 'I promise I'll look after you, but I need you to do something else for me too. When we say goodbye, you mustn't cry. Not a single tear. Do you hear me? This is important. I need you to be brave. Can you do that?'

Kieu glanced at the bedroom door, as if pleading for her mother to come out and save her, but the noise of the rain had kept them hidden. The door stayed shut. She looked at Phuc for a moment and nodded weakly, before her sobs began to spill again.

Phuc grasped her tighter. 'Do you trust me?' he said,

almost shaking her. 'Do you understand that I will never let you come to harm?'

Kieu's lips puckered and a cry escaped from the back of her throat.

'I need you to tell me you trust me, Kieu.'

She wiped her eyes with the back of her hand. 'I trust you,' she whispered.

Phuc released Kieu's shoulders and slumped back with a sigh and throb of fleeting relief. From beside his chair, he grabbed her sandals and clothes and pushed them towards her. 'Get dressed and wash your face,' he said. 'We have to go.'

Phuc held Kieu's trembling hand and knocked on the glass panel that covered the door to Cheung Hu's secret office at the back of the tobacco store. He stared ahead, holding his breath and concentrating on the rows of cigarette packets with all his might. He couldn't bring himself to look at his daughter. The sound of her rapid, shallow breathing was enough to torture him; he didn't need to see her face. From the opposite side of the door, a low voice rumbled.

'Who's there?'

Phuc answered and waited – his jaw clenched rigid – then the door split open. The round, sallow face of Cheung Hu glared out from the gloom.

'What are you doing here?' he said. His voice was brisk and icy.

'I've come to settle my debt,' replied Phuc.

'We agreed to meet at the market.'

'I know.'

'You're early.'

'Yes, I know.'

There was a pause, and Cheung Hu's eyes flicked momentarily beyond Phuc's shoulder and into the store. Phuc glanced back too. It was still early, but the Cholon shops were starting to trade and the streets were busying.

'Get in,' Cheung Hu hissed.

Phuc stepped forward and Kieu stumbled clumsily beside him. He heard her gasp as she saw where she was, and he gripped her harder. The room was just as threatening as it had been before; cool, dim and tomb-like, and stacked from floor to ceiling with racks of poised, glistening weaponry. An enormous, suited bodyguard towered above them at the door. A second hung in the gloom against the back wall, looking even meaner.

Cheung Hu was sitting at his desk in the centre of the floor. He knitted his fingers together beneath his chin and eyed Phuc coolly. 'Is this your daughter?' he said.

Phuc nodded.

'Did you not understand our arrangements, Mr Phuc?'

He shook his head. 'No, Brother. I understood.'

'So you thought you knew better?'

'No, Brother.'

'What then?'

Phuc glanced at Kieu. She was staring at her feet and hair had fallen to cover her face like a dark, heavy veil. He swallowed hard, but the words he wanted to say were stuck in his throat. Look how he'd broken her! Every previous moment they'd shared was irrelevant, now. She would never forgive him. Still, for the sake of all his family, this had to be done. He tore his eyes away and regained himself. Cheung Hu's impatience burned on his cheeks.

'I can't stand the waiting,' Phuc stammered at last. He could hear his voice on the cusp of breaking. 'Just take her now. Please. Don't make me suffer any longer.'

Cheung Hu hesitated, then rose up from his chair and crept around the desk and stared, like a stalking cat. 'It concerns me when plans change,' he said suspiciously.

'You have no reason to be concerned,' said Phuc. He kept hold of Cheung Hu's eye and tried to calm the pummelling of his heart in his chest. 'I just want this over.'

For a second more, Cheung Hu seemed to consider him, then he perched on the corner of his desk and pointed a beckoning finger at Kieu. 'Come here.'

Kieu lifted her head and looked at Phuc, who forced a painful smile and released her hand. She walked towards Cheung Hu and Phuc could see that her legs were shaking.

'What's your name, girl?' Cheung Hu asked her.

'My name is Kieu,' she whispered back.

Cheung Hu clapped his hands together and almost smiled. 'Ah! Kieu the heroine!' he cried to the room. 'How appropriate! Do you know why you're here, Kieu? Do you know what your father has done to you?'

'Yes,' Kieu replied and she tipped her chin at him. She looked fierce and defiant, but her eyes were dry.

Good girl, thought Phuc. Good girl. Be strong! He rammed his hands in his pockets and clenched them to fists as

Cheung Hu wrapped his long fingers around Kieu's tiny arm. She was staring at his hand, frozen. He pulled her towards him and she took a stiff, stumbling step. She glanced at Phuc, her face terrified. Cheung Hu lifted her arm and held it out to the side, inspecting her as if she were an animal in the market. He drew her lightly around, so her body would follow, and he examined her from behind. He folded his top lip back over his teeth and Phuc saw the pointed tip of his flickering tongue. Stay calm, he told himself, though he felt his insides fit to burst. He wanted to hit Cheung Hu, to explode across the room and scream, *'Don't fucking touch her!'*

Cheung Hu began slowly to nod in approval, then he sniffed and snapped his fingers at Phuc. 'Say goodbye.'

Phuc leapt forward and grabbed his daughter, hugging her tightly and feeling her sharp in-breath. In his arms, she slackened briefly, and he could smell the sweetness of soap on her young, soft skin as he buried his head in the crook of her neck. He dragged his face up and – over her shoulder – he shot a pointed look at Cheung Hu's desk. Just as they were when he'd been here before, the vials of iridescent orange diesel glittered from their shallow dish. He kept hold of Kieu while he counted them and through her thick black hair, he whispered in her ear.

'Remember not to cry, little bear cub,' he said, then he let her go and left the room without looking back.

Outside the tobacco store, bright daylight hit him and so did a sense of red-hot resolve. He marched to the end of the street, forcing his desperate feet not to twitch into a run and glancing urgently back as he rounded the corner. The front of Cheung Hu's shop was empty and no one was watching. He had done it! Out of sight, he broke into a sprint; quicker and more frantic than he'd ever run before. There wasn't much time! He needed to get Kieu back before any harm could come to her!

Head down and heart spitting, Phuc tore through Saigon's teeming Chinatown. His lungs flamed as he ripped across the market courtyard, darting through the narrow, unpaved backstreets and stopping just beyond the shadowed opening of Fán T'án Alley. With all his strength, he pummelled his fists against the locked door of the Herder's bar. The metal gave a thunderous rumble and shuddered on its hinges. He stepped backwards into the street and squinted at the dim light in the upstairs window.

'Let me in!' he bellowed breathlessly, launching his body back into the door. He kicked with his feet and his knees, as if he were fighting a man. 'Let me in or I'll break down the door!'

THIRTY

The dry taste of yesterday's alcohol was gritted across Alexander's tongue. Sitting on the Herder's bed, with his body half-propped, half-slouched against the wall and his legs splayed out in front of him, he heaved an inward breath and sour, prickling sickness set his jaw. His head was throbbing and the room smelled rancid. Stale sleep, dirty sheets, drink and his dripping body mixed in the air, and the tang of the Herder was lingering, hostile, beneath it all. He rested one hand on his thigh and stretched and flexed his quivering fingers. The light of the electric bulb spluttered over his skin as the ceiling fan sliced through its glare. He flicked his thumbnail against the metal lid of his baby's jar.

Hanh was awake too. Alexander's stomach had pitched when he heard the quiet click of her door, carefully opened, an hour earlier. He shouldn't have done what he did, last night; he shouldn't have touched her. He'd fucked this all up. As soon as his knees began to grind against the tiled floor and he looked down at her tiny rigid body beneath him, he knew he was wrong, but it had been so long since he'd had a woman and he couldn't stop. He groaned and smeared his hands across the bed-sheets. He'd thought about going to her room last night to say he was sorry. He'd stood outside for a while and listened to her half-sobbed, frantic breathing, but he just couldn't face going in there. He was disgusting. A filthy mongrel dog. He didn't deserve her forgiveness. He'd killed her father and stolen her home. If she knew who he was, she would hate him. If she knew what he was going to do to her next, she would scream and run.

He pressed his fist to his lips and drew a woozy breath. Hanh was as good as worthless, now, and the Herder would punish him for it. This was worse than any mistake he'd made before. They'd probably never work together again, and he'd be on his own, and then what would he do? He slipped down in the bed and let out another self-pitying moan. Would it be better if he told the Herder what he had done? Perhaps he would never find out, though. Perhaps Cheung Hu wouldn't drag Hanh off to the back-street doctors to have her checked with her legs askew. Phuc hadn't said that he needed a virgin, had he? He clenched his knuckles and thrust them down on to the lid of the jar, frustrated. He didn't care where Hanh went any more. He just wanted her gone.

Suddenly, there was an enormous crash of sound from the main room. What the fuck had she done? Alexander threw back the sheets and staggered from the bedroom, just in time to see the villa's front doors swing open and slam against the crisp, white walls.

'What are you doing here?' Alexander cried.

'It's my house,' replied the Herder. He marched inside and was glaring meanly. 'If you're going to wear my robe,

Alexander, at least tie it up. You put all men to shame with that mangy winkie.'

Alexander winced and snatched the robe tight around him. 'I wasn't expecting you.'

'It wouldn't be any fun if you were.' The Herder threw a sharp look about the room. 'Where's the girl?'

Alexander glanced anxiously at the closed door of the kitchen veranda. The Herder had a knack for timing. Somehow, he knew just when to appear and check up on him. 'I don't know where she is,' he replied and he chucked a shake of his head as though he didn't care a sniff for her.

'You don't know?' spat the Herder. 'That's careless.'

'She's probably in the courtyard. She's doing housework.'

'You should keep a closer watch on her.'

'Don't worry. There's nowhere for her to go.'

'Piss always finds a crack in the pan, Alexander.' The Herder's stare skimmed around the room again, and then settled coolly back on Alexander. 'Is there anything you want to tell me?' he asked suspiciously.

Alexander's heart gave a buck. How the fuck did he know already? His eyes darted to the corners and the ceiling cornices as if he were being watched. 'What do you mean?' he stammered.

'I mean you seem wired – even for you. Is everything all right?'

'Of course,' Alexander lied. He snatched the cigarette packet from the table beside him and pushed a smoke to his rigid lips. He bent his head to his hand and sparked the lighter with a nervy strike of his thumb.

'Good.' The Herder grinned. He seized the cigarette from Alexander's mouth and plugged it to his own. 'We've got work to do.'

The Herder rummaged in his pocket and pulled out a crumpled ball of paper. He thrust it into Alexander's chest so hard that he staggered backwards.

'What's this?'

'It's a message from Phuc. That luckless bastard nearly battered my door down this morning. The plan's changed.'

Alexander unpicked the note and read it quickly. The instructions were brief and blunt; but clear as a dice. He looked at the Herder, surprised. 'Phuc's daughter's gone?'

'Apparently so.'

He read the message again, his finger following along the lines of scrawled writing. 'Will it work?'

The Herder shrugged. 'Probably. Cheung Hu's an arrogant cockerel. Who cares anyway, if Phuc pays us?'

Alexander nodded, uneasy. He didn't feel sure and he didn't trust Phuc, but he wanted Hanh gone, and given the change in circumstance, he had to admit that the plan seemed clever. With one more task, all this would be done. He felt the Herder watching him closely. 'Fine,' he said, and he hauled an awkward smile to his lips. 'I'll do it.'

'Good.' The Herder sucked on his cigarette and stared, unmoving.

Alexander stared back, and he didn't move either. It wasn't just Hanh and Phuc that bothered him, now. Something else was prodding him. He knew he should have felt happy that the Herder was here, but he didn't, and he didn't know why. This was what he wanted, wasn't it – to work together? But it didn't feel right. An insect flustered in the air at his face and he brushed it aside bitterly. Hanh had never found him any lemongrass. He never gave her the chance. 'You don't need to stay,' he said, drily.

The Herder gave another casual shrug. 'I don't mind. I'm here now.'

Alexander clamped his teeth to his cheek. *I'm here now.* The journey he'd taken to get to the villa was just a few minutes, though he spoke as if it had been a right chore. He could have paid for a messenger to bring Phuc's note, if he'd wanted. The truth hit Alexander's chest, like a punch. He knew then why the Herder was here and why he felt troubled; he still didn't trust him. 'I can handle this,' he said, frowning down at the dark wooden floor.

'I'm sure you can,' the Herder replied. 'It's only a telephone call, Alexander. Even you can manage that.'

'So why are you waiting?'

'Moral support.'

'I don't need support.'

'Fine!' cried the Herder, and he threw up his hand, grinning. 'I promise to you give you no support whatsoever.'

'That's not what I meant.'

'Well, if you said what you meant, Alexander, you might find life simpler.' He lunged suddenly forward and slung his arm around Alexander's shoulder, steering him towards the telephone in the corner of the room. 'Shall we get on with it?'

Alexander tried to keep his head high and stride purpose-fully, but his legs felt slow and heavy. The Herder stayed tight to his heels. He couldn't even leave Alexander alone to make one phone call. Alexander didn't speak. He just clutched Phuc's note in his hand and smoothed it flat against the sideboard. He pinned it down, his finger stabbed below the line of numbers. He'd show him! Wedging the receiver between his ear and shoulder, he began to dial. The Herder leaned against the wall, smoked, and studied him, arms folded.

The line clicked alive. 'Yes?' said a crisp, Chinese voice.

Alexander pressed the telephone to his ear and strained to hear above the pound of his heart. 'Cheung Hu?'

'Who is this?'

'My name is Alexander.'

'How did you get this number?'

'I'm a friend of the Herder,' he said, and his eyes flick-ered sideways. The Herder didn't flinch.

'That smug Russian?' snapped Cheung Hu and Alexander could hear the scowl in his voice. 'A friend of his is no friend of mine. What do you want?'

'I have some information that you may find interesting. It's regarding Mr Phuc.' Alexander tightened his grip on the note in his hand. He looked again at the Herder, who threw him a nod. Alexander flicked a nod right back, and took a deep breath. 'Last week, I sold Phuc a girl. He told me that he was planning to give this girl to you. I under-stand he came to your office, this morning. I think you should know, Brother, you do not have his daughter. You have one of my whores.'

There was a silence on the line. 'I don't believe you.' Cheung Hu's tone was soft, but a hint of rage was simmering beneath it.

'It's true,' Alexander replied. 'He brought her to you early, didn't he? Does that feel right, Brother?'

'Weak men can't wait.'

'Are you certain?'

Cheung Hu paused again and Alexander heard a thin-drawn, brooding breath. He held the tip of his tongue against his lip in anticipation. When Cheung Hu spoke again, his voice was a whipcrack.

'That snake!' he cried, so loud and sudden that Alexander jerked the receiver away from him. A delighted grin broke out on the Herder's face.

Alexander eased the telephone back to his ear. 'I can tell you where Mr Phuc's real daughter is,' he said, and the Herder grinned more widely.

'What do you want from me?' Cheung Hu demanded.

'I'm afraid that Mr Phuc has tricked us both. He paid for my girl with counterfeit money. I would like to be rewarded for the information I give you. I would also like you to return my girl.' Alexander glanced at the Herder and then added, thoughtfully, 'She was a good earner.'

Cheung Hu considered for a moment. 'Do you know where Phuc is?'

'No,' replied Alexander. 'But if you have his daughter, you won't need to find him. He'll come to you.'

'Tell me where she is.'

Alexander stood up straighter. He was doing well. He knew he was. 'It will cost you five thousand dong.'

'That's thievery!'

'That's the price.'

'Fine,' spat Cheung Hu. 'Where is she?'

The Herder raised his hand and placed it down on Alexander's shoulder. He tapped his fingers and rocked his head in approval. Alexander stared at him. Was it real? Had he done enough, this time? He dragged an itching smile to his lips. Cheung Hu was a hungry fish, chewing on the line, just like the Herder had said that he would. The Herder was always right about things like this. He was smart. Whether his approval was genuine or not, Alexander knew for certain that he was better with him by his side than alone. The Herder was the best thing for him. He stared back into the Herder's eyes and clutched the telephone tighter.

'I have her,' he said. 'Meet me at the Notre Dame Basilica in thirty minutes, and I'll give her to you. Bring the money and my girl.'

The next pause that came was enormous, heavy and menacing. 'Thirty minutes,' said Cheung Hu, at last. His voice was suddenly, chillingly calm. 'I'll be there.'

THIRTY-ONE

Hanh pressed the length of her body to the slim veranda door, as much to steady her trembling legs as to listen. Hot panic swam in her cheeks. With the squally wind and the birds agitating through the trees, she could barely catch cut snippets of words and they weren't making sense, but with all that had happened she knew in her gut that this didn't feel right. With one eye closed, she squashed her nose to the doorframe and strained to see through the crack that winked above the hinge. Alexander was standing with his side to her, barefooted and naked beneath a billowing robe, but he didn't look balanced. His neck and head were down. He was leaning sideways like a drunk, and she thought she saw a slight, unsteady waver. His face looked ashen. It did nothing to soothe her.

'Tell me you'll get this done, Alexander,' barked the fat Russian. He was standing beside him, as big as a bear. Despite his smirk, the look in his eye was black and un–flinching.

Alexander frowned. 'I know what I'm doing.'

The Russian prodded his finger at Alexander's face. 'Do you?' he said, bluntly. 'This is not an ordinary situation. I don't want a mess when we get there.'

'I can handle it.'

'And this girl of yours will behave?'

'Yes.'

'You've told her what to say?'

Alexander hesitated and clawed at his neck. He looked like a schoolboy, all sullen and shamed. 'Not yet.'

The Russian's grin disappeared, as if a switch had been flicked. 'You've cut this too fucking fine, Alexander.'

'It's not a problem. She'll do what I tell her.'

'She'd better.'

Hanh squeezed closer against the door. Her belly was twisted tighter than a spring, and her breath ripped so shrill through her head that she needed to hold it to hear them. They were talking about *her* – they had to be – but they sounded so cold and aggressive! What in heaven or on earth were they going to tell her to do?

Alexander mumbled something inaudible and slipped away into the bedroom. He emerged just a few seconds later, ramming a T-shirt into the band of his jeans. He spoke to the Russian again, who thumped his shoulder and roared a laugh, and then Hanh watched with horror as they turned to face the veranda, and she felt four ruthless, bloodshot eyes on top of her. She leapt backwards, falling into the iron table and chairs and shoving them across the tiles with a bone-crunching clatter. They were coming to get her!

The veranda door threw itself open.

'What are you doing?' Alexander scowled from the doorway. The Russian stood at his back like a guard.

'I was cleaning!' Hanh cried, scrabbling up and snatching a dishcloth from the sink.

She started to move towards the courtyard steps and the Russian circled round, trapping her in. She stepped towards the door instead, but Alexander's hands had whipped to the frame on each side and he gripped it so tightly that she could see the veins in his arms bulge blue. His voice was cool as river water, hollow as eddies.

'We're going into the city.'

Hanh looked quickly around. There was nowhere for her to go. She took a tiny, snatched step back.

'Hurry up, Alexander,' hissed the Russian.

Alexander didn't move. He kept his hands clutched around the doorframe. His face looked in pain – as if he were wrestling some terror of his own. 'I need you to do something before we go,' he said to Hanh, his eyes skimming over her.

Hanh glanced from Alexander's face to the Russian. His grey tongue was running along his lips and his stare was as hot and filthy as Dinh's, and she thought of last night and imagined his sickening weight on top of her, just like Alexander's had been. She couldn't do it again! Not quietly, not without crying, or shouting out in pain. 'What do you want?' she asked, afraid.

'I want you to agree to take a job.'

'You've found me work?' she said, surprised.

'Yes, and somewhere to live.'

Hanh hesitated. 'Thank you,' she said, warily. She wasn't sure what else to say. A job was good news. Somewhere else to live was good too. She couldn't wait to leave here. She watched Alexander's hand slip down the doorframe. He twisted his finger into the bolthole and chipped out a large splinter of wood. He flicked it away and his eyes shot back to her.

'In the city we'll be meeting a man called Cheung Hu. You will be working for him on behalf of our associate, Mr Phuc. Mr Phuc would like you to tell Cheung Hu that you are his daughter.'

Hanh wrung the damp cloth in her hands, feeling a swell of wetness. The charge on Alexander's face was sparking electrically. 'I don't understand.'

'You don't need to understand. You just need to agree.'

'What type of work have you got me?'

Alexander paused. 'You'll be a waitress. There will be other girls there too. You'll like it. It's a good job.'

Hanh's thoughts stumbled. This was wrong. She shouldn't have to lie to be a waitress. 'I don't want to do it,' she said.

'I've done you a big favour, Hanh. I've helped you. Don't embarrass me.'

Alexander's voice crept across the veranda. The Russian kept licking his lips and Thuy's warning beat through her head. She knew what was happening. She knew what Saigon waitresses did. *She knew.*

'What kind of trader are you, Alexander? What do you do for your business?'

Alexander bared his teeth. 'My business is none of your business.'

Hanh stepped backwards, bracing her body against the

sink. Her legs were shuddering. From the claws of the tiger, to the mouth of the crocodile, she thought. 'Don't make me do it,' she said and she shook her head.

'We don't want to make you do anything,' Alexander replied. 'Just agree.'

Hanh shook her head, more urgently this time. 'No.'

Like an explosion, Alexander burst suddenly from the doorway and lunged at her. Hanh cried out and threw herself aside, scrambling through the Russian's flailing grasp and tearing down the veranda steps. She sprinted across the slippery, uneven courtyard tiles, tripping as she ran towards the bathhouse in the distance. She ran around its corner, snatching a look back and catching Alexander's furious face chasing after her, and she hurled her body at the tree trunk on the back perimeter. As she tried to clamber madly up and over the wall he grabbed at her ankles and she kicked her legs against his face, frantic and scurrying.

'Let go of me!' she screamed, but his grip was too strong and he yanked her to the ground.

'You will do as I tell you,' he shouted back, pinning her to the mud by her throat and clambering over her. The Russian stood above them both. His stare was fixed and impassive.

'I won't!' Hanh cried, trying to turn away from them. A root rammed into her kidney and she thrashed, whimpering.

'If you don't agree, I'll kill you,' said Alexander, tightening his grip on her neck. He held his face just an inch from hers and all that Hanh could do was gasp. She couldn't speak: he was holding her too hard. She felt the hot blast of his breath on her cheek. As he clamped his arm straight, the back of her head thumped against the earth and the light before her eyes began to cough and fade, and she tugged at him uselessly. 'Tell me you agree!' he bellowed.

Hanh forced a sound from deep inside her – not words – but a howl of panic from the depths of her stomach. Alexander loosened his grip.

'What did you say?'

'I agree,' she cried.

'Your name is Kieu!' Alexander yelled as if he were a general in the army. 'Say it! Say your name is Kieu!'

'My name is Kieu.'

'Who are you?'

'I am Mr Phuc's daughter!'

Alexander released Hanh's neck and stood up, and she crumpled to a ball at his feet. He kept his boot on her ankle so she couldn't move, and she felt like a rabbit in a trap. He ripped his canvas belt from its loops and leaned back over her. She yelped and her body went rigid as he grabbed her arms and wrapped the belt around her wrists, jerking her roughly and tying her hands so tight that they throbbed. He collapsed on the ground beside her, his chest heaving, and wiped his hand through the sweat that was balling from his head. He looked at Hanh, right into her eyes and she stared back, searching for anything to help her understand.

'Let's go,' said the Russian, already walking away.

Alexander hauled himself up and scooped his arm beneath

Hanh's knees. He picked her up and carried her back across the courtyard and through the yawning belly of the house. Ten strides or more behind the Russian, he marched along the garden path and out through the villa's front gates.

There was a rickshaw waiting on the tarmac. Alexander pushed Hanh in. Both men climbed into the cab behind her, shoving her to the well at their feet. The rickshaw driver scurried rat-like from his shade on the curb, clearly shocked at the sight of them and suddenness, but the Russian bellowed and he jumped on his bike and fired hurriedly at the kick-start, and Hanh knew that he wouldn't help her. She sat awkwardly on the floor as the rickshaw sped away, her legs and arms screwed around her and her joints jarred by the shunts of the road. She tried to nudge her bound hands so they sat less painfully, but the knots were unforgiving and burned her skin with the twist. Closing her eyes and concentrating, she tried to drag her shallow breath back from the brink of a gasp.

Alexander was selling her. He was selling her, as if she were a pig or a dog! It had been his intention from the moment they met. She could see it now; it was as clear as the sky. He had picked her out and slipped a rope around her neck, and meeting by meeting, lie by lie, he had inched her towards the market. She had let him do it. She had *wanted* him to do it. What a fool! The paddy fields slipped past her and the city began, and she struggled to keep her focus. None of this was real. Not the rickshaw, nor the beauty of the villa, nor the charm and venom of Alexander. *My name is Kieu.* She soundlessly mouthed the words. She

THIRTY-TWO

The rickshaw arrived early at the Notre Dame Basilica and the sky was a deep, expectant grey. Alexander tucked himself and Hanh against a side wall and waited impatiently, stubbing the toe of his boot through the gravel and chain-smoking. He had covered her bound hands with his jacket so as not to cause suspicion, but still, he felt so conspicuous. Every few moments, he patrolled a step or two forward and stole a furtive glance at the garden square on the opposite side of the road before slinking back to the safety of the wall. The Herder was sitting on the grass, in full view of the seething city, picking crumbs from the cracks of his teeth and studying him.

It was far too crowded here for Alexander's liking. The square was littered with all sorts of Party men; uniformed officials playing *cò tuóng* on the benches and soldiers patrolling the pavements with guns. In the pointed shade of the tall white bell towers, a dozen or more vendors touted their bread and broth, and the beggars were working like pack mules. The spin of bicycle spokes sizzled in the air. Yet, despite the crowds, Cheung Hu was easy to spot. His was the only pale Chinese face and his red silk shirt fluttered from his back as he pounded along the street. Against the backdrop of the light-brown brick of the Basilica, brown faces and dusty-brown clothes, he stood out like a polished ruby.

Alexander dragged his hands over the skin of his arms. Cheung Hu looked so much like the Herder. The likeness was not in his face, his body or his clothes, but in the way he cut through the hordes of people. With his head down, eyes up and long, driving steps, the crowd seemed to part before he reached them. Alexander took a last fat pull on his cigarette and chucked the butt into the gutter. Grabbing Hanh's wrist, he left the shelter of the basilica, pulling her with him but not looking at her face. They dodged through the streaming bicycles and into the square and he steered her to an empty bench and pushed her down.

'Don't move,' he snarled. 'I'll be watching you.'

The Herder heaved himself from the grass and moved after Alexander. They dipped through the crowds towards Cheung Hu, Alexander's eyes following the flashes of red silk that came through the shifting walls of people. He sunk his hands to the bottom of his pockets. His fingers skimmed the edge of Phuc's note and hovered there momentarily before coming to rest on his flick-knife.

In the centre of the square by the Virgin Mary, they met Cheung Hu. Alexander clocked a single bodyguard. He was loitering just a few steps back: thick-necked and chip-toothed, with fists clenched tightly.

Cheung Hu's eyes twitched distrustfully. 'What are you doing here?' he said to the Herder. His voice was as cold and blunt as it was on the telephone.

'Still breathing fire, you Chinese dragon,' the Herder grinned. He grabbed Cheung Hu's hand and flicked a hard shake along the length of his arm. 'How are you?'

Cheung Hu ripped his hand away and raised an angry finger at Alexander. 'You didn't say he would be here.'

'You didn't ask.' The Herder stepped forward and gave a huge, sarcastic shrug. He tipped his eyes to the body-guard. 'You've brought your minder . . .'

'Enough jokes!' Cheung Hu shouted. 'What's going on?'

The Herder gave a conciliatory nod, lowered his voice and leaned close to Cheung Hu. A gaunt vendor tugged on his cuff and he batted her away like a pestering fly. 'This is a big deal today, isn't it, Brother . . . ? Righting the wrongs? Why would I leave something so important to a measly greenhorn?' He slapped Alexander's back and spat him forward. 'I'm here to make sure everything goes to plan.'

Cheung Hu twisted his head, eyes narrowing. 'What's in it for you?'

'You and I are the same, Brother. I understand how you feel. This Phuc is a swindler. Such vile, brazen trickery from peasants must not be tolerated. You're showing Saigon that men like us aren't for slighting.'

Cheung Hu's glare slipped to Alexander. Alexander's eyes plummeted to the ground and his cheeks flared – a mix of embarrassment and white-hot burning rage. *Measly fucking greenhorn*. He knew it. The Herder really didn't trust him. He wasn't even trying to hide it any more.

'Fine,' said Cheung Hu, after a moment of cruel, shameless staring. 'Where's Phuc's daughter?'

'Do you have the money?' asked the Herder.

'You'll get your money when I get my girl.'

The Herder shook his head. 'Show it to me.'

Cheung Hu turned away for a moment and called to his bodyguard in brisk Cantonese. The Herder reached out suddenly and clamped his hand around Alexander's wrist, dragging him in. 'Get a grip, Alexander,' he hissed in his ear. 'This is your deal, remember? Take charge.' He jerked him forwards and kicked at his heel as Cheung Hu turned back.

The bodyguard sidled up and eased his hand partway from his pocket. Cupped in his palm, Alexander could see the blue-green corners of a wad of banknotes. As the man slipped back away, Alexander pulled his cheeks gently inwards and shifted a glance at Hanh. She was still on the bench where he'd left her, clutching her elbows and staring at her lap. Even from this distance, he could see the mud and cuts on her shins. Her whole body trembled. Before the gaping Basilica archways, she seemed so small and break-able. Five thousand dong was her price. It felt a pittance. He tried to look away again, but found that his eyes were snagged on her, and it hurt when he tried to move them. An ache was beginning to form in his head.

'Are you satisfied?' asked Cheung Hu, snapping Alexander reluctantly back.

'Yes,' he said, and he forced a nod to shake Hanh off. 'Where's our girl?'

'At my office.'

'I told you to bring her.'

'And I didn't listen. You'll have to excuse my suspicion, Brother, but I don't trust you either. How the fuck did you end up with Phuc's daughter? It doesn't make sense. Surely you must understand that I need reassurance? I'll give you the money now and I'll take your girl too, but you're not getting hold of the other one until I'm sure that she's right.'

Alexander shook his head. 'I can't let you do that.'

'Why not? If you're telling the truth, it won't matter; you have my word that I'll give your girl back.' Cheung Hu sniffed and the wind whipped his hair around his face like a black storm. In the sky above them, black gulls were wheeling. 'I have to say, a part of me hopes that you're lying. I was going to put her to work in the port bars. Those sailors come off the ships with a fist full of cash and a dick like an elephant. A pretty little lotus like her would have made me a fortune. What's the other girl like?'

Alexander's heart jerked in his throat. 'You want to send her to the bars?'

'I'll see what state she's in.'

'There's nothing wrong with her.'

'There's nothing wrong with her *now*.' Cheung Hu scratched his nose with the tip of a long, clouded finger-nail and his expression stayed straight as a banner. He took his pointed nail and prodded it sharply into Alexander's shoulder. 'I'll teach that snake Phuc I can't be tricked.'

Cheung Hu's words blew a shiver across Alexander. He looked at the ground and tried to shove an image of Hanh to the back of his mind. He could feel the warm skin of her neck in his hands and the flex and gulp of her throat as she struggled for air. He rubbed his palms roughly together. 'I'd keep her for myself, if I were you,' he said, but his voice was shaking.

Cheung Hu puckered his lips, disgusted. 'I wouldn't keep a girl like her.'

'She's a good girl.'

Cheung Hu laughed. 'A good girl! Tell me, Brother. What makes a girl good?'

Alexander squirmed and backed a step away from him. 'You can just tell,' he stammered.

Cheung Hu turned to the Herder, still laughing. 'I thought this boy was your apprentice? You haven't taught him anything!'

The Herder shook his head and stared at Alexander, scowling. 'You can throw an ass in a river, but you can't make it swim,' he said. 'This little ass will never understand women. You wouldn't believe the shit he spurts about what makes them *good*.'

Cheung Hu shuffled back close. Alexander felt spit on his cheeks as he spoke. 'Let me explain it to you. A girl is good if she serves her purpose. This little one's purpose is to settle my score, not to make my supper.' He paused and looked around the square. 'So do we have a deal?'

Alexander looked at the Herder and exhaled. The breath shuddered through his lips. He couldn't make a decision like this. He felt too drained.

'Fine,' said the Herder, with a sniff and a scowl.

'So where is she?'

'Don't worry. She's close.'

Alexander's gaze sloped helplessly back to Hanh. He didn't want to listen any more. Shards of rain were beginning to cut through the air; cold, hard slaps on his cheeks, spotting his glasses and blocking his vision. Just get this over, he thought. Get it done. He was so close now to getting rid of Hanh, forgetting what had happened and starting again, but his stomach felt sick. This was what he needed to do; it was what the Herder wanted. He was almost back to where he had craved to be for so long, but it didn't feel like it was supposed to. Doubt leaked through him. It was greasy on his skin. Control and relief and freedom, he had held them in his hands when he left the war, solid and certain as rock, but now he couldn't be sure they were ever there for more than a wing-beat moment. He couldn't remember what they felt like at all. As the sky shrunk behind the clouds and the rain beat down, and the noise of the crowds in the street grew thicker, and Cheung Hu gripped his shoulder and grinned, Alexander felt like a tripwire, like it would only take half a pound of pressure, then that would be it. Boom.

Cheung Hu caught Alexander staring. 'Ah,' he said, with amusement. 'We've found her.'

Alexander nodded feebly.

'What are you waiting for, then? Bring her here.'

Alexander didn't move. He hated the thought of having to speak to Hanh again, of having to listen to her desperate questions and her stubborn, pitiful snivelling. He wasn't ready. Not yet. He pulled his T-shirt around his body and twisted the gathered hem to a ball in his hands.

The Herder struck Alexander on the arm. 'The dragon's not stopping for coffee, Alexander,' he said, smearing the dripping rats' tails back from his eyes with his fat wet hand. 'Get the girl.'

Alexander slid his hand into his pocket, unfolded his flick-knife and ran his fingertip along the smooth, cool blade. He could just go over there and bring Hanh back. He could cut the knots from her wrists, tell her to follow him and then lead her over here. He wouldn't have to touch her. He didn't have to answer her questions. He could do that. It wouldn't be difficult. 'Fine,' he said. 'But I want the money first.' He pointed at the bodyguard. Seeing that his arm was shaking, he snatched it back down to his side. 'I get the money, then you get your girl, and then you're free to go.'

'I'm free to go?' Cheung Hu raised his eyebrows and looked at the Herder.

The Herder shrugged and smirked. Alexander swallowed hard. 'We're all free to go,' he muttered.

Cheung Hu paused and then nodded to his bodyguard, who sidled up, checked for Party men and then slipped Alexander the wad of cash.

Alexander tucked the money into his pocket. He couldn't delay any longer. He sunk his hands to the bottom of his pockets and paced across the garden square, trying not to run. Glancing back, he caught the Herder watching. His heavy frame was leaning against the Virgin Mary. His arms were folded and his stare was fixed on Alexander, warlike.

Hanh's face sprung upwards as Alexander crashed down on the bench. 'What's happening?' she asked him. Her voice was a rasping whimper.

Alexander didn't answer. He wrenched her hands towards him beneath their jacket-veil and whipped his knife from his pocket. It slipped in the wetness of his hands and Hanh flinched as the metal touched her. Alexander gripped the knife harder, turning the blade so that it lay flat against her skin and slipping it between her wrist and the tight belt-bind. He slung his eyes downwards, staring at her quivering hands and the knife as it ripped back and forth through the knotted material. There were quick, shallow jolts of air firing between them. Was it her breath or his? Feeling warmth on his thighs, he scanned down and saw that Hanh's skirt was sodden and a puddle of urine was dripping from the seat. He looked up at her face, at her swollen eyes and her mouth, stretched wide and thin in anguish. Her head lolled on her neck with each terrified breath. He looked back down and gave one more upward yank of the knife. The last threads of the bindings split open. He stood up and dragged her to standing.

'Where are you taking me?'

'You're being collected.'

She pulled herself backwards. 'I don't want to go.'

Alexander gripped tighter. He was conscious of the bustling square, the prying crowds and the eyes of the Party upon them. 'It's not your choice.'

'Don't make me. Please! Do you know what they'll do to me?'

Alexander's jaw gritted and he stiffened his grip on Hanh's wrist. He knew too well what they'd do to her. Cheung Hu had made sure that he couldn't pretend. 'Shut up,' he said and he quickened his step.

Hanh wrenched back on his arm, her feet slipping on the wet pavement. 'I thought you were a good man!' she pleaded. 'I thought you were going to help me.'

'Shut up!' he hissed again.

'You're a dog! A lying dog! I trusted you!'

Hanh's words were piercing knife points. He snatched his blade back out from his pocket and held it hard to the flesh at her hip, pulling her into him.

'Don't struggle,' he growled as she tugged against him, and he could feel her hot, swift breath on his chest. He was walking fast now, holding her firm to stop her flailing limbs, and he knew he was hurting her, and his head was pounding, and then all of a sudden he was facing Cheung Hu and the Herder, and the sight of them both in the rain stopped him dead.

Cheung Hu glared back at him. 'What are you waiting for?' he said. 'Bring her here.'

Alexander didn't move. He stood on the brink of the garden, ten feet or so from Cheung Hu, clutching Hanh tightly. The Herder was still pitched against the statue, and he craned his thick neck round to stare. Their faces were calm, detached and impassive. The chill of it kept him rooted still.

Cheung Hu took a few strides forward, opening his arms wide. 'What's wrong with you? Come here!'

The Herder straightened too, turning to Alexander. 'What are you doing, Alexander? Give him the girl.'

Alexander didn't respond. His knife was still pressing into Hanh's haunches, but when he had stopped walking her struggles had stopped too. He eased his grip. He was holding her in his arms, like she was his baby. He looked at the stone-faced men in front of him. All those girls he had helped in the past . . . where were they now? Tied up in the back of a Chinaman's office or a grim Hanoi brothel, most likely. He hadn't helped them; he had rounded them up and sent them to hell. Hanh was right. He wasn't a good man. He was a liar and a dog. He could still make it right, though, couldn't he? It wasn't too late to be good. He didn't need to send Hanh to hell. Perhaps he shouldn't hand her over. Perhaps he should *keep her*. He could look after her. He could do it properly, this time. She could make his suppers, like she did before, and they could sit together and eat and talk, and they could forget this ever happened. He could help her. *Really* help her. He looked at the Herder, standing at the feet of the Virgin Mary with his hands on his hips and fuming eyes. He wouldn't approve, but he'd gotten over worse before, and Alexander could deal with that later. He squared up and stared at Cheung Hu. 'I made a mistake,' he shouted.

Cheung Hu stared back. 'What do you mean?'

'You already have the right girl,' Alexander cried. 'Your girl is Phuc's daughter, not this one.'

'What the fuck are you doing, Alexander?' the Herder hissed.

Cheung Hu glanced at his bodyguard, then looked at Hanh, and then at Alexander. His face was a thundercloud. 'How do you make a mistake like that?'

'It's just a mistake.'

'Are you lying to me?'

'It's the truth,' he said, and he pointed again. 'You already have Kieu.'

'What's your man doing, Herder?' Cheung Hu yelled.

The Herder shook his head. 'I've no fucking clue.'

'This is madness,' Cheung Hu snarled. He spun on his heels and barked at his bodyguard. 'Get the car.'

'What are you doing?' said Alexander as the bodyguard begun to stride away.

'I'm leaving.' Cheung Hu clicked his fingers at Alexander. 'Give me the girl.'

Alexander shook his head and pulled Hanh closer. 'No. You can't have her.'

'Wrong,' spat Cheung Hu. He marched at Alexander and seized Hanh's wrist.

'She's mine!' Alexander bellowed, releasing Hanh and slashing his knife hard along the length of Cheung Hu's grabbing arm.

'Fuck!' he cried, recoiling. His jacket was torn, and he snarled at Alexander, clutching his forearm and staring at the two gaping pleats of flesh and their dribbling redness. He staggered back in furious shock. 'You shouldn't have done that!'

'You shouldn't have tried to take my girl.'

Cheung Hu stepped back again and jabbed his finger at

the Herder. 'Your greenhorn should be in a fucking asylum, Herder!'

'I know,' said the Herder, raising his hands and shooting an anxious look around the bustling square. His voice was brisk and wary. 'I'm sorry.'

'What the fuck are you going to do about it?'

'We can come to a deal.'

Cheung Hu shook his head. 'No more deals. You prick-eyed Russian liars can't be trusted to deal any better than the Fán T'án peasants.'

'He'll give you back the money.'

'I don't give a shit about the money.'

'He'll work for you.'

'Are you fucking joking?'

'No! Tell me what you want.'

'I want the girl.'

'Take her. She's yours.'

Cheung Hu's eyes skipped to Hanh and he waved his un-injured hand in the air. 'Come here!'

Hanh stayed still. She was trapped in the centre of the three men, confused and terrified, unable to run.

'Listen to me, little flower,' he said, more sternly. 'My name is Cheung Hu. I own businesses in Saigon. I'm a very rich man. I'll look after you. Come to the car with me.'

Alexander hitched himself up from staggering. His mind reeled and his vision was blurred. 'Don't move, Hanh,' he said. 'He's lying.'

'Shut up, Alexander,' bit the Herder.

Cheung Hu roared and hit his fist to his ribcage. His white face was twisted and angry and he stamped his heeled boot on ground. 'He doesn't know when to stop, does he, Herder? Does he wish he was dead?' He ripped open the clasp of his jacket, revealing his belt, and through the rain and the fog in his head Alexander caught the glistening black metal of a gun-barrel. 'Give me one reason why I shouldn't grant his wish and be done with this.'

The Herder raised his palms slowly higher and shook his head. 'I haven't got a reason,' he said. 'I agree you can't stand for this. I wouldn't stand for it either.'

'You don't care about your man?'

'I don't care to make you my enemy, Brother. I'd shoot him myself to prove it if I had a gun.'

The Herder glanced around and stepped back a few slow, cautious paces. His arms began to lower. Cheung Hu's eyes chased after him, flashing through the rain. The square was still crammed and meddlesome stares were starting to find the commotion, and with the soldiers on the corners each of them knew that they couldn't do a thing. Cheung Hu's dark-green UAZ jeep flew aside them suddenly, the body-guard at the wheel, and Cheung Hu flicked his blooded hand at Alexander's face and spat at his feet before snatching open the door.

'If a dog bites, you'd blame his owner, wouldn't you?' he growled at the Herder as he clambered inside. The engine gave a threatening rev. 'You mark my words, my friend: this isn't done.'

THIRTY-THREE

Phuc leaned out from the slender opening of the Cholon side street and peered along the road to Bin Tay Market. He pushed his hand to the wall to steady himself and scanned the writhing courtyard mob. It was hard to see any faces. A line of parasols blocked the spilling stall-fronts and the concrete was a web of overladen, teetering bikes. He turned to Tam in the shadow behind him. 'They're still not here, Brother,' he cried, dismayed. 'They're not fucking here!'

Tam rammed his hands into his pockets and carried on pacing the length of the alleyway. 'Give them a chance, Phuc.'

'How long since I called them?'

He glanced at his watch. 'Twenty minutes.'

'Twenty minutes! What the fuck is taking them so long?'

'They'll be here, Brother. Stay calm.'

'How can I stay calm, Tam? I've given my daughter to a Chinese mobster!'

'We'll get her back.'

'You should have seen her face. She was petrified.'

'I fucking bet she was.'

Phuc paused suddenly, his eye-line shooting towards the

tobacco store in the opposite direction. 'Did you hear that, Brother?'

'Hear what?'

'It's a motor car!' he shouted. 'Cheung Hu's back already!'

Tam lunged forward as Phuc went to run from the alley, grabbing his shirt and yanking him backwards, out of sight. 'You're hearing things, Brother!' he cried, throwing Phuc against the wall. He pinned him by his shoulders and shook him roughly. 'Cheung Hu's jeep left barely ten minutes ago. He won't be back for an hour. Now get a fucking grip or you'll fuck this all up!'

Phuc collapsed – his hands on his knees and breathing deeply – as Tam let go. He thought he was going to vomit. 'What have I done, Tam?' he mumbled at his feet.

Tam crouched beside him, looked up and gave a small, sad smile. 'You've done all you could, Brother.'

Phuc nodded, weakly. His friend was right. As soon as Phuc had left the Herder's bar, he had run straight back here. Tam had been waiting – just like he had said – and together they had watched, smoked and gnawed on their fingers, but just as they hoped, Cheung Hu snatched the bait. Phuc's heart had skipped with relief as one of Cheung Hu's bodyguards rushed from the shop and clambered into the jeep on the kerb outside. He fired it up with a sudden roar, ripping around the street corner and into the back alley with the secret office entrance, before appearing again just a minute later and speeding away. The windows of the jeep were blacked out though, and it moved so fast that Phuc couldn't see if Kieu was with them. That was what distressed him most.

'Are you sure you couldn't see if Kieu was in the car?' he asked Tam again, for at least the fifth time.

Tam shook his head. 'No, Brother. I'm sorry. He won't have done, though – he's not honest enough. And even if by some fluke he did take her with him, you've got insurance. He'll give her to the Russian and you'll still get her back. You're prepared, Phuc. You've thought it through this time. Don't worry.'

'But what if I'm wrong?'

'You've been right so far, haven't you? You knew for certain that Cheung Hu would meet the Russian. You knew he was too proud to let an insult lie. You and that little girl of yours were smart enough and brave enough to leave doubt in his mind. Have faith, Brother.' Tam dragged Phuc up by his elbow and steered him calmly back to their vantage point at the neck of the alley. He pointed towards the market. 'Look!'

Phuc followed the line of his sight and a set of crisp, brown uniforms caught his eye suddenly. Three armed Party officials were prowling against the yellow market facade. They stopped by the man who sold ducks' eggs – the ones with their shells packed in salted black ash – and looked around, mean-eyed and expectant.

Phuc gave a sober nod. 'It's them.'

'I told you they'd be here,' Tam replied, still smiling. He hugged his friend and then shoved him out of the alleyway. 'Good luck.'

Phuc stumbled forward. He snatched a last precautionary glance at the tobacco store and then strode towards them.

301

A familiar, ominous scar-face firmed in his view. It was the Party official who had called at his home, just one week earlier.

'Do you have my file?' Phuc demanded. There wasn't time for fear or hesitation.

The official stiffened. He was taken aback for the briefest moment, but then he nodded and flicked open his satchel, so Phuc could see. 'Do you have our payment?'

Phuc stared at the bulging brown folder that winked up from the bag. All of his past and his future was tucked neatly in there. It looked so innocent, just waiting to be taken. So utterly, deceitfully harmless. He wiped his mouth and drew a breath. 'No,' he said, 'but I've got something better.'

The official's eyes hardened to rock. 'Don't fuck with me, Comrade.'

'I'm not. It's true.'

'We made a deal. You owe me five hundred dong.'

'I know, but just listen—'

'Mercy pleas won't pay my bills.'

Phuc shook his head, quick and firm. 'I'm not asking for mercy.'

'You've dragged me into filthy Chinatown for nothing!'

'No! The offer I have is far more valuable.'

The official's expression was crumpled by rage and the scar of his cheek was swollen and reddening. He whipped a steaming look at his henchmen, gave a menacing sniff and then leaned at Phuc. He stabbed his long, sharp finger-nail in the sliver of air between their faces. 'You're a fool, Comrade,' he hissed. 'You're as good as dead! Don't you think I've heard excuses from a thousand scrabbling rats? A man like you has *nothing* to give me.' He spat at Phuc's feet, shoved him aside and marched away.

Phuc darted after him. 'You're wrong,' he cried. 'I can give you Cheung Hu!'

Across the yard, the official froze. He turned sharply back. His face was alert, his expression ablaze with anger and anticipation. 'What did you say?'

Phuc ran beside him. 'I can give you Cheung Hu,' he said, more gently. 'You know him, Brother . . . don't you?'

The official's eyes flickered, suspiciously. 'Every Party man knows him.'

'Wouldn't you like to bring him in?'

'He's not my business.'

'He's a thief and a criminal.'

'Of course he is,' the official said, sneering. 'A hundred of my bosses are fat with bribes from his brothels and game-dens . . . and their bosses too. Who cares if he robs a few peasants? Why would I want to bring him in? Nobody I know would thank me.'

Phuc stepped forward and took hold of the official's arm. 'He's robbing the Party far worse than the peasants, Brother,' he whispered. 'He's tapped the pipes at the Government shipyard. He's been syphoning fuel every night for a week.'

The official frowned and stared at Phuc's grip. His eyes kept twitching. 'Cheung Hu wouldn't touch the Party,' he said, shaking his head. 'We have truces.'

Phuc shook his head right back. 'He's broken them, Brother.'

'He wouldn't dare.'

'Are you certain?' pushed Phuc. 'The man has no conscience. He's a foreigner . . . no respect for our flag. I understand you can let him slide for a whore and gambler, but surely the Party can't tolerate this? You can be the one who stops him, Brother; the hero who slays the traitorous Chinese dragon! Think how your bosses will thank you for that. Think how they'll reward you for your patriotism, for being so loyal and courageous. You'll be promoted. You'll get a new house, perhaps . . . bigger rations. Cheung Hu's scalp is worth much more than five hundred dong.'

Phuc stepped back and paused, watching desperately as his words soaked in. All Party men were greedy and shallow and Phuc knew this prize was too sweet to resist, but it couldn't come quick enough!

The official made a last attempt at shabby resistance. 'You're lying,' he muttered, uncertain.

'I can prove it,' cried Phuc, and he nodded to the hovering henchmen to pull them in. 'I know where he steals from. I've been to his office too. I've seen vials of fuel there! You'll have more than enough evidence to shop him.'

The official's eyes sprung wide and black. He was snared! 'You know where Cheung Hu's office is?' he asked, surprised.

'Yes,' replied Phuc. 'And I know he's not in it.'

'Tell me where it is.'

'Clear my debt and give me my file.'

The official paused and then grabbed Phuc's hand and shook it. 'It's done.'

Phuc held him tight, not letting go. 'There's one more

thing I want,' he said, with as much boldness and courage as he could. 'If I take you there and we find a girl, I get to keep her.'

The official's gaze thinned, suddenly mistrustful. 'A girl?' he asked. 'Who is she?'

Phuc clenched his jaw at the official, rebellious. 'If you want Cheung Hu the girl is not your concern.'

The official glanced at his each of his henchman. A second of silent consideration passed between them and then one of them shrugged and the official turned back. 'Fine,' he said. 'Now show me the office.'

Phuc led the men away from the market courtyard and through the bustling streets of Cholon. They slipped by the shaded side street where Phuc had hid and he glanced stealthily sideways and caught the reassuring glint of Tam's green eyes. Phuc's heart throbbed in his mouth. He was almost there! With all that he was and ever would be he hoped his daughter was still in that room! If Cheung Hu had left her there like he hoped he would have her back in just a few minutes. The official would get his evidence, and Cheung Hu would be arrested and sent to the camps. Phuc would be free!

On the pavement outside the tobacco store, there was still no jeep. Phuc marched bravely inside, the officials following keenly. The shop assistant was leaning on the cabinet in the doorway and she burst up at the sudden sight of them in her empty store. She scuttled after them as they as they barged to the back of the long thin room.

Phuc pointed to the rows of cigarette boxes on the back wall. 'It's a door,' he said. His whole body was tingling.

'No! You can't go in there!' cried the panicking assistant.

The scar-faced official ignored her, bringing the butt of his rifle into the glass panel. It shattered on Phuc's feet. He swept the boxes from the shelves to the floor and they saw the crack of a doorframe, and he whipped a bayonet from his belt and thrust it into the fissure.

'Fuck!' he cried as the door belted open. Grey daylight spilled into the secret room and row upon row of sparkling guns flashed back at them.

The bodyguard that Phuc had seen against the back wall earlier was standing by the desk in the centre of the floor. In his hand was a gun, but it wasn't upheld. Alone and off guard, he seemed unsure of what to do. Phuc strained to peer past the gawping officials to look for Kieu, but the room was still dim and they blocked his view. The body-guard's wide white eyes skimmed between the three officials and the gun-barrels that were trained to his worried face.

'Comrades!' he muttered as he placed his weapon down and took a stumbling, slight step back. His voice was low and wary. 'I'm a friend of yours. I promise.'

'Bullshit.'

'Cheung Hu is my master. He has many brothers in the Party. Good friends. Let me call them. You'll see we've been kind to you for many years.'

The scar-faced official shook his head. 'We know what you Chinese rats have been up to. Your years of bribes and trickery won't help you. Every man in the Party's your enemy now.'

The scar-faced official stepped forward into the secret room. His comrades followed after him, one holding the bodyguard against the back wall with the line of his weapon and the other clamping a set of handcuffs around his fat wrists. For the first time, Phuc could see in properly.

'Daddy?'

The high trill of Kieu's voice jumped up from the gloom. She was curled on the floor in the corner of the office, knees clutched to her chest and trembling wildly. Phuc shoved in and hurdled down beside her and she pressed herself desperately against him, grabbing at his arms and butting her head into the safety of his chest. He prised her back from his body, holding her by her shoulders and study-ing her face. She thrust at his arms and tried to pull herself back to him, and he grabbed her wrists to hold her still.

'What did he do to you, Kieu?' he said, staring into her terrified face. Kieu's eyes puckered and she began to sob, her sharp, wheezing draws of breath piercing the air. He tightened his grip on her shuddering shoulders. 'Tell me what happened, Kieu. Did he touch you?'

Kieu gave a feeble half-shake of her head. 'I want to go home, Daddy,' she mumbled. 'Take me home.'

Phuc exhaled deeply and let his daughter clutch back against him. He closed his arms around her and rested his cheek on her soft black hair. He watched the officials slink around the room and circle outwards like a pack of dogs, teeth bared and drooling.

'Look on the desk,' Phuc said, and he pointed. The dish of vials was hidden beneath a pile of messy paper. 'There!'

The official shifted the papers aside and examined the bowl of sparkling test tubes. He held one aloft in the light of the doorway and orange liquid glittered like silk. He uncorked it and sniffed, recoiling at its strength. 'How do we tell where they came from?' he said, looking sceptical.

'Go to the West Quay,' said Phuc. 'Search along the bottom of the fuel pipe, and at the farthest end from the guard-house – behind the containers – you'll find a tapped valve. Take a sample from there and you'll see it's the same.'

'Do you give me your word?'

'Yes! You know where I live. If I lie, you can find me! They're from the Government shipyard. I swear to you, Brother.'

The official paused and then nodded, tipping the dish of vials carefully into his satchel. He rummaged for a second and took out Phuc's file. Phuc hauled himself up, lifting Kieu with him, and reached out to take it. The official grabbed his hand and shook it hard.

'You're a good Comrade, Brother Phuc,' he said, squeez-ing him tightly. 'I give you my word, too: no man from the Party will trouble you again.'

Phuc gave an uneasy nod. With years of fear unravelling behind him, with all he had seen and done in the past week, all that he had put his family through, approval from the Party felt a messy, merciful blessing. He tugged his hand and his file free and looked at the ground. 'Cheung Hu will be back any minute,' he mumbled.

The scar-faced official walked away and plucked a Makarov revolver from a pin on the wall, weighing it in his hand. He slumped into Cheung Hu's chair and kicked his feet on top of the desk. 'We'll wait,' he said, grinning.

Phuc lifted his arm and wrapped it around Kieu's shoulders, gathering her into him. He wanted to take her home now, to see Phuong and the boys and start their new life. There was nothing left to do here and he felt so worn and weary. Without another word or look, he tucked the heavy file beneath his arm and slipped from the back door of the secret office, guiding his daughter out through the alleyway. As they left the crowded streets of Cholon and headed toward their home in the Zones, he raised his face to the sunless grey sky. Cool, fresh wind beat on his cheeks and began to numb him. His relief was complete and elating.

THIRTY-FOUR

Alexander slumped on a bench at the Herder's side and watched Cheung Hu's jeep rip away into the rain. The punch of the engine echoed across the tarmac like a stone that had been skipped. It struck the high basilica walls and shook in his chest. He stared as the car swerved around the sharp cathedral corner, disappearing from sight, and then dipped his head and looked at the ground beneath him. His mind was so thick and heavy he felt as though he'd been drugged. The Herder's huge booted foot was only an inch from his own; he could rock on his heels, twist and stamp and crush him. Alexander would not have been surprised to see the solid leather boot close down on him. He knew he was in for a lashing. It would probably be worse than any the Herder had whipped him with before. But at least he still had Hanh.

She was beside the bench, on the opposite side of the Herder. Fixed still by shock, her poise was alert and animal. Her drenched hair clung to her cheeks, and the muscles in her neck were strained tighter than rope. Flecks of Cheung Hu's blood specked her blouse. She stared at the Herder, and then at Alexander, with wide black eyes. She looked so ruined and fearful. It made him feel sad. Later, he would explain it to her. He would sit her down on the veranda steps, hold her hand and tell her that he was going to keep her. He would find them a house outside Saigon and it could be like their first few days together, and he would promise to look after her properly this time. He'd say he was sorry about what had happened, last night and today. He knew she was a good girl really. She'd understand.

The last traces of the jeep's motor dropped from the air and Alexander's gaze crept warily up to the Herder. The Herder was already staring down.

'You've surpassed yourself today, Alexander,' he said. His eyes were fireballs.

Alexander winced. He knew what was coming. He would have to ride out the Herder's wrath before he could talk to Hanh. 'I know,' he mumbled, and glanced away as he heaved himself to standing.

'You don't know anything.' The Herder shook his head and scowled. He dragged both hands through his hair and let out a sigh so deep it was almost a growl. 'Just when I thought you couldn't be covered in any more crazy, you find a fucking vat to sink yourself in.'

'I'm sorry,' said Alexander, clawing at the flesh in the bend of his elbow behind his back.

'Sorry doesn't begin to cut it.'

'I can explain.'

'Don't!' The Herder vented a bellow so loud that the vendors around them all stopped and stared. He spun away and stormed across the square towards the basilica, shoving through the swarm of ogling people without breaking his stride. His feet thumped on the sodden grass. 'Your explanations make me *ache*, Alexander.'

Alexander snatched Hanh from where she was rooted and slung her rigid-tense bundle of bone and muscle over his shoulder. He scampered after the Herder, his heart walloping inside his head. 'I knew what I was doing!'

'Bullshit!' cried the Herder.' No man has ever been so deluded as you.'

The Herder strode across the street and down the side of the Basilica, his eyes raging back and forth in search of a cab. He stopped at the crossroads and flailed an arm at a passing rickshaw, but it sped quickly by and kicked wet dirt up his trousers. He cursed and wrenched a hipflask from his jacket pocket, knocking back a vast angry swig.

'Let's recap your achievements today, shall we, Alexander?' he said. He spun away from the road and brandished the metal bottle furiously in Alexander's face. 'You went all doe-eyed over a scraggy little whore and you ruined our deal. You robbed Cheung Hu, the most powerful Chinese man in Saigon, if not the whole of Vietnam. You did your level best to sever his arm with a tiny fucking flick-knife. You had me held at gunpoint in Saigon's most crowded city square. You humiliated me. Well done, Alexander. That's a good day's work, even for you. You've screwed us both.'

Alexander squirmed and shunted Hanh's weight on his shoulder. He could feel her trembling, the lick of her shaking hair and her hot, quick breath. 'I haven't screwed you,' he said.

'Wrong,' spat the Herder, and he pointed his finger and a harsh blunt stare at him. 'You hung a noose around both our necks the moment you refused to hand over the girl. You're my man, Alexander. My responsibility. What do you think Cheung Hu will do now?'

'He'll calm down.'

'Did he look like a man to practise forgiveness?'

'I'll explain what happened. I'll tell him about Phuc.'

The Herder chucked out a mocking laugh. 'Will you? When he knocks on your door and asks politely? How fucking stupid are you?'

Alexander writhed. Hanh's weight felt heavier and heavier on his shoulder and neck, and his head was pounding. He lowered her to the floor and she scrambled into a basilica archway, pushing her body against the wall, her head crooked down like a damaged bird. 'I'm not stupid,' he said, and he pressed his palm to his brow and stumbled a few unsteady steps backwards.

'Well, there's something seriously wrong with you,' said the Herder, wielding his hipflask wildly again. He shook his head in despair, and his long hair swayed and shuddered. 'You're nothing but trouble, Alexander. I should have let Cheung Hu kill you when I had the chance.'

Alexander's memory limped back to the square, to the oily blood on the knife in his hand, to the splicing rain, to his aching eyes fixed on Cheung Hu's gun, to the Herder's cruel glare and emotionless tone. *I'd shoot him myself to prove it if I had a gun.* He looked down at his cuff, stained red and wet with Cheung Hu's blood. He could smell himself, like uncooked meat, like the market-stalls with butchered limbs strung up and bloodied slicks beneath their tables. Like war. Like camps after battles, where skin hung gashed. Like the ruby paddy-waters in the setting sun on the nights when Americans had hurricaned by. His lips began to pucker and pinch. This could have been his own blood, so easily, if the Herder had gotten his way. 'You were going to let Cheung Hu kill me,' he mumbled uncertainly.

The Herder's eyes shot up and he paused for the faintest, shrillest moment. 'Don't be ridiculous, Alexander,' he said. 'What do you think he would have done if I hadn't been there? I saved you.'

Alexander clenched his eyes shut and tried to remember what had happened, to force his mind to focus in the moments of clarity that blinked through each beat of the pulse in his head. He knew he was right. His mind wasn't tricking him. 'No,' he said, opening his eyes. 'You didn't defend me.'

The Herder paused again. It was a pause as broad, brash and bullying as the man himself, and then he raised his flask and toasted Alexander. 'You're right. Today you have been truly indefensible.'

'You said you'd shoot me.'

'And I would have done too, if we weren't in that damned public square.'

'I thought we were a team.'

The Herder sprung suddenly forward and hurled his flask against the basilica wall. He roared at Alexander, his spine stooped, his shoulders rolled and his eyes flaring. 'A team implies we are equal, Alexander. It implies we both con-

314

tribute. You give me nothing. You add no shred of value. We have *never* been a team.'

Alexander backed away and glanced at Hanh still scrunched on the floor. Her spine was strained and spiked by bone at the tightness of her coil.

'Fine!' he yelled, and he meant it. He could take her and go away from here and start his new life and never see the Herder again. The way he felt right now, that would be just perfect! He'd had enough of trying to please, of doubt, of failing, of never quite living up to expectations. At once, he felt a chip of relief. 'I'll leave!' he cried. 'We won't work together any more.'

'Wrong again, Alexander,' snarled the Herder, pounding into the middle of the street and finally flagging his rickshaw. The driver veered to the kerb with a look of surprise and the Herder threw himself roughly in. 'You'll be working for me for a very long time. After all you've done today, you owe me. Every night from now on, you'll be sat outside my bedroom door. Wherever I go, you'll come with me. Whichever girl I choose to fuck, you'll listen. You are now my personal guard dog, and you'll keep that job until every man who gives a shit for Cheung Hu's pride is dead and buried, or until his brothers kill you – whichever comes first. If it's your death, I expect your mangy dog ghost to guard me some more. You're mine for eternity, Alexander.'

Alexander shook his head. 'No. I won't do it.'

'Yes, you will,' said the Herder, threateningly. 'This isn't a choice. You'll start right now. Give me your girlfriend and get in the cab.'

'No.'

'Don't fucking start with me, Alexander. Bring her here.'

'No! We're leaving!'

The Herder's face swelled a bright, fearsome purple. 'You're fucking insane! Where are you going to go, Alexander? I didn't drag you out from the war and spend years of my life moulding your weak little brain, and putting up with your utter, trolloping bullshit just for you to defy me! I own you, Alexander. You can't come and go as you please. Now, do what I tell you and get in the cab!'

As the Herder raged and swore from the back seat of the quivering rickshaw, Alexander was hit by a moment of brutal, crushing lucidity. It wasn't a pain, but a blunt, violent pressure that exploded inside his skull, like a pound of dynamite, but still, it was fresher and far more true than anything he'd felt in his lifetime before. All those things the Herder had offered had never been real. The escape and opportunity, control and liberation: they didn't exist. They never would. The Herder had used him. He had rolled him out across the land like a tank, to do his bidding. He glanced at Hanh on the ground in the arch; she clung to the wall as if she feared a gust of wind might blow her away. She wasn't real either. He had tricked himself too. He would never be able to help her. Not like this. Not ever, really. She hated him. Of course she did; he had shattered her into a million tiny unfixable pieces. He gave a rancid, guttural moan and ripped his eyes away from her, just in time to see the Herder's brawling body lunge from the cab. His hand reached out and grabbed for Alexander's neck.

Alexander thrashed away and dodged the plunging grasp and before he had a chance to think, he had bundled Hanh up from her terrified pile and started to run. He slung her over his shoulder and tore along the basilica wall and his feet streaked through the deep, spitting puddles – cold, sharp and fresh – and he reached the corner and snatched a look back, and shot a hard and *wonderful* glare right between the Herder's snarling eyes.

EPILOGUE

Hanh walked along the ridge of the paddy, holding out her arms for balance. She stopped in the shade of a wilting palm, placed down her basket and sat on the ground. Dangling her ankles beneath the water, she sunk her feet into the soft cool mud. The rice was growing quick and strong, and it tickled her bare skin. When she pushed her soles down to the hard earth, the bright green crop reached almost to her knees. It felt good to be home, to be a part of her hamlet again. There would be a rich harvest this year.

Thuy was already in the fields. Hanh watched as she moved slowly through the mud, pulling weeds from between the seedlings. With her head dipped forward and the early evening sunlight bouncing golden from her *nón lá* hat, she looked like a glistening sun. On the horizon, Thuy's brother was standing on the roof of Hanh's home. With his hands on his hips, he admired the reward of his labour. For days, he had been spreading crisp, brown palm leaves over the bamboo beams and knotting them together tightly. There were just a few loops left to tie and the thatch would be finished by sundown. All of Thuy's family had given their time to help Hanh fix up her home. Together, they had mended the wire on her broken window, fastened new bolts to her doors and thickened her roof, ready for the coldness of winter. They had cared for the house while she was gone too, making sure the scavenging neighbours let everything be. Hanh had never felt so grateful for anything else in her life. The family had welcomed her home, without judgement or spite. They had sheltered her from the eyes of the hamlet until she was ready to face their scorn, and kept her warm and safe and fed as though she were made of the very same blood. They had never asked for a word of her story. She loved them for it.

Alexander had brought Hanh back to the hamlet. That day in Saigon, he had promised he would, though she hadn't believed him. In the roads beyond the basilica, he had flagged down a rickshaw and then driven her around the city for hours without an aim: just escaping. When the cold, the rain and her shock made her shake, he had wrapped his arms around her shoulders. At first, she had struggled against him, but then, as he gripped her tightly and she heard the breathless sound of his sobs in her hair, she had known that he wouldn't hurt her, and she wasn't afraid. They had slept in a park until the dawn light peeped up and then flown in an aeroplane back to Hanoi. An aeroplane! Hanh had held the surge of her heart in her mouth and clutched the arms of her seat with all her might as the plane rumbled along the runway, shuddered beneath her and lifted away into the clear blue air. Once before, Alexander had told her how calm the earth could seem from the sky. When she looked down at the swept vastness of the land, at the sparkling silver threads of rivers tracing through a hundred fields of lush, green rice, she understood him perfectly. This was where she belonged. She had felt such pride and peace in every part of it.

Alexander had given her money too, as well as bringing her home. When they had stood at the entrance to the hamlet's pathway and said goodbye, he had stared at the ground and held out a wedge of banknotes, thick as a fist and bigger than any she'd ever seen. She had said she wouldn't take any – she didn't want to be in his debt – but the next morning she had found the bundle tucked beside her porch-stove, tied to a rock with a length of red string.

From the field where she worked, Thuy looked up and waved at Hanh. Thuy had invited her for supper to celebrate finishing the work to her home. Hanh squinted into the sun and waved back as Thuy bent to the ground. She was searching for paddy-crabs to take home to her mother, picking them up from the water and collecting them in the wicker basket slung on her hip. This evening, her mother would boil the crabs and make soup, with asparagus and noodles. Hanh had already bought pâté, wrapped up in a pandan leaf. She had made sweet *chè* pudding and brewed her own fresh lotus tea. Tonight's supper was going to be a feast.

Hanh pushed the sleeves of her blouse up to her elbows, ready for work. As she folded the material back from her wrists, she paused and looked down with satisfaction. Two thin lines of cotton nodded up and down though the beige linen cuff. She had stitched them herself, perfectly straight.

With the money Alexander had given her she had started a course as a seamstress. She had paid for Thuy to have classes too. When the girls had learned to sew, Hanh hoped she would have enough money left to start a business. They could buy silk and cotton and thread and rent a small shop in Hanoi's Old Quarter, if they liked. Being a seamstress was a good profession. If she worked hard, she would earn enough money for food and shop rent. Her mother would have been happy.

In the distance, when Hanh looked towards the river, she could see the white peak of her mother's headstone. It was a bright, clean stone, with her mother's name in gold lettering. Hanh was glad she'd been able to give her mother something special. Still, as she had cleared away the dry, browning flowers and the spent stubs of red incense from where she had left them, she felt a little regret. She had given her mother a good burial with the help of Alexander.

Sometimes Hanh still thought of him. When the night air was as cool and damp as it was at the house in the Mekong Delta, she would lie awake and think of what might have been. When the blossom was pale enough pink to be almost white, when it fell from the peach trees and spread thickly on the ground, Hanh would crouch in the flowers, let her eyes slip into a blur and imagine the earth was covered in deep Russian snow. Once or twice, she had crouched on her porch to cook her supper and thought she saw his dark eyes peering out from the trees at the paddies' edge. She didn't mind though. She slept a little better even, knowing he was out there. For a while, she

321

had wondered if there would be a child. Each morning, she had woken and touched her hand to her belly, smoothed it over her bare skin, felt for a curve. She imagined a child with beautiful milky skin and bright blue eyes, someone to love, who would love her back unconditionally. Someone who made her feel worthwhile.

There wasn't a child though. When Hanh went to the river to wash at night, she talked to her mother and father. She told them about Alexander and asked their advice. In her heart, when she lay in the water, she knew it was better this way. It felt peaceful, being back with her parents. This was where she was meant to be. Hanh smiled and took her hat from her basket, and with one last glance towards the river, she waded into the shimmering green rice.

Alexander waited patiently beneath the sprawling bows of a sycamore and dragged slow on the cigarette cupped in his palm. The night was moonless and the street was bare. A slight breeze slipped through the trees, and the leaves spurred him on with their whispers. For hours, he had been here. One by one, he had watched the brothel windows drop from lighted yellow to thick-sleeping black. The punters had long since left, the front doors were still and now just one bulb was flickering weakly. He didn't care how long it took, though. For the last few months, he had felt almost weightless; the pressure of time had deserted his side. Night after night, he'd slept soundly – without visions or sweats or wakeful screams – and now his mind was clear and fresh. The ache that had lain in his stomach was gone. Instead, a

sense of triumph was brewing: a deep achievement – unen-
cumbered by guilt – that he had never imagined existed.
He could wait all night.

The darkness swelled suddenly when the last bulb snuffed.
Alexander paused for a moment more, at peace with the
solitude, and then crumpled his cigarette out on the trunk
of the tree. It dropped to the floor, still smouldering. He
plucked his rucksack from his feet and slung it over his
shoulder, then checked both ways for hidden watchers and
stole across the empty street.

Inside the slumbering town house, Alexander moved
swiftly. Light-footed and smooth, he climbed the staircase
at the end of the cool, tiled corridor, keeping his feet to
the sides of the wood to stop their creak. How many times
had he trod these steps towards the Herder? A thousand or
more. And yet, tonight, it wasn't quite real. It felt like one
of his memories, one that had wriggled free and floated
above him, but content and placid as the clouds. It was as
though he had reached up and captured it in an empty
liquor bottle, then corked it quickly in. He had left his
memory in the sun, then shaken it up, and now he peered
at himself through misted glass. It felt surreally calm, distant
and untouchable. It was thrilling all the same though; it
was something entirely for him.

The drapes were all drawn when he reached the upstairs
hallway; they were sheathed across each gaping doorway
and tacked on by pins. As he crept along the narrow passage,
he could see through their seams, and the thin shapes of
bodies appeared before him. They were lying stretched out,

hair strewn across pillows, little black soles to protruding feet. In each grubby bed was a sleeping Hanh. He let slip a smile. He had paid a piece of his debt to them all, by helping her. Though he hadn't managed to say he was sorry, he felt sure that she knew. When he'd taken her home, her stare had been kinder. When he gave her Cheung Hu's money, he didn't see fear. Forgiveness would be too much to expect, but she'd given enough for now to let his shame slumber.

At the end of the hallway, Alexander pressed his ear to the thick heavy wood. He had stood here, too, so many times before – assessing and waiting – but never with such unruffled belief. From the opposite side of the Herder's door, there was silence. Slowly and carefully, he pushed the handle and broke open the door. The smell of drink and stale sex hit him as he edged across the threshold and stood beside the Herder's bed. He peered down expectantly and examined the enormous body like he would a powerful beast in the zoo, but asleep and off-guard, the Herder seemed different. The muscles in his face were sagging and limp. His breath was laboured, and the effort it took to drag a wheeze from the back of his throat made his body twitch. He lay there, slack and greasy, and Alexander felt his confidence surge. Up close, the Herder looked old and vulnerable. He wasn't a bear, or a wolf, or a saviour. He was only a man.

Alexander crouched down and took his rucksack from his shoulder, inching open the zip as quietly as possible. The Herder spat a snort and rolled heavily over, his face coming to rest so near to Alexander's that he could smell his rotten breath. Alexander didn't flinch. He kept his eyes trained on the Herder's steaming nostrils as he peeled open the rucksack and eased out his heavy glass jar. He placed it gently down on the Herder's bedside table, sliding it to the edge of the bed and twisting it so that the face of his sleeping baby watched the Herder – staunch and indignant – and then he grabbed his bag, gave a satisfied grin, and slipped soundlessly from the room.

AUTHOR'S NOTE

The Trader of Saigon started life on a flight between Singapore and Ho Chi Minh City (formerly Saigon) in 2007, though I was not aware of this fact at the time. I was travelling with my husband Scott, and we were seated beside a well-fed Asian man in a sharp grey suit and tinted glasses. The plane took off and he hailed the stewardess for a whiskey, then he pulled out his wallet, presented his business card, and casually told us how he made his fortune selling women. He said he'd sat next to a missionary couple on his previous flight and was delighted to have better company this time. It quickly became clear that this was an exaggeration – he was not at all interested in talking to me – but I filtered my questions through Scott and listened intently. His business was strictly legitimate, of course; he sold nothing but brides. His women were young, beautiful, smart and ambitious. From across the continent, they had sought him out and were looking for love. These days, the market was mostly in China, where men outnumbered women and it was often difficult to find a wife, but he had sold his girls all over the world. American, German and British customers were not uncommon. Asian brides were the best wives a man could get – so loyal and obedient.

Demand was unprecedented. He'd been clever to capitalise. Business boomed.

I continued my travels with his card as my bookmark for the rest of our trip. I had no intention of writing a book about this (or anything else) at the time, but several years later when I did sit down to write, the man on the plane was the character I just couldn't shift.

What struck me most was his flippancy, and the pride he plainly felt getting rich through means I found simply astonishing. I wanted to know if my unease was a matter of cultural perspective. Was I being naïve, filtering my judgements through an idealised western concept of what marriage should be? I began to research the Asian bride industry, (he was right: it was booming) and discovered that whilst some legitimate 'match-making' companies do operate, these are exceptions. The overwhelming majority are fronts for something much grimmer. Across the world, there exists an extensive, sophisticated and extremely lucrative industry in human trafficking. The scale of exploitation is vast. At its mildest, women and girls are misled about their future husband's wealth or status. Kidnapping, forced marriage, child prostitution, violence and sexual slavery dominate at its most extreme.

The man I met did make it into the novel, though broken down and reassembled into more than one part. In the end, he became split between Alexander and the Herder; who he presented himself as, perhaps, and who he may have really been. Alexander is the embodiment of his self-importance, and the denial I can't help but believe must be buried inside him. The Herder is an amalgamation of the most alarming facts and cynical comments I collected throughout my research. Many of the phrases he uses in fact, (referring to the girls as 'stray cows', offering '100% virgins' and refunds if they run away within a year, jokes about 'pretty girls for brides, ugly girls for brothels', for example) are drawn straight from the lips of traffickers – from interviews and articles, and even from the promotional videos they post themselves on their company websites.

Trafficking is a global concern, but I always wanted to set the novel in Vietnam. My experience on that flight and on visits to the country had rooted the issue there in my mind. The scale of American involvement in the Vietnamese civil war meant I could sit the story on the peripheries of western consciousness; it was a country readers knew a little about, but was still remote and intriguing. The war itself is well-documented. What happened next, when the soldiers, film crews and journalists left, is much less so. I felt there was scope to explore what came after.

On April 30th 1975, after more than two decades of continual fighting, the North Vietnamese Army finally overran Saigon and the South surrendered. Official reunification occurred the following year, giving birth to The Socialist Republic of Vietnam as we know it today. The cultural and historical barriers to reunification were compounded by the clear social gulf that became immediately apparent as North met South. The North was poor and ill-developed, while the South, bolstered by the Americans, was comparatively rich. The task of restoring order and stability and unifying these two conflicting societies was enormous. Hanoi swiftly confiscated private land, collectivised agriculture and declared state ownership of trade and industry across the South. It's estimated that up to three million people were interred in camps for 're-education' – those deemed to have had 'connections' to the US, plus monks, priests, intellectuals, businessmen and thousands of men and women who had found themselves living on the wrong side of a conflict they had little to do with.

In the years that followed, the Vietnamese economy collapsed, inflation rocketed and the Government was forced to rely on Soviet aid to keep it afloat. The mix of scarce jobs, food and money, together with the rampant corruption and elitism, came together and formed a perfect storm for black market activity, including the mushrooming sex trade.

Today, the Vietnamese government has liberalised, and built diplomatic relationships worldwide. Economic growth in Vietnam is amongst the fastest in the world; tourism is flourishing and investment has helped to create jobs and prosperity for increasing numbers of people. Despite this, however, there is still widespread poverty and gender inequality, and the country continues to struggle against an epidemic of human trafficking that only a truly global attack can ever fix.

ACKNOWLEDGEMENTS

I am extremely grateful to everyone who has helped bring this novel to publication. Thank you to Scott, firstly and mostly. I wouldn't have written one word without you and this book belongs to you as much as me. Thank you to the family and friends on whom I inflicted repeated drafts and persistently neglected, especially Mum, Dad, Annette, Andrew, Nyree, Sooze and Moon. I deeply appreciate your honesty, encouragement and endless patience. Thank you to Elsie Anderton for helping me to return to Vietnam, to the staff and students on the MA in Creative Writing at Bath Spa for getting me off the starting blocks, and the kind and knowledgeable people at Ships Nostalgia for giving such enthusiastic advice on how best to steal fuel, without asking questions. Thank you to my agent Rob Dinsdale for being so generous with his time and for such continually thoughtful feedback, and to Jon Watt and the team at Quercus. I appreciate the consideration and support you have given me.

I am also grateful for the information and inspiration contained within the writings of Duong Thu Huong, Bao Ninh, Nyugyen Du and Duong Van Mai Elliott.